SPACESHIPS
AND
SPELLCASTERS

SPACESHIPS
AND
SPELLCASTERS

GLYNN STEWART

FAOLAN'S PEN
PUBLISHING
faolanspen.com

This edition published in 2018 by:

Faolan's Pen Publishing Inc.

22 King St. S, Suite 300

Waterloo, Ontario

N2J 1N8 Canada

ISBN-13: 978-1-988035-76-5 (print)

A record of this book is available from Library and Archives Canada.

Printed in the United States of America

1 2 3 4 5 6 7 8 9 10

First edition

First printing: May 2018

Cover art © 2018 Rocking Book Covers

Faolan's Pen Publishing logo is a trademark of Faolan's Pen Publishing Inc.

Read more books from Glynn Stewart at faolanspen.com

ONSET: MURDER BY MAGIC

An ONSET universe novella

1

"SOME OF YOU already know why you're here," someone said in the silent conference room at the FBI National Academy.

The speaker was a man dressed in a plain black suit, similar to though more tightly tailored than those worn by each of the twenty-three men and women sitting at classroom-style desks in the brightly lit room. All of them had just completed the gruelling twenty weeks of training to be FBI Special Agents. They'd received their badges and credentials from the director of the FBI that morning, but all they'd received for assignments was an instruction to be in this room at this time.

"The rest of you, I am certain, realize that all five of the members of your class who joined late are sitting in this room," he continued. "You have also, given the talents that led to you sitting in this room, heard rumours of a group within the FBI named 'Division O.'

"To lay your mind at ease, I will tell you that those rumours are completely false," he said with a straight face. "My name is Kyle Ardent, and I do not work for the FBI. If you accept the offer I'm here to present, neither will you.

"This is Nineteen-Ninety-Nine, however, and I am no longer allowed to draft you," he told them as concerned mutters rippled through the room. "There are, in the desks in front of you, detailed non-disclosure agreements. Breaking these agreements is treason.

"If you do not wish to sign these agreements, you may leave," Ardent concluded. "Report to Special Agent Jason Miller, and he will make certain you are given a regular FBI assignment. If you remain, you will become part of something... more."

The agents shuffled. The tone of this meeting seemed as if it belonged in a stuffy room buried in a basement somewhere, not this skylight-lit conference room on the top of the FBI National Academy.

Jamie Riley smiled at his fellow agents' consternation as he quickly skimmed the non-disclosure agreement. It was the third such document the dark-haired twenty-year-old had signed in the last six months, and it was completely identical to the first two.

After signing it, he looked up to watch five members of the assembled group slowly make their way from the room, leaving the papers unsigned on their desks. When the door shut behind the last of them, no one in the room made a move. It seemed to Jamie that everyone was holding their breath.

"Agent Riley, could you collect the forms for me, please?" Ardent asked, sounding unconcerned that he'd just lost almost a quarter of his audience.

Jamie, who had been one of the five late joiners to the regular class due to, among other things, classes Ardent had taught, stood up at the older man's instruction. He collected the agreements, quickly checking that each Agent had signed it and giving his former classmates reassuring smiles. The four other "special" recruits looked more comfortable than the rest but still awkward.

The tall young man delivered the stack of papers to Ardent, who gestured for him to remain standing up with him.

"Very well," the older man said quietly. "If everyone is sure this is where they belong, let's begin with a more complete introduction of myself.

"I am Senior Special Inspector Kyle Ardent of the Office of Supernatural Policing and Investigation," he said in a flat, crisp tone that brought the roomful of agents to straight-backed attention before they could even question the word "supernatural."

"The office is what is often referred to as Division O in FBI operations, but it is, in fact, a completely separate entity—an entity to which you may be transferred.

"Since the most common response to this speech is the claim that the supernatural does not exist, I have asked Jamie to remain up here with me," the Inspector continued with a small gesture at Riley. "Could you alleviate your fellows' doubts, Mr. Riley?"

Jamie had suspected that was why Ardent had kept him up at the front. Like the other four recruits who'd undergone additional training, he was a supernatural—in his case, a Mage.

With a deep breath, Jamie reached inside himself and muttered a nonsense phrase under his breath as he exhaled and lift his right hand. Considering a visual to be best, he conjured a six-inch-tall pillar of blue flame on his extended palm.

A ripple of confusion, surprise, and fear ran through his former classmates, all but four looking at him with new, horrified eyes. He let the magic flame flutter over his hand for a moment and then blew on it, tossing it to Emily Rossum, the other Mage among the five supernaturals in the class.

She caught it with a smile, turned it pink, and then scattered it in sparkles across the room.

"Now that you're done showing off, take your seat, Inspector Riley," Ardent told Jamie.

A shiver ran down his spine—technically, he was an FBI Special Agent until later that day, and Ardent was the first to refer to him by that title.

"As Riley has competently demonstrated, magic is, to a certain extent, very real," the Senior Inspector told the agents quietly. "He, Ms. Rossum, Mr. O'Conner, Ms. Groen, and Mr. Riesling were all inserted into your classes by OSPI upon completion of *our* specialty training course. They are all supernaturals.

"As you can imagine, this does not remain secret without the action and co-operation of the United States government. A number of offices, code-named the Omicron Branch, wield the full power and authority of the United States in domestic affairs of the supernatural.

"Such authority includes investigative and law enforcement

responsibilities and powers very similar to those of the FBI," Ardent continued. "To fulfil the need for appropriate personnel, we both run supernatural volunteers for OSPI through the National Academy and make an offer of recruitment to some of the top students from the regular course.

"Mr. Riley and the other supernaturals in your class were the first group," he concluded. "The rest of you in this room are the second. The agreement you have signed means that if you refuse this offer, you would be well-served to simply forget that this meeting ever happened —chalk it up to a post-graduation celebration.

"Those of you who accept are going back to school for another fifteen weeks, to learn everything about the Omicron Offices and the nature of the supernatural we can possibly teach you.

"If you accept, I have travel papers and tickets here for each of you," he told them. "If you do not, feel free to leave to avoid any accidental pressure by your peers."

Three more of the group, muttering about "stage tricks" and "lunacy" quickly left. Jamie, followed quickly by the other four OSPI volunteers, was the first to pick up the manila envelope with his name on it.

———

THE ONLY CONTENTS of the envelope turned out to be three taxi chits, a printed online hotel room booking, and an embossed reservation card for a five-star restaurant in downtown Washington.

The first chit delivered Jamie and the single suitcase that contained all his worldly possessions to the hotel, where he changed into another black suit. He'd gone directly from his parents' house to college and directly from college to OSPI's training program when he'd been identified as a Mage and recruited.

Somewhere along the way, most of his things had ended up at his parents' home in Baton Rouge, Louisiana, and he'd never recollected them. His suitcase contained two sets of athletics gear, four black suits, six dress shirts, and a semi-automatic pistol.

The pistol stayed in the suitcase as he pulled out a small black box and removed the one item in the suitcase that *wasn't* standard-issue special agent: a three-inch-long bronze brooch in the form of a leaf.

Delicately carved into the face of the brooch was a series of blessings written in Sindarin—one of the two elvish languages created by J.R.R. Tolkien when he wrote The Lord of the Rings. The brooch, its blessings, and Jamie's ability to read the blessings (and to, though he'd rarely admit it, *speak* the fictional language) were gifts from his mother, who was obsessed with Tolkien's fictional world.

He pinned the brooch to the lapel of the clean suit then hung the other up for the hotel room service to clean and press, before calling the cab to take him to the restaurant, where, unless he was severely mistaken, he would finally, officially, become an OSPI Inspector.

————

THE SECOND TAXI chit delivered Riley to a genteelly pseudo-French building in southern Washington, DC, only about fifteen minutes from the hotel the agency had booked him in at.

He was met at the front door of the restaurant by the tuxedoed maître d', who apparently had mastered looking down his nose at people who shopped at even the expensive end of Walmart's suit section.

"May I help you?" he asked, somehow managing to look down his nose while still having to look up at Jamie, who had at least three inches on the man.

"Special Agent Jamie Riley," Jamie said softly, handing the man the reservation card. "I'm meeting a party."

First the title and then the embossed card took the haughtiness out of the man in a flash. He bowed slightly over the card.

"Of course. Right this way," he said, his voice suddenly as smooth as silk.

Jamie followed the tuxedoed man through the gorgeously decorated restaurant. The main dining room, despite being the same size as most major restaurants, had a total of eighteen tables in it. Each table was secluded away from the others by decorative fountains and potted trees, allowing privacy even in this public space.

The maître d' led him through the restaurant to a set of double doors and opened one of them, gesturing Jamie through. The private room on the far side of the doors had been set up with a stage and a dozen round tables, all covered in the same white tablecloths as outside. This room lacked the privacy screen of plants and fountains to keep the tables private, though.

He knew he was in the right place, as he spotted Kyle Ardent immediately. The instructor was one of the fifteen people already in the room, none of them Jamie's classmates from the academy.

Ardent spotted him in turn and gestured Jamie over to join him where he stood talking to a looming giant of a dark-haired man.

"Jamie Riley, this is Brigadier Michael O'Brien," he introduced the new graduate to the looming man. O'Brien was easily Riley's own six-foot height but far broader and heavier with it. "Brigadier, this is one of our new graduates, Jamie Riley. He's one of the supernatural volunteers we sent to the FBI Academy."

Jamie, like most Mages, had a touch of the Second Sight, and the brigadier's aura glowed brightly to his eyes as the commander of OSPI's High Threat Response teams—the name had come up in his courses—offered his hand.

"It's always good to see new blood," the brigadier rumbled. "Especially supernaturals—of the twenty Inspectors we're commissioning tonight, only you and your classmates have gifts worth mentioning in that area."

The brigadier shook Jamie's hand firmly and then caught a glimpse of someone else across the room. "Excuse me, Mr. Riley, Mr. Ardent. I need to speak with Senator Cardston."

And with that, the second most senior OSPI officer in the United States separated from Jamie and Ardent, heading across towards a graying black man in a perfectly tailored suit.

"It looks like some of your classmates are joining us," Ardent told Jamie after the brigadier had moved on, gesturing to the door. Damien Riesling had arrived side by side with Emily Rossum in a manner that clearly had Ardent wondering about their level of friendship.

Jamie, who knew perfectly well that Damien and Emily were both completely gay, smiled at his teacher's discomfort and walked over to join them, collecting a swift handshake from Damien and a peck on the cheek from Emily.

"I can't believe we've actually made it this far," Damien murmured. The Inspector-to-be rivalled Jamie's height but had a weightlifter's breadth to go with it. Jamie's hand almost vanished in the fair-haired man's impeccably groomed paw. Unlike Jamie and Emily, Damien was not a Mage—his primary supernatural ability boiled down to getting about five times the result from any degree of physical exercise, and having skin that rivalled Kevlar for its resistance to damage.

"I wish I could disagree," Emily said with a nod. The Mage was shorter than either man, petite and frail in a way that belied her magical strength. "I thought that after we'd passed the OSPI training, they'd almost wave us through the academy training."

"I think they forgot to tell our instructors we were supposed to be special," Jamie told her, remembering the brutal slogging of physical and mental education that had filled the last ten weeks. Unlike the potential Inspectors recruited earlier in the day after the FBI graduation ceremony and the fifteen non-supernatural Inspectors graduating that day, the five supernaturals had spent twenty-five weeks at an OSPI training facility before heading to the National Academy to finish off the FBI training.

The non-supernaturals would add fifteen weeks at that OSPI training facility to their FBI training and then graduate. The reasoning, as Jamie understood it, was that non-supernatural Inspectors mainly need a crash course in the supernatural and the US government systems that dealt with it, whereas the supernaturals often needed detailed training in their own powers.

The three had moved away from the door, so they missed their last two classmates entering. They didn't miss the microphone turning on as the graying black senator, accompanied by a redhaired woman in a dark-blue skirt and suit jacket, took the stage.

"Good evening, everyone," the man said, cutting through the scattered conversations in the room. "The last of our new Inspectors has arrived, so if I can get you all to take a seat, we can get things started."

The five supernatural students ended up sitting together, with Senior Special Inspector Ardent taking up the sixth seat at their table.

Jamie exchanged quick nods with the two classmates he hadn't managed to speak to, but he didn't have time to do any more before Cardston spoke again.

"For those of you who don't know me, I am Senator Larry Cardston, and I am the longest-serving member of the Special Committee for Supernatural Affairs," the politician introduced himself. "This"—he gestured graciously to the redhead standing with him—"is Congresswoman Valerie Shuler, the most recent addition to our ranks after Congressman Deville's unfortunate heart attack.

"You all, I am sure, know of our group as 'The Committee of Thirteen,'" he concluded the introductions, earning a small chuckle from the crowd. "We were created in the fifties in response to a number of supernatural incidents that led to locked sessions of Congress—and the realization that this could not continue.

"We are the brain of Omicron, the directing intelligence behind everything we all do with regard to the supernatural in America, but we cannot act alone. Like any agency, we are bound by checks and balances, the laws of our great nation.

"To enforce those laws upon the supernatural citizens of our country, upon the Omicron Agencies, and if necessary, upon the Committee itself, we created the Office of Supernatural Policing and Investigation.

"OSPI is the beating heart of Omicron!" Cardston declared to the gathered crowd of officers. "Without you, those to whom God gave great power but not great control would be unfettered, left only to their own morals and faith to keep them to the path of right.

"To the Committee and the Omicron Offices we lead, many powers are given," he said quietly. "We are all entrusted to wield greater power than others, and so we are given greater responsibility. But when asked, 'How do we know this power is wielded rightly and justly?' the Committee has an answer. When we are asked, 'Who guards these guardians of America's citizens against the dark?' the Committee answers: the first and greatest Omicron Office. Your office. The Office of Supernatural Policing and Investigation."

Jamie knew, on a conscious level, that Cardston was playing the crowd he faced. That didn't really matter, as the old senator's words hit the chords that had drawn the young Mage to OSPI when his powers had been discovered by his anthropology professor half a year before. He was applauding with everyone else.

"We are gathered here to pass on that burden," Cardston reminded them. "That part of this gathering is for others. I am here to remind you why you serve, and to bear witness. To present our graduates with their official papers, I give you Omicron's greatest legend: Brigadier Michael O'Brien!"

O'Brien looked vaguely embarrassed, clearly not meeting the senator's gaze as he joined the two Committee members on stage, but he shook Cardston's hand gamely and took the microphone as the senator took a seat beside Shuler.

"I'm not nearly as pretty a speaker as Senator Cardston," the officer rumbled. "So I'll say this: I know what each of you, supernatural or mundane, went through to stand here today. Thank you.

"If you can approach the stage when your name is called," he continued, "we can get through this quickly and get to the food."

2

────────

THE NEXT MORNING saw a bleary-eyed and hungover Jamie Riley bidding his former classmates farewell in the main concourse of the Washington National Airport. All five had stayed up long after the official graduation had finished and were all varying degrees of worse for wear. Except Emily, who was as perky and happy as ever, earning the petite blonde Mage looks of disgust from the others.

"Where are you heading?" she asked them all.

"Montana," Riesling said with a grimace. "Hopefully I can get a transfer to somewhere warmer eventually. It's not like they're sending me to somewhere I have family."

"Los Angeles," Jamie told them with a smile. "It's beaches, and Hollywood stars for me, folks."

He suspected he'd be lucky if he saw a beach, let alone a Hollywood star in the seaside city. The first six months on the job as an OSPI Inspector were notorious for being utterly overwhelming.

"Where are you?" he asked Emily.

"The Big Apple," she replied with a smile. "I'm heading right to the head office for a stint with Thaumaturgical Research."

That made sense to Jamie. He was, as Mages ranked these things, a Second Circle Master. He was strong, with a natural gift for wielding that power. Emily was a Fourth Circle Initiate, one of the fifty or so strongest Mages in the United States. Part of it was training, part was natural gift—and Thaumaturgical Research would want to break down how much was which.

"Researcher or lab rat?" Liam O'Conner asked pointedly, and Jamie gave the broad redheaded man a dirty look. Liam was the reason the students knew that Emily was gay, as he'd been persistent in pursuing her—despite the efforts of the rest of the other two men—until a very public fight in which she'd flat-out told him she had no interest in men. He didn't seem to be over it.

"Both," Emily responded with a toss of her hair. A boarding call rang out through the concourse for Jamie's flight before the conversation could continue.

"That's me," he told the others, hefting his small carry-on. The suitcase that had followed him around for the last year or so had already been checked in, his Colt M1911-Silver service side arm and the three clips of silver bullets that came with it in a lockbox at the bottom of the case. The black leather folio with the silver badge in it he'd received with the gun was tucked into the breast pocket of his shirt.

Emily gave him a quick hug, and he traded handshakes with the others.

"Good luck," he wished them all and then set off for his new city.

———

Four hours later found him in the concourse of the Los Angeles airport, pushing the cart with his carry-on and suitcase while looking for the man he was supposed to meet. Finally, he spotted a short, swarthy gentleman in a navy-blue suit, holding a sign with "Riley" on it.

"I'm Jamie Riley," he introduced himself, hoping this was the right person.

"Good to meet you," the suited man responded with a bright grin and a flash of pleasure in his aura. "I'm Adrian Pattakos. The boss is assigning you to me, so she figured I should come pick you up."

"I appreciate it," Jamie told him, shaking the man's hand gratefully. "I've never actually been to LA before."

"I'll give you the rundown on the way to the office," Adrian offered. "The rest of your stuff is being shipped over?" he asked with a gesture at Jamie's suitcase.

The new Inspector flushed slightly. "I've been living out of college dorms and FBI training quarters for the last two years," he told the older man. "This is everything."

The older OSPI man whistled quietly as he appropriated the cart from Jamie, leading him towards the exit.

"I see I'll have to get Laura to take you shopping," Adrian said with a laugh. "She'll like that. I apologize in advance."

"Laura?" Jamie asked, following the senior Inspector out into the parkade.

Pattakos popped the trunk on a boxy blue Lincoln and easily loaded the two bags in before answering.

"Laura is the other junior Inspector assigned to our 'team,' such as it is," he explained. "She's a redheaded spitfire, one of the best investigators I've worked with—and she *adores* shopping."

Jamie hopped in the passenger seat of the Lincoln when Adrian popped it open. With the door closed, he breathed a small sigh of relief. It was more than a little worrying to talk work in public.

"You have a team?" he asked the senior Inspector as they left the parkade.

"Not really," Adrian admitted. "One of my cases is more complex than I can handle on my own with the rest of my caseload, so the boss assigned two of our new Inspectors to support me—Laura and you. Laura's only been with the Office for a year or so, and you're brand new."

"What's the case?" Jamie asked, eager to get to work.

The older Inspector laughed. "I think you need a bit more LA background before you dive into Empowered drug distribution," he told Jamie. "What do you know about LA?"

"In all honesty?" Jamie considered for a moment. "A handful of specific case studies with regard to supernatural affairs, high school American history, and what Hollywood tells us."

"So, not much," Adrian concluded. "The big thing to realize about Los Angeles is that this is one of the most ethnically diverse cities in the world—so we've got a lot of poor black fucks who think gang life is cool thanks to idiot rappers."

Jamie opened his mouth to disagree with the older man's assessment of the impact of LA's multi-ethnicity but closed it again. The other man's tone made him uncomfortable, but he couldn't argue with his new boss. Not yet, anyway—and not when Pattakos himself was dark-skinned enough that most people would have figured the Inspector for an immigrant, if not one of the kids he was disparaging.

"Both the Crips and the Bloods were born here, and LA is still a stronghold for both of them," Adrian continued. "The two gangs are fighting a pretty constant low-level war. Mostly that, and the crack cocaine issues that come along with it, are an FBI or LAPD issue. The PD has 'Community Resource Against Street Hoodlums'—CRASH— units that are doing a pretty good job of keeping things under control, despite what some would tell you!

"Both sides have a handful of supernaturals 'on staff,' though, and those bad boys turn into our problem," the senior Inspector explained. "It's also starting to look like their distribution networks are being used to run something *else* into the city."

"What's that?"

Adrian grunted in response. "That's something you'll get a full briefing on at the office. I wouldn't want to spoil the surprise," he told him.

"A lot of the imports brought various traditions of varying levels of real power along with them too," Adrian continued, changing the subject back to the general tone of LA. "We're one of the supernatural hotspots of the country, so the office is kept busy. There's only fifty or so of us, ten real supernaturals including you and me. Expect to be busy."

Jamie nodded agreement with Adrian's last comment as they pulled up to a small four-story glass-and-chrome building with a sign outside that declared it to be an FBI REGIONAL OFFICE.

"We're here," Adrian told him.

———

THE BRIGHT AFTERNOON sun reflected painfully from the glass building as Jamie followed Adrian into the office. The main doors led into an artfully adorned reception area, blocked from the rest of the building by solid walls decorated in black walnut. There was a door on either side of the room, and the floor was covered in a thick blue carpet.

A young Hispanic woman in a pristine blue suit sat behind a large desk of the same dark wood as the walls. The desk was flanked by a pair of US flags. The symbol behind the desk was the only clue this was not a standard FBI office—a stylized Omicron in silver.

"Welcome back, Inspector Pattakos," the raven-haired receptionist greeted Jamie's companion cheerfully. "The chief said to send you and Inspector Riley up to see her as soon as you got in."

She slid a plain dark-blue pass card across the table. "This is your personal card, Inspector," she told Jamie. "It'll let you into the first three floors and the basement. The top floor and most sections of the basement are restricted to senior Inspectors and the chief—you'll need permission from the chief to enter those areas. Ms. Wilson's office is on the third floor."

Jamie blinked for a moment, processing the young woman's rapid-fire delivery of information, and Adrian laughed.

"Slow down a moment and let the poor man listen, Lily," the older Inspector told the receptionist. "I'll get him up to Karina."

Lily giggled with a sheepish smile. "Of course," she agreed. "Welcome to LA, Inspector Riley. I'm Lily Matter. Call me Lily. Everyone here does."

Jamie took her hand and shook it carefully as he returned the smile. "Thank you, Lily. Call me Jamie," he requested. "I'm sure I'll be seeing you around."

"Of course! I'll let Ms. Wilson know you're on your way up," Lily told them, reaching for the phone on her desk.

"Stairs are that way," Adrian told Jamie, gesturing to the right-hand door. As they passed through into the main offices, Jamie realized that the apparent transparency of the glass outer walls was something of an illusion. There was a single set of cubicles against the glass and then an interior wall concealing most of the building from the outside.

Adrian led Jamie to a door in that interior wall that revealed a stairwell heading up. Eager to get started, Jamie took the lead, taking the steps two at a time up to the third floor, where his security card unlocked the door.

On the third floor, a slightly out of breath Adrian pointed him to the door leading into the interior of the building. Stepping into the central core of the office, Jamie could see that this door led a corridor that linked four parallel corridors, each lined with offices.

"Far-right corridor," Adrian told him. "Center office. Each of the inspectors has their own office on the third floor. First floor is administration staff. Second floor is Forensics, Thaumaturgics, and the clinic—you'll probably be spending a good chunk of time there. You're only our second Mage. The armoury, morgue, and detention are in the basement."

"What's the fourth floor?" Jamie asked, wondering what was up there that even Inspectors were barred from it.

"Secured conference rooms, interrogation, and a special research lab," Adrian replied. "It's nothing special or amazing, just stuff we don't normally have use for, so there's no point in us having access."

Jamie nodded as they approached the office Adrian had specified. Most of the doors, he'd noted along the way, were wide open, allowing him to glance in at offices in various states of organization and setups, mostly occupied at this time of day.

Senior Special Inspector Karina Wilson's door, however, was closed. A brass nameplate on the door stated her rank and name with the subheader of STATION CHIEF.

Adrian rapped on the door, and Jamie's eagerness dropped out of the bottom of his stomach like a stone as a wave of nervousness hit him. Suddenly, it sank in that this was real, and he was about to meet his first OSPI station chief—his first real boss.

"It's Pattakos," Adrian said through the door in response to a query Jamie hadn't heard. "I'm here with Riley."

"Lily said you were coming. Come on in," Wilson responded. With a deep breath, he followed Adrian into Ms. Wilson's office.

3

___

Station Chief Karina Wilson's office was a windowless box nearly at the center of the building. It was perfectly clean, without a single stray paper on the immaculately polished wooden desk. Four gray filing cabinets lined one wall, and a large whiteboard covered the other. A dark-blue screen with the stylized silver Omicron on it had been pulled down to cover most of the whiteboard.

Wilson herself sat behind the desk, half-concealed by the computer. Jamie's first impression of her was of a stocky, heavyset woman. She was perhaps five feet five and heavy with it, but with enough muscle to still look like she could snap him one-handed.

Her graying hair was knotted behind her head in a tight bun, and her blue eyes were flat as she looked at him, her lips slightly curled as if ready to launch into a sneer at a moment's notice. Her aura was plain and mundane, without a drop of power, woven through with a degree of exhaustion and bitterness that could never quite heal.

"Come in, gentlemen," she instructed, her voice hoarse as if from too many cigarettes.

There were two uncomfortable-looking chairs in front of her desk. Jamie waited for Adrian to sit down to be sure he should and then followed suit.

"Welcome to the Los Angeles OSPI station," Wilson told Jamie, who started to relax somewhat. "As I'm sure you've established by now, I have assigned you to operate as Inspector Pattakos's partner. I don't expect much from a new graduate supernatural, but I hope you at least don't drag his investigations down too much."

Any hint of relaxation left Jamie halfway through her sentence, his back rigid. He didn't *think* he'd done anything to make Wilson angry with him, but something seemed to have upset her.

"Do I have a case load of my own?" he asked, carefully turning his best professional gaze on the station chief, who hesitated halfway through her sneer.

"We do have two cases that should be simple enough," she allowed carefully. She slid open the drawer in her desk and removed two dark-blue file folders. "I intended to assign them to Laura."

"Laura is already jointly responsible for eleven cases with me and Inspector Lager," Adrian suggested, his voice respectful. "I can, of course, provide appropriate support to Inspector Riley with his cases."

Hesitant for a moment longer, Wilson finally slid the folders across the empty desk to Jamie. "Very well, Inspector Riley," she told him. "These will be your first cases. Both are quite simple, and you should be able to present us with enough evidence for an arrest within the week."

"Thank you, ma'am," Jamie said quite honestly. He hadn't joined OSPI to run errands for others.

"That said, you will also be Adrian's partner, and you will also need to focus on supporting his cases, which are by and large more complex and longer term," she continued, ignoring his words in a way he wasn't used to.

"The largest of these is what he has sensationally codenamed the 'Black Dream' file," Wilson explained, turning her flat gaze on Adrian, whom Jamie saw smile slightly out of the corner of his eye.

"Black Dream, to be clear," the Inspector told Jamie, though the words were also directed at Wilson, "is the street name of the drug whose distribution I'm investigating."

"Mostly, OSPI leaves the gangs and their drug networks to the FBI and the LAPD's CRASH teams," Wilson continued, acknowledging

Adrian's words with a small nod. "In this case, Black Dream is both Empowered and extremely dangerous. We don't know the drug's source, and we have only the vaguest notion of how it's manufactured, but so far, it hasn't expanded far beyond Los Angeles, which means we can probably stop it here before it spreads farther."

"What *do* we know?" Jamie asked before he could catch himself. Wilson continued to ignore him, but he saw the flash of irritation in her aura and regretted speaking.

"It seems to have been moved into either the Crips' or the Bloods' distribution network and fully integrated alongside crack cocaine, at least locally," she told him.

"Black Dream's effects are threefold. Firstly, it significantly increases the user's physical strength and speed. Secondly, it gives the user... delusions of grandeur, basically. Impressions of their strength and speed above the augmented levels they *do* possess. Lastly," she finished, her voice softening with an edge of sadness, "they suffer from extremely detailed, hyper-real hallucinations.

"The combination makes them a deadly threat to those around them and extremely difficult to stop. The use of deadly force has been authorized in all cases of Black Dream usage," she concluded.

"Some of the dealers see the danger as much as we do," Adrian added. "They've set up 'dreamhouses' where they lock the users in—trapped in a room while the drug runs them through whatever power fantasy is locked in the back of their brain."

Jamie could imagine the idea quite well. It probably worked well for stopping the users from hurting others, but...

"I can't imagine that does a lot for stopping the users hurting themselves," he said quietly.

For the first time since starting her lecture, Wilson acknowledged him with a curt nod. "If nothing else, using the excess speed and strength the drug gives them leaves them drained for days and quite possibly injured."

"So far, we've had almost no luck tracking the chain past individual dealers," Adrian told Jamie. "At least one has dosed himself on Black Dream when we caught him and tried to use the increased strength to escape."

"Has anyone had the chance to thaumaturgically examine samples of the drug?" Jamie asked carefully, hoping that he was allowed to ask questions now.

"Inspector Lager has taken a look, but the Inspector's Sight is below par," Wilson replied, the disapproval in her voice and aura *probably* not directed at Jamie. "I hope a second look will reveal more."

Jamie nodded. His own Second Sight was nothing incredible, but it was certainly enough that he should be able to learn *something* from examining the drug.

"Your office is 317," she told him. "Review those files this afternoon, and be ready to get to work tomorrow. Dismissed!"

———

Jamie followed Pattakos to office 317, the middle office of the corridor on the opposite end of the floor from Wilson's. His new workspace consisted of a plain desk with a black computer and monitor, two corkboards, and a row of filing cabinets that were empty when he checked them.

He closed the filing cabinets then slid the folders onto his desk and dropped into the chair, gesturing for Adrian to take the single uncomfortable chair across from him.

"What," he asked quietly, "was that about?" He didn't think he'd done anything to upset Wilson, but she'd treated him like a half-dead rat her cat had dragged in, when she wasn't ignoring him completely.

"I'd ask what you meant, but I'm guessing you mean the chief's treatment of you," Adrian said dryly, dropping into the chair. "Ms. Wilson feels—with some justification, mind you—that supernaturals are given a soft hand through training and arrive in the field under-qualified to perform the roles expected of them."

"I see," Jamie answered, flipping open his two files. The first was a series of thefts from museums. A quick glance at the age of the artefacts answered why OSPI had the case—all of them pre-dated the estimated date of the ritual enacted by King Solomon to seal magic from the world. A ritual with some obvious flaws, but artefacts from before that date were far more likely to have magical properties.

The second was a thaumaturgical murder, first degree—premeditated murder by magic. A man murdered by having his heart crushed, his minor Mage wife the primary suspect.

He closed the files and slid them into the top drawer of his desk. He'd review them more completely later.

"Is this going to cause me problems?" he asked his new partner bluntly.

The older Inspector shrugged eloquently. "When I came to LA two years ago, she'd already been running the branch for three years, and I had six years in OSPI," Adrian said. "Because I was Empowered, she treated me like an idiot child for six months. I'm your partner and senior, so let me deal with her—it'll probably be easier for everyone that way."

"I'll need to meet Inspector Lager," Jamie said, changing the subject. "Are they in the office today?"

"She's in the field today," his partner answered. "Violet Lager was our only Mage prior to you showing up, so she's been run ragged doing Second Sight sweeps of crime scenes, on top of her normal duties. Some of that will get dumped on you now," the senior Inspector told him with a grin.

"Wonderful," the new agent said dryly. "Anything else I should be aware of?"

"As one of our two Mages, you have free access to the thaum lab," Adrian told him. "Wilson is actually the only one other than you and Lager who has access on her card."

That sounded like a situation in which Jamie wanted to sort out the split for time and space in the lab with Lager—*soon*.

"We don't have much on the Dream file at the moment," the older man admitted, "so take the afternoon to review the files Wilson gave you. Do you have somewhere to stay?"

"All I own is in the duffel bag we left in your car," Jamie told him with a smile. "I figured I'd grab a hotel room for the next couple of weeks and sort out getting a place as fast as I can."

"Laura's brother is a real estate agent in the area," his partner told him. "Have her put you in touch with him; he should be able to find you something quickly."

"Laura was... the other junior assigned to you?" Jamie asked, straining his memory. He had a good memory for names when he had faces to attach them to, but those dropped in passing were harder for him.

"That's right," Adrian confirmed with a snap of his fingers. "In fact, I should introduce her to you. Let's go."

Feeling overwhelmed by the cascade of new people and names, Jamie followed Pattakos out into the corridors of OSPI's LA office once more.

4

———

Laura's office turned out to be four doors down from Jamie's, though she wasn't there. The tiny room was identical to his, except hers was clearly in use. The corkboard was covered with news articles, surveillance photos, and clips of biographies. A giant map of the city had been taped over the wall next to the door and covered with small flags of multiple different colours. At least four files were open on the junior agent's desk.

"She'll be on the second floor if she isn't here," Adrian told Jamie, leading the way back to the stairs they'd originally climbed.

The second floor was split into quarters. The northeast quarter that they emerged by was clearly labelled as Thaumaturgical Laboratory, Restricted Access. Adrian led the way to the northwest corner, labelled Forensics.

The lab was currently mostly empty, except for a single young woman in a black suit and skirt and with red hair hanging down to her waist in a tightly knit braid.

"Howdy, Laura," Adrian greeted her, causing her to turn around from whatever she'd been reviewing on the lab's computer.

At the sight of Jamie, she smiled brightly and stood. Her eyes, Jamie noted distantly, were a sparkling green set in an adorable button-nosed face with a scattering of freckles. Her conservative suit and blouse did nothing to reduce her attractiveness and he barely managed to avoid freezing like a deer in headlights.

"Hi, Adrian," she greeted the senior Inspector, though her gaze didn't move from Jamie's. "I take it this is our new Inspector."

"Exactly. Laura Sutcliffe, meet Jamie Riley," Adrian introduced them.

It wasn't until they shook hands that Jamie finally managed to disengage his gaze from Laura's. He wasn't sure what it was about the woman's eyes, but the sparkle in them fascinated him.

"You're both assigned to assist me with the Black Dream file," the senior Inspector noted, "so you'll be working together quite a bit. Do we have anything new?" he asked Laura.

"Nothing significant," she answered with a shrug. "I'm reviewing the autopsies on the last few overdoses, trying to get a feel for what concentrations of the drug were in their systems."

"Do we get anything useful from a mundane autopsy?" Jamie asked, curious. Most of the drug's impacts sounded as if they came from its supernatural aspects, which were unlikely to show up in most examinations.

"Therein lies the problem," Laura agreed. "There are a few chemical traces we've identified as being from the Dream, which lets us identify our 'Dreamers' in the general pool of autopsies in the city, but we're not seeing any other commonalities."

"Any common cause of death?" Jamie asked, his mind racing for possibilities.

"Yeah," the woman responded with a snort. "Stupidity. You've got the rundown on the effects?" Jamie nodded. "Well, between hallucinations and thinking they're Achilles reborn, Dreamers walk into all sorts of shit they shouldn't. Broken necks are high on the list—so are gunshot wounds, knife wounds, and about fifteen different kinds of fall-induced trauma. The heart attacks are about the only ones we're really sure are actual overdoses."

"So we're pulling the files on any death with the chemical traces?" he asked and considered when she nodded. "False positives?"

"About forty percent is my current estimate," Laura replied with a deep sigh and a fetching flip of her hair. "Without sending an autopsy-trained Mage to reperform the surgeries, I have no way of being sure." She eyed Jamie for a moment.

"No such luck. My pre-OSPI education is in economics," Jamie told her with a smile. He hadn't *finished* the degree, but that was a different story altogether.

"Laura, Jamie is new in town," Adrian interjected. "He's staying at a hotel tonight on the office's tab, but I suggested he get in touch with Ryan."

Laura nodded brightly. "Of course! Here." She quickly scribbled a number on a pad of paper by the computer. "I also put together a summary of our current findings on the Dream for the chief last week. I'll forward it to your email so you can review it."

"Thank you," Jamie told her. "I look forward to working with you."

"Likewise, Jamie," she answered.

―――

Following Adrian, Jamie returned to his office. He turned the computer on and glanced over at the senior agent as the machine booted up.

"Anything specific I should be getting up to today?" he asked.

"Go over the two files Wilson gave you and put together a plan of attack," Adrian suggested. "Touch base with me before you go charging off, but they're your cases. Otherwise, look at the Black Dream data and see if you can set up house showings. I've got my own cases to get back to working on, so I'm going to have to leave you to it."

"If I have questions?" Jamie asked. He was pretty sure he'd have *some* kind of question. "For that matter, what's my login?" He looked at the Windows login screen blankly for a moment.

"JRILEY," Adrian replied. "Password1, capital P. I'm in office 311, at the end of the corridor. If I'm not there, Laura can probably help you—or you can bounce me an email, and I'll check in on you when I'm back from wherever."

"Thank you, Inspector," Jamie told him with a grateful smile.

"Please, Jamie—call me Adrian," Pattakos told him on his way out the office door.

———

WITH ADRIAN GONE, Jamie opened the first of the two files on his desk. It was a sparse file—an autopsy report, a Supernatural Registration file, and a copy of a travel restriction order on the woman in the file.

Mrs. Emma Sharp was a low-level Mage, a Class One Initiate with some training but no major Gift. She was properly registered, fully aware of the legal limitations and requirements of her unusual nature, completely cooperative, and an apparently perfect supernatural citizen of the United States.

As such, when Mr. Robert Sharp passed away unexpectedly, his autopsy was performed by an in-the-know physician. That physician had identified Mr. Sharp's "heart attack" as his heart being crushed by telekinetic force—a murder by magic.

The case hadn't progressed much beyond that as the coroner's report was dated the previous day. Wilson had arranged the court order restricting Mrs. Sharp to the city as a "person of interest" and then dropped the file on her newest Inspector.

Contact information for the Omicron Defender appointed as Mrs. Sharp's lawyer was in the file. Unlike normal cases, in which the state only appointed a lawyer if the accused could not afford one, Omicron *always* appointed a lawyer for each accused. The lawyers also got involved somewhat earlier than in normal cases—there would be at least two Defenders on duty in the OSPI office Jamie worked in at all times. The rights of someone charged with a supernatural offence were sufficiently different that they needed a specially-trained lawyer—and that lawyer had to be in the know about the supernatural.

Based on the two pieces of data Jamie had to go on, he agreed with Wilson that Mrs. Sharp seemed to be the most likely suspect, but he'd need more to go on before he made an arrest. The first step was to interview her.

He called the lawyer.

"Mr. Steeple," he greeted the man. "I am Inspector Jamie Riley with the LA OSPI detachment."

"Mr. Riley," the lawyer greeted him, his voice tired. "How can I help you?"

"I have been assigned the Sharp case," Jamie told him. "Have you been in touch with Mrs. Sharp and advised her of her rights?"

"Mrs. Sharp is well aware of her rights," Steeple told him dryly. "But yes, I have spoken to her since she was declared a person of interest in her husband's death."

"I would like to interview her as soon as reasonably possible," Jamie said. "I imagine the autopsy report was something of a shock to her, but I'd like to discuss the circumstances of her husband's death with her before they fade any more."

"You're asking me if you can speak to her?" Steeple asked, sounding surprised.

"You will of course need to attend yourself," Jamie reminded him, "plus regulations require me to go through you."

The lawyer actually laughed. "Would you believe me, Inspector, if I told you I'd forgotten that regulation?"

Jamie took a sharp breath, surprised in turn. That was an important rule, to make sure that the rights of the accused were respected.

"Be that as it may," he said slowly, "could you arrange the interview?"

"I can," the lawyer confirmed. "I have a two-hour slot free tomorrow at one. I'll confirm with Mrs. Sharp, but I imagine she'll be available."

"I will book an interview room here," Jamie told the man. "The receptionist will tell you which one when you arrive."

"I look forward to meeting you," Steeple replied, and Jamie could almost hear the lawyer shaking his head as the man hung up.

Jamie quickly set up the appointment in the calendar on his computer and sent an email to Lily Matter to request an interview room—yet another airless box in the hidden core to the glass-sided office building, he was sure—for one p.m. the next day.

Taking a breath to ground himself, he turned to the second case file and began to review the list of potentially-linked thefts.

5

———————

ONE O'CLOCK THE next day saw Jamie meeting Mrs. Sharp at the reception desk of the building. He was sure that Ms. Matter would have made sure the woman and her Omicron-appointed lawyer got to the interview room without problems, but he wanted to put the woman at least somewhat at ease.

He'd spent the morning canvassing the condo complex the Sharps had lived in, interviewing the people—mostly stay-at-home spouses—who were there on a Thursday morning. The image he'd put together from those interviews fit neatly with the impression he'd received from Emma Sharp's file: a well-put-together couple, good citizens. The couple had served on the condo board and helped coordinate social events. Emma's job at a small thaumaturgical consulting agency could not, under the laws Omicron enforced, be talked about. This had left her often working from home during the day, and she'd happily babysat and helped out around the community.

To add to the picture, the neighbours described a couple that acted like newlyweds after ten years of marriage, wandering around the local parks hand in hand. The only thing missing from the image was children, and that was hardly rare for a professional couple these days.

Nothing that Jamie had learned about the couple remotely

suggested a reason for Emma to have crushed her husband's heart. For that matter, Jamie's review of her file suggested that she wouldn't have had the magical strength to *do* it.

Which left him wondering, as he met the primly dressed Californian woman, whether her husband had done something horrible to trigger one of the bursts of extra magical power any Mage could show —or if there was another Mage in the Sharps' life.

"Mr. Riley, this is Mrs. Sharp." Steeple, the defender, looked almost exactly as Jamie had pictured him from the phone conversation: a tall, skinny, balding man with worry lines worn into a face aged far beyond his years.

"Mr. Steeple," Jamie returned the lawyer's greeting and offered his hand to the only suspect in his case. "Mrs. Sharp, thank you for agreeing to meet with me on such short notice."

"Anything I can do to help find the truth behind Robert's death," the short blonde woman in the dark-blue skirt-suit told him.

Jamie swallowed the urge to correct her to "murder" and gestured for the two to follow him. "Please, come with me," he instructed.

The pair followed him in silence to the interview room, and it hit Jamie with a bit of a shock to remember that in this building, speaking to someone suspected of a crime and her lawyer, the power lay almost entirely with him. He hoped neither of them saw his shiver, and he was suddenly glad for the laws and regulations that restricted that power.

The interview room was as much what he was expecting as Mr. Steeple had been: a windowless box with a video camera and a table. There were four chairs in the room, and Adrian Pattakos was sitting in the extra one.

As Jamie's partner, the senior Inspector was there as much as a double check on Jamie as anything else. Jamie would have preferred to interview Mrs. Sharp alone, but he had to admit that the presence of the more experienced investigator couldn't hurt. It was, after all, his first live interview.

"Please, Mrs. Sharp, Mr. Steeple, have a seat," Jamie instructed as he sat next to his partner, facing his "person of interest" across the table.

The aged lawyer waited for his client to sit and then carefully folded himself into the plain chair, setting his briefcase down beside him.

"Mrs. Sharp," Jamie said quietly, "you are not under arrest, but you understand, I'm sure, that you are under significant suspicion here—hence the presence of Mr. Steeple.

"You have at all times the right to refuse to answer a question," he continued. "You have at all times the right to consult in private with Mr. Steeple *before* you answer a question. Everything said in this room is recorded, so we will provide you with another room for such consultations.

"Lastly, I do possess the ability to view your aura under Second Sight. I will not use this ability except with your permission," Jamie told her. The reason for that legal requirement was more due to the Sight's unreliability as a lie detector than any moral standing. All it really showed was mood, so it was roughly as reliable as a polygraph for that purpose.

"Do you understand these rights?" he asked.

The suited blonde nodded carefully.

"This is my partner, Adrian Pattakos," Jamie said, gesturing to where Adrian sat quietly beside him. Adrian nodded politely to the lawyer and suspect but remained silent.

"Let's start with something simple, Mrs. Sharp," the junior Inspector continued after a moment. "How did you meet your husband?"

Emma Sharp took a deep breath, wiping incipient tears from her eyes, and then laid her hands flat on the table as she faced Jamie. He didn't need the Sight to know that she was either honestly grieving—or a phenomenal actress.

"We met in late '87," she explained slowly. "It was shortly after I had my accident and I was starting to learn my new powers. Robert was my physical therapist for my physical injuries. We hit it off, and we ended up getting married in '89."

"So Mr. Sharp was a physical therapist?" Jamie questioned.

"Yes," Mrs. Sharp said with a sad smile. "He loved to help people.

It was such a huge part of him. It was an inspiration for me, helped me get through my therapy and learning my powers."

"Was Mr. Sharp aware you were a Mage?" he asked.

Mrs. Sharp glanced quickly over at Mr. Steeple. Technically, it was illegal for Emma Sharp to have told Robert Sharp, who was not in the know about magic, about her powers. In truth, Omicron assumed that any mundane spouse of a supernatural was told as a matter of course, so Mr. Steeple just gave her a small nod.

"He was," she admitted. "I told him when he asked me to marry him—I didn't think he deserved to marry into the supernatural without knowing what he was getting into."

"And how did your husband feel about it?"

"Honestly? It made him uncomfortable when he thought about it, so he didn't," Emma answered, the first touch of bitterness in her sadness. "He knew about it, but I couldn't talk to him about it—or about my work."

Jamie nodded. Emma's work, like that of many registered supernaturals', was intimately tied to her powers. If her husband hadn't been comfortable with her powers, she couldn't have talked to him about work at all.

"So who did you talk to about your powers and work?"

"My co-workers, mainly," she answered a little too quickly.

"Anyone else?" he asked, sensing a nerve.

For a moment, she looked as if she was going to say something, and then Emma shook her head no. Jamie considered pushing further, but if she wasn't willing to say yet, it would only make her a more difficult witness.

"Okay," he accepted with a short sigh, feeling Adrian twitch in the chair next to him. "Can you tell me how you discovered your husband was dead?"

"I always wake up earlier than him, so I thought he was still sleeping that morning," she said very, very slowly. "I got up to make coffee and brought him back a cup, and he didn't respond. I couldn't get him to wake up, and when I realized he had no pulse, I called 911."

"Did you attempt any form of magical healing?"

"I don't have the power or the training," Emma told him. "Dear God, do I wish that I did."

"When did you discover he'd been murdered?" Jamie asked.

"When the lovely young officer showed up at my door yesterday morning to tell me I wasn't allowed to leave the city," she said dryly. "I'm told his heart was crushed by telekinesis," she finished, choking up.

Jamie slid the box of tissues on the table across to her, waiting for a moment while she recovered her composure.

"Had you and your husband argued recently?" he asked her quietly. It was within the realm of possibility for her to have unconsciously used magic fuelled by anger to kill Robert. Extremely unlikely but possible.

"Not over anything *serious*," she exclaimed. "He didn't like one of my friends."

"Why not?" the Inspector asked, but Mrs. Sharp remained silent. Jamie looked askance at her as she shook her head silently, but a quick glance at Mr. Steeple's stony expression suggested he shouldn't demand an answer.

"Was this one of the friends you discussed magic with?" he asked. "Was this friend also a Mage?"

Emma was now shaking her head continuously, a distressed look on her face. Steeple laid a firm hand on her shoulder and turned a glare on Jamie.

"My client is unprepared to answer those questions," he said flatly, and Jamie met the man's gaze for a moment and then glanced back at Emma as a sudden horrifying thought struck him.

"Emma," he said softly, gently, trying to pierce the sudden tears. "I have one last question for you. Are you unwilling to answer my questions... or unable?"

Steeple started to open his mouth to protest, but Emma managed to squeak out one word past the tears.

"Unable." Her voice was much quieter than before, strained with exertion and choked with tears.

"Unable," Jamie repeated, and Emma lifted her tearful gaze to meet his. "Mrs. Sharp, may I examine you with the Sight?" He raised a hand to stop Mr. Steeple speaking until the woman had answered.

Slowly, as if she was fighting to do it, Emma Sharp nodded her consent.

"Mr. Steeple, Inspector Pattakos, I would like you both to confirm that Mrs. Sharp has given her permission," Jamie said formally to the lawyer and his partner.

"She has," Adrian said instantly.

"It appears so," the lawyer said coolly.

With a soft sigh, Jamie released the hold he'd kept on his Sight since starting the interview—the Sight was not something easily turned on or off, and he suspected the men who'd said it couldn't be used in OSPI interviews didn't realize how hard it was *not* to.

Steeple's aura caught Jamie's eye first. Its base was the plain dull gray of a mundane, laced through with colours marking irritation and deep concern. His focus was clearly on his client, and he was worried about her, despite having barely met her. Jamie approved.

He focused his Sight on Mrs. Sharp next, and her aura was a mess. The pale blue marking her as a Mage was almost hidden beneath the swirling hurricane of her emotions. The deep purplish black of grief mixed with the crimson red of anger—which Jamie was pretty sure wasn't directed at him. Grief, loss, anger, fear, pain... all of these had their own colours and their own place in the multicoloured hurricane that swept across her aura.

And in the middle of that hurricane, attached to her aura but not part of it, was exactly what Jamie had feared. Wrapped around her head, her aura was marred by bars of a blue so dark as to be almost black. Forged of power, forged of magic, those bars marked where the will of a powerful Mage had been imposed on Emma Sharp's mind.

Jamie himself could never have cast the spells that bound Emma. Only a Fourth Circle Mage, like Emily Rossum, could even *begin* to manipulate the human mind to that level.

"Mrs. Sharp, Mr. Steeple," he said finally. "Your mind has been affected," he said bluntly. "I suspect that whatever you have been blocked from speaking about is extremely important to the truth behind your husband's murder.

"I need to consult with one of my colleagues," he continued. He couldn't break the spell alone, but depending on Inspector Lager's level of skill and power, it was *possible* they could do it together. "We may be able to break the spell, but there is some risk to you, and you *must* consent," he told Emma, to an almost imperceptible approving nod from the lawyer. "If you are prepared to take on the risk, I will consult with the other Mage in this office and then set up an appointment with you for the attempt."

Emma nodded, still clearly struggling against the power of the spell. "Anything to find who killed my Robert," she said through her tears.

———

JAMIE FOUND INSPECTOR LAGER, the LA office's other Mage, in the Thaumaturgy Lab on the second floor. The room showed the inherent contradiction of its nature. The floor was plain white tile, the walls painted the same institutional color. Multiple cameras were set up to capture everything occurring in the room, feeding to a small server rack along one wall with three workstations set up.

The frame of the room was a perfectly modern forensics lab. And then... there was a black wrought-iron pentagram mounted in the floor. A pair of taxidermied ravens separated the workstation monitors. A Native American dreamcatcher, clearly handmade with real wolf's fur and bear's teeth and easily six feet across, hung on the wall across from the server rack. Even from the door, Jamie was sure that the store cabinet was heavier on depleted uranium dust and formaldehyde than "eye of newt," but he suspected the reptile parts were in there too.

Violet Lager looked up as he stepped into the quiet room. The Mage was probably in her late forties, graying early and heavy with the kind of weight no amount of exercise could ever clear away. Her aura ached with a bone-deep weariness and marked her as a Second Circle Initiate Mage—more experienced than Jamie, clearly, but magically weaker.

"Inspector Lager," Jamie greeted her, turning his most charming smile on the older woman and offering his hand.

"You would be Inspector Riley," she said coldly, ignoring the smile and extended hand. "Were you looking for me or to use the lab?"

"Looking for you," he told her, letting his hand hang out for a moment before dropping it back to his side. "I wanted to discuss sharing lab time so we didn't get in each other's way, and I have a case I'm going to need your help with."

A certain degree of stiffness seemed to go out of Lager's shoulders, and she turned away from Jamie to check on the bench she'd been working at. There was a tiny flash of magic, and then she turned back.

"That should hold for a few hours," she told Jamie. "Pull up a chair."

There were four cheap rolling office chairs in the room. One had taken some kind of blade through half of its back at one point, but all of them were structurally intact.

"If you're in the middle of something, I can come back later," Jamie offered.

"That won't be necessary, Inspector," Lager told him. "I'm not used to anyone other than me using the lab, though I did know you were joining us."

"You were here first. I'm perfectly willing to let you know when I need the lab and work around your schedule," the new Inspector told her and earned a flash of a smile through the older woman's weariness.

"I've got a few forensic cases and tests ongoing, so I'd actually appreciate that," she admitted. "By no means do I need the lab even half of the time, so we shouldn't have too many issues."

After her initial semi-hostility, the smile and ready agreement caught Jamie a bit off guard, and he paused for a moment to regroup his thoughts.

"You said you had a case you would need my help on?" she asked. "I have a lot of files on the go at once—until we can get you up to speed so you can take over some of the forensic duties, that's all sitting on my plate."

"I hope to get up to speed fast," Jamie assured her. "But this is something I can't do alone. I just finished interviewing Emma Sharp—the Mage whose husband was murdered—and *someone* has set up blocks on her mind. I suspect whatever's behind them is relevant to the case," he finished drily. "But that kind of mental manipulation is way out of my depth."

Lager nodded slowly and turned to eye the dreamcatcher on the wall. "Out of mine too," she admitted. "Creating that is... Fourth Circle magic. Even the two of us working ritual magic together couldn't do it."

"I know," Jamie told her. "But in my experience, it's easier to break things than build them. I *think* I can find the fault lines in the spell with the Sight."

"You're right that it should be easier to break than build," she agreed, somewhat distracted, and gestured at the dreamcatcher. "That will also help—it was a gift from my original teacher. It blocks mental or visual scrying of this room—it would weaken any such spell on a person who came in here."

"So if we work together, we should be able to break the spell on her?" Jamie asked, optimistic about the case.

"We should," Lager said slowly. "I'll need the rest of the day to wrap up a couple of things I have on the go in here that could interfere, and then you and I will need most of tomorrow to set up the room for the ritual. Have her—and her lawyer, I suppose—come by tomorrow evening, and we should be ready."

For a moment, Jamie was irritated by Lager taking charge but then mentally laughed at himself. It was his case, and he was the stronger Mage, but *she* had a far better idea what they were actually going to do!

"I'll get in touch with her and set it up."

6

MORNING SAW Jamie better rested than he had been in some time. It was as much the psychological effect of finally getting to work, he was sure, but it still helped.

Despite his late night, he was at the office and the thaumaturgic lab before Lager was. He spent the time opening up the small leather bag of crystals that made up his ritual toolkit. He didn't have nearly enough for any major working—hence his need for a crystal supplier—but he had five perfect six-inch points to mark the corners of the working pentagram.

"What's this I hear about you pulling Lager off of her duties?" Karina Wilson demanded harshly from the door, reminding Jamie that the station chief was the only person other than the two mages with access to the thaumaturgy lab. "And why is Mrs. Sharp not under arrest? You should have all the evidence to charge her by now."

Jamie straightened from where he'd been kneeling over the quartz crystals and faced his boss.

"I have interviewed Mrs. Sharp," he told her quietly. "I have interviewed her neighbours, the only people around when Mr. Sharp died. I have also reviewed the autopsy report. So, if Mrs. Sharp was the murderer, I agree that I would have enough evidence to arrest her."

"Of course she murdered him," Wilson told him bluntly, maneuvering her bulk carefully around the iron pentagram in the middle of the lab. "He was murdered with magic. His wife is a Mage. Who else would have done it?"

"Ma'am," Jamie answered, pausing for a moment to wonder if he could explain this without getting into trouble. "As I said, I reviewed the autopsy report. I know exactly how Robert Sharp died. To kill a man the way he was killed is a complex piece of magic, requiring a significant degree of power, an extremely precise degree of control, and detailed knowledge of human anatomy."

"Anatomy?" Wilson demanded, latching on to what clearly seemed out of place to her.

"Very little magic is 'plug and play,'" Jamie told her, hoping his patient explanation wasn't going to irritate her further. "Mrs. Sharp couldn't simply cast a spell to 'kill him without being obvious.' Magic, with some exceptions, requires more direction than that. Whoever cast this spell needed to know *exactly* how a human heart worked."

"Given some time to research human anatomy, I could have cast the spell that killed Robert," Jamie continued. "It would have taken me two or three *hours*, with constant access to a restrained or unconscious victim. Inspector Lager—" He chose to presume that Wilson knew he was a more powerful mage than Lager. "—could *not*. Mrs. Sharp is significantly weaker than Lager.

"To cast this spell would have required specialized mundane knowledge, significant magical power, and skill and training with that power. Emma Sharp possesses none of these things—nor, from my interviews, does she have a reason to acquire them. Of means, motive, and opportunity, she only had opportunity."

"And how does this explain pulling Inspector Lager from her other duties for a full day?" Wilson demanded, dropping the argument over Sharp completely.

"Mrs. Sharp's mind has been magically affected," Jamie explained. "She has been prevented from speaking about certain matters—and, I believe, certain people. The only reason I can think of to block her from speaking about someone would be if they were involved in Robert's murder.

"To break this kind of magical conditioning will require both Lager and me and a full day of preparation and a ritual spell, as neither of us could break it on our own."

"And you believe that this is worth the effort?" Wilson demanded, and Jamie wasn't sure if she was condemning him or honestly asking.

"If it works, it will provide a very clear lead and allow us to catch Robert Sharp's murderer," he answered slowly. "So yes, I think it's worth it."

The station chief harrumphed and then glanced up as Lager arrived, the older Mage looking at the pair in the lab questioningly.

"Then I'll leave you to it," she told them.

Lager stepped comfortably over the pentagram as Wilson skirted it on her way out of the room, exchanging a polite nod with the station chief, and paused by Jamie to glance down at the quartz points.

"I use feathers," she told him. "These are impressive. Where did you get them?"

"Washington," Jamie told her. "They were expensive but worth it."

Lager quickly glanced over her shoulder as the door shut behind them. "What was that about?"

"Chief Wilson wanted an update on how I was handling the case," he told her.

"Well, then we should get on with handling this part of it."

———

FOR THE NEXT EIGHT HOURS, Jamie and Violet cleaned the lab, packing away everything unnecessary for the ritual. Jamie placed his quartz points at the tips of the pentagram, and Violet matched each of them with a feather from a different bird, starting at the top, with eagle, horned owl, peregrine, albatross, and raven.

All of the modern computing equipment was covered in plain black cloths kept in the room for just this purpose. Omicron often combined technology and magic, but for something like this, restricting the room to items of magic and simplicity was wisest.

By mid-afternoon, the two Mages had killed the artificial lights and set up large three-wick candles in each corner of the room. Continuing by candlelight, they fully purified the room with incense, salt water, and power.

Finally, everything was ready, just in time for their subject to arrive. Lily led Mrs. Sharp and Mr. Steeple up to the lab, where Jamie let them and Adrian in.

"Inspector Pattakos, Mr. Steeple, we'll need you to sit out of the way," Jamie told them. "You are here as observers, and if you interfere, you could cause Mrs. Sharp injury."

Jamie watched until the two men had settled themselves down against one of the walls, away from the dreamcatcher, which glowed, ever so slightly, in the dark room, and turned to Mrs. Sharp.

"Mrs. Sharp, once again, I must warn you that there is a distinct risk to both your physical and mental health from this process," he told her softly. "Neither I nor Inspector Lager are fully qualified to carry out this ritual, though we are confident in our ability to do so. Nonetheless, the choice is yours."

"Call me Emma, Inspector," the grieving woman told him. "Like I told you before, I want this... I *need* this. I *need* to talk about..." She winced as she touched on the subjects blocked to her.

Steeple gave Jamie one firm nod, acknowledging he'd heard Emma's confirmation before Jamie could ask.

"Then take a seat in the center of the pentagram," Jamie told her.

Obediently, the widow stepped into the center of the room, careful even in the flickering light of the candles to avoid the crystals and feathers. She took a cross-legged seat in the center area of the iron five-pointed star.

Jamie exchanged a look with Lager and took a deep breath. To his Sight, the whole room glowed with their preparations, a gentle construct of light and breath including the dreamcatcher, the pentagram, and the two Mages.

Closing his mind to the outside world, he reached for his Power and linked it into the spell construct. A moment later, he felt Lager's Power join in, focusing through his Sight. They'd decided before that he would be the lead, as his Sight was stronger than hers, if anemic by any objective standard.

Using the construct and her Power as a guide, Jamie's Sight settled on Emma, ruthlessly cutting everything else out of his field of view.

Emma shivered as the construct settled around her like a gentle blanket. To Jamie's eyes, it accentuated her aura, picking out the differences, showing her nervousness and courage like bright stars, and picking out the indigo contrast of the chains on her mind against a background of energy.

Jamie stepped into the pentagram at last and loomed over Emma. Lager stepped in on the other side, and they faced each other over Emma's sitting figure. Tendrils of Jamie's Power wove over Emma's aura, touching, weighing. There was strength in this woman, buried under the grief of the moment. She was weakened, as much of her strength had been founded on her love, but somehow he knew she would overcome.

That made the marks on her aura dirtier somehow. It wasn't just the spell that bound her from thinking or speaking, Jamie saw now. Deep scars cut into her aura, into her *Power*. Someone had touched her aura, much as Jamie did now, but had twisted it—damaged it, trying to achieve some eldritch goal.

Some of the scars marked her Power, twisted remainders of some attempt to grow it, to strengthen the magic she commanded. Others marked the surface of her deep, abiding love for her husband. Those scars, in their own way, were both shallower and deeper than those on her magic, as if the twisting had been harsher, but her love had resisted it.

Even if Jamie had known *how*, these scars were too old, too metaphorically scabbed over, for him to heal, so his tendrils of power withdrew from the blue light of Emma's core.

They touched the dark-blue bars of Power locked in an iron cage around her mind. Words and symbols flowed along those indigo bars, he saw now. Those words and symbols would mean something to Emma's unconscious mind but nothing to anyone else—including the spell's creator.

Gently, carefully, with every ounce of the clarity and power their construct and Lager's aid gave him, Jamie wrapped his tendril of power around one end of the first of these bars. With a deep breath, he lifted it, pulling it apart from her aura.

After several tense seconds, it lifted, the spell beginning to release her.

———

THE RITUAL SEEMED to only take a few minutes to Jamie, as he gently pulled back each of the bars from Emma's aura. Even knowing that time inevitably compressed like this, he was stunned when he and Lager finally stepped out of the circle and he checked his watch. Over three hours had passed.

Adrian had been watching and passed both Lager and Jamie bottles of water as soon as they were outside the circle. Steeple, holding a third bottle, glanced questioningly at Jamie. Jamie nodded, gesturing for the man to give it to Emma.

"We're done. Whoever cast this had tried to do more before," he said quietly. "If he hadn't, he wouldn't have had the base from which to work."

A moment of quiet passed in the candlelit lab.

"I think I can answer your questions now," Emma Sharp told the OSPI officers, unsteadily lifting herself to her feet with Steeple's help. "Can I get a chair?"

Lager was already pulling one of the lab's much-abused rolling chairs out before Emma asked, and wordlessly passed it to the woman. She gratefully sat, looking up at the others.

"I'm not sure I want to tell this more than once," she admitted. "Can you get a recorder or something?"

Jamie glanced at Lager, who nodded and pointed to a drawer in one of the room's cabinets. Adrian pulled the device out as Lager blew out the candles and turned the lights back on.

"Do you have some way of confirming I'm telling the truth?" Emma asked as everyone gathered around her again. "I think it might save us some time later."

"I am trained in the use of the Omicron standard Truth spell,"

Jamie admitted with a cautious glance at Steeple. "I am not certain I can use it without a court order. Mr. Steeple?"

Jamie was pretty sure he *could* use the spell at the request of an interview subject, but he wanted the Omicron Defender's opinion on record as well.

"You can use it with the explicit permission and voluntary agreement of the interviewee," the lawyer confirmed. "I confirm for the record," he told the now-active recorder, "that Mrs. Emma Sharp has knowingly and voluntarily requested the Truth Spell."

"It's not as simple as knowing if you're lying or not," Jamie told her. "The spell is, in its own way, as harsh an intrusion as what we removed. It will prevent you from saying anything you know or believe to be a lie."

It was an incredibly complex piece of magic, one Jamie could only use because it had been subject to more analysis than any other spell in the history of Omicron and standardized down to the point that it had court-admissible uses.

Emma nodded sharply. "Do it," she ordered.

Jamie picked up one of his quartz points, quickly cleared it of the remnants of the previous spell, and then charged it for the Truth Spell. It took him several minutes, and he was grateful for the chair to sink into when it was done.

"Hold the crystal, and the spell is in effect," he told Emma, who took the quartz point in her hands. Bone-deep weariness struck him, almost all of his energy expended by now. But he still had a duty to fulfil.

Emma breathed deeply, steeling herself, and began.

"You asked if there was anyone other than my co-workers I discussed the supernatural with. There was one other man.

"His company came to us for supernatural consulting, as he wanted a second opinion on an assessment he'd made himself—he was a Mage but the only one in his practice.

"When the contract was done, he and I kept in touch. It was nice to talk about all of this stuff to someone who wasn't a co-worker or"—she gestured at the two OSPI officers—"an Omicron suit. He was sympathetic, sweet, extremely knowledgeable about magic," she told them.

"After a few months, we met up for coffee and continued discussions in person.

"Discussions eventually turned into experimentation. He believed he could induce a trial for me, increase my power levels. God forgive me, I agreed. We did a number of rituals over a few weeks, with no success.

"Robert… didn't like him. He figured he was after more than just a partner in magic. We argued about it a few times, but he'd never tried anything, so I figured it was just jealousy. Two weeks ago, after another failed attempt to raise my power, he tried to seduce me. I was weak. I almost let him."

The scars on her aura told Jamie the truth about that weakness. Her "friend" had been spending as much time trying to break down her love for her husband as increase her power.

"I confessed everything to Robert," she continued, choking back tears. "If I'd ever doubted he loved me before, I never would again. He wasn't angry at me. He even understood why I needed someone to talk to about magic. And he *asked* me not to see him again. Didn't yell, didn't demand, didn't order—he *asked*.

"How could I say no? *I* didn't want to see him again. So I called him. And I told him never to contact me again, that I couldn't trust him. He said that I would contact him. That I'd see the light soon enough." Choked by tears, Emma fell silent, her face resting on the crystal in her hands.

"And a week later, Robert died," Jamie said quietly. "Who was he, Emma?"

He knew that she'd spoken in generics due to the remnants of the spell, but he needed a name.

"Dr. Alex Donovan."

The only sound in the silent room was Adrian's sharp intake of breath.

$$7$$

Adrian waited until Jamie had finished taking his immediate notes and seen Emma Sharp and her lawyer out of the office. But when Jamie returned to his office with the recorder, having promised Lager he'd clean up the lab in the morning, he found his partner sitting on his desk, eyeing him.

"You don't even know who Dr. Donovan is, do you?" Adrian asked.

"Other than the name on the top of my current list of suspects, no," Jamie admitted. "And seeing as how it's after eleven at night and I just led a multi-hour ritual, I don't intend to find out more until the morning," he continued.

"Dr. Alex Donovan is one of exactly *twenty-three* recognized Doctors of Thaumaturgical Medicine in the United States," his partner told him.

"So he would definitely have the knowledge and skill to pull this off," Jamie said with a sigh.

"Jamie, this is the man the *Committee of Thirteen* goes to for medical care," Adrian said sharply. "He's wealthier than Croesus and is owed more favours by the government than *God*. There's no way he'd risk all of that over a moderately pretty forty-something woman!"

Jamie sighed. "How long have you been a cop, Adrian?" he asked.

"Long enough to know that pursuing this is a bad idea!"

"In your time as a cop, when was the last time someone was *logical* about the kind of passions that drive them to murder?"

"That's not the *point!*" Jamie's partner snapped. "Honestly, I think this is some fantasy about the most well-known supernatural in America she's managed to convince herself is true!"

"Even if she only *subconsciously* knew it to be false, she still couldn't say it under the truth spell," Jamie told him tiredly.

"All you have is one woman's testimony!"

"And I will look to see if I can find anything to corroborate it," Jamie snapped back at him. "In the morning. But I will *not* refuse to charge a murderer because he is politically powerful!"

———

Jamie walked into Adrian's office just before lunch the next day and dropped two sets of papers on his desk. His partner looked up from the email he was reading with a closed look on his face.

"What's this?"

"This"—Jamie tapped the topmost paper—"is a fax from the LAPD. It's a speeding ticket issued to Dr. Donovan the night Robert Sharp was murdered—in the Sharps' neighbourhood. The good doctor's mansion is on the other side of the city, according to his Registered Supernatural file."

Adrian looked the fax over and set it to the side. "And this?" he asked, looking at the internet printout underneath.

"It's an article released by Dr. Donovan about three weeks ago on methods and rituals for inducing trials and increasing the power levels of First and Second Circle Mages," Jamie told him. He'd actually taken a few tips from the article for his own studies, not that he'd tell Adrian that. "He repeatedly mentions his 'lovely and ever-willing' assistant and volunteer, whom he doesn't name."

Adrian skimmed the first page of the article and then dropped the papers on his desk and looked across them at Jamie.

"I can't convince you to drop this, can I?"

"Everything I have says Alex Donovan murdered Robert Sharp," Jamie told him grimly. "He had the means. We *know* he had the medical knowledge for as specific a method as was used, and the power. The man cures cancer for a living, for crying out loud! He also, it seems, had the opportunity—we now *know* he was in the neighbourhood."

"And you think his motive was jealousy?"

"Can you really say it doesn't add up?" Jamie asked Adrian, who sighed and shook his head.

"It does," he confessed. "But this is a political shitstorm you're stirring up. You know that, right?"

"That's for the courts to deal with at this point," Jamie told him. "I'm going to need your support to get a warrant—I've been on the job a *week*. No judge is going to sign off on a warrant for this man for me, no matter my evidence."

"Jamie, I don't want to touch this with a ten-foot pole!" Adrian told him. "Get your name or face in Donovan's mind, and even if you succeed in putting him away, your career has a good chance of being *over*."

"We're not talking about just putting him away, Adrian," Jamie reminded him. "This is life and death. Life for Aggravated Psyche Invasion—and the chair for Thaumaturgical Murder in the First. I'll make the arrest, keep you out of whatever cameras come up," he promised, to Adrian's shocked expression. "But we need to bring him in."

"All right," Adrian whispered.

———

Despite his hesitation, Adrian managed to get the appointment set up with the Los Angeles Omicron Justice for later that day. While his partner was on the phone with various flunkies, Jamie wrote up the affidavit summarizing their findings.

They met again at four, an hour before they were supposed to meet the Justice, and Adrian reviewed the affidavit.

"Bobby is *not* going to believe I wrote this," he said sourly after reading it. "Which may be for the best—it reads like it came from a textbook, Jamie."

"Are you surprised?" Jamie asked in response. "A textbook is the only place I've *seen* one of these."

Adrian shook his head. "It'll do. Don't worry. Bobby—Justice Robert Stuart, sorry—is just used to us throwing together the affidavits in a rush." The Senior Inspector checked his watch and shook his head. "Let's go."

The Supernatural State Court of California was on the thirty-fourth floor of a downtown skyscraper, listed on the directory as simply SSC OF CALIFORNIA. Access was via elevator into a reception area sealed with bulletproof glass.

"Inspectors Pattakos and Riley?" the primly clad blonde receptionist asked when they approached her desk in the empty waiting area. "You're His Excellency's last appointment; everyone else has cleared out for the day. Go on through, second door on the left."

The second door on the left of the plushly-appointed "courthouse" turned out to be a small hearing room. Four chairs faced a single table, behind which sat an aging man with steel-gray hair and a dark-blue eyepatch.

"You've signed and sworn the affidavit?" Robert Stuart asked gruffly.

"Yes, Your Excellency," Jamie and Adrian said, almost in unison.

"Let me see it," he said.

Jamie dropped the short document on the Justice's desk. Stuart waved the two Omicron agents to their seats as he skimmed the handful of pages.

He sighed.

"If there was anyone in the world I would not have believed this of, it would have been Alex Donovan," the judge said quietly. "But you've given me probable cause, so I will suspend my personal judgment until a court of law can decide."

He pulled a manila folder across the desk and extracted a sheet of paper. He skimmed it, signed it, and then did the same to a second sheet before sliding them across the table to Jamie.

"Warrants to search Dr. Donovan's house and to arrest his person," the Justice told them simply. "I am sustaining the charges of Psyche Invasion and Thaumaturgical Murder, both premeditated and in the first degree. Bring him in, gentlemen."

"Yes, sir."

8

———————

Jamie stopped at the black government sedan Adrian was driving and looked at his partner. "We have his address and the warrants," he told the Senior Inspector. "We should get this over with, before Donovan can get a hint of this from his contacts and make a run for it."

Adrian sighed.

"I still think this is a damn stupid idea, kid," he said flatly. "But if we're going to do it, then we should do it fast."

"You can stay in the car," Jamie offered, dropping into the passenger seat. "If he's half as connected as you think he is, Donovan'll figure his connections can get him out of this. He'll come quietly."

His partner didn't answer for several minutes, the only sign of his mood the sharp cuts and turns he made as he drove the black sedan through the streets of Los Angeles. Jamie tightened his grip on the handle of his door as Adrian made a particularly tight turn between two taxis, onto a highway heading towards the wealthy suburb Dr. Donovan lived in.

"Sure, you can take the bullet for this if you're so goddamn self-sacrificing," he finally told Jamie. "I'll be in the car with the safety off in case something goes to shit."

Jamie nodded wordlessly. It was pointless to tell Adrian that if something went "to shit," Alex Donovan was a Third Circle Master Mage to Jamie's Second Circle. It was unlikely Jamie could get into the house in time to make a difference in the ensuing duel.

He corrected his sentence slightly as they pulled up to Dr. Donovan's home. The sprawling red-brick villa was no mere "house." Two wings stretched back into a neatly-landscaped orchard of apple trees, and the driveway delivered them to a grand entranceway.

Jamie exchanged a nod with his partner and checked that the strap was off on his shoulder holster, freeing the silver-loaded sidearm there, and approached the house, warrants in hand.

The late-spring sun was setting behind him, and the smell of the blossoms in the apples trees hit him like a wall. Enjoying the smell, Jamie smiled slightly as he rang the doorbell on the mansion's front door.

Thirty seconds later, he was debating between ringing the doorbell again or forcing his way into the home the way his warrants authorized him to do. Before he could do permanent damage to the front of the building, the door finally opened.

The young man in the neat suit who stood behind it was clearly not Alex Donovan. He looked Jamie up and down, a slight sneer to his lips.

"I'm sorry, Dr. Donovan is not accepting visitors and has no appointments tonight," the butler told Jamie.

"Is Dr. Donovan home?" Jamie asked, calmly ignoring the supercilious sneer.

"That is irrelevant," the young man replied, his sneer expanding. "Whatever you are selling, we do not want it."

"The question is relevant," Jamie told the butler, overriding his attempt to continue speaking, "because it decides whether I am showing you my warrant to search the house or my warrant to arrest Dr. Donovan."

He'd opened the black leather badge case with his OSPI badge before the butler had finished the first sentence, but the servant only now *saw* what the man on his doorstep was holding. Someone personally working for a registered Doctor of Thaumaturgical Medicine would know what OSPI was, and the butler's eyes showed his realization.

"I am Inspector Jamie Riley, OSPI, and I am here to arrest Dr. Donovan," Jamie told the no-longer-sneering man. "I will repeat myself once: is he home?"

"He is," the butler, now white under his Californian tan, squeaked.

"Where is he?"

"His office," the butler answered quickly. "Take the double doors on the right, fourth door on the left. He never closes it."

"Do you live here?" Jamie asked gently, and the servant shook his head. "Go home," the Inspector ordered. "You're not being paid enough for this."

With a shake only perceptible to Jamie's Sight, Dr. Donovan's assistant vanished out the front door, barely squeezing around the Inspector.

Jamie drew his wards and Sight around himself and entered the home of a murderer.

———

THE MANSION WAS LUXURIOUS, richly appointed in dark hardwood flooring and furniture. A stereotypical wide marble staircase led up to the second floor, and an antique grandfather clock ticked away against the wall by the double doors the butler had directed Jamie to. Only the dark metallic silhouettes of a trio of security cameras looked as if they belonged to the modern day.

An eerie silence filled the grand house. For all of its scale and grandeur, it was empty, and even Jamie's Sight picked up only a few touches of personal feeling. In a world that always faintly glittered under his gaze, Donovan's mansion was sterile.

Something about it made him nervous, and he drew his service automatic as he nudged the double doors quietly open. The hallway beyond continued the themes of antique clocks and hardwood. A wall-mounted cuckoo clock faced the open fourth door of the hallway, its mechanisms still running.

Jamie made it three quarters of the way of the way to the open door to Donovan's office before the cuckoo clock went off.

A carved wooden hawk burst out of the gaudily painted wooden doors of the clock, rotated on the end of its support to face Jamie, and screamed, *"Intruder! Intruder!"*

With a muttered curse, Jamie finally saw the alarm spell wrapped around the clock. It bellowed, *"Intruder!"* a third time and then stopped as Dr. Alex Donovan stepped out into the hallway.

The handful of seconds it had taken the doctor to come out were enough for Jamie to have his badge open in one hand and his gun raised in the other, unwaveringly focused on the doctor.

Donovan was a tall, dark-haired man in a navy-blue suit and looked much younger than the forty-odd Jamie knew him to be. Magic had smoothed away the impacts of aging, leaving the man looking in his early twenties.

His confident demeanor suggested the lie to that, and his eyes screamed it. They were ice blue, cold, and flat as he stared Jamie down.

"What is the meaning of…" he began before Jamie cut him off.

"OSPI," Jamie said flatly. "Hands up."

Shocked into silence, the suited doctor obeyed.

"Doctor Alex Donovan?" the Inspector demanded, and the doctor nodded sharply.

"You are under arrest for the murder by magic of Robert Sharp," Jamie told him. "You have the right to remain silent. You have the right to an attorney. Due to the circumstances of the charges, one *will* be provided for you by the Courts. Do you understand these rights?"

"Do *you* understand who I *am*?" Donovan demanded, lowering his hands slightly but keeping them visible. "I'd suggest you get out of my house and pursue real criminals, not figments."

"I repeat," Jamie told him determinedly, "you are under arrest. Do you understand these rights as I have read them to you?" Keeping the gun trained on Donovan, he slid his other hand into a pocket and unclipped the pair of silver-coated handcuffs he carried.

Donovan looked at the cuffs contemptuously.

"Do you know who I *am*?" he asked again. "I don't know what delusion you're operating under, Inspector, but I will not submit to this indignity." He dropped his hands completely, placing them on his hips as he glared at the agent.

Jamie stepped forward, keeping the gun trained on the man's center of mass.

"You are not being asked," he told Donovan flatly. "Put your hands back up and turn around."

The tiny smile that suddenly flickered over the doctor's lips was the only warning Jamie had before the man stepped back slightly and said: "No."

A moment later, a blast wave of telekinetic force threw Jamie back down the hallway.

———

Very few spells had any level of complexity—they did one thing, with no criteria or thought to them. The first complex spell Jamie had ever learned was a ward that required a fixed location and a number of quartz crystal points. It recognized threats to the protected area semi-autonomously and blocked them.

The most recent complex spell Jamie had learned was a modified version of that same ward—shorter term but mobile and linked to a single anchor.

The silver Sindarin brooch from his mother flashed hot, felt even through the shirt he'd pinned it to, as the spell anchored to it recognized the attack. As the blast hit Jamie, the ward split it, deflecting much of its force away from him.

The dark-panelled walls around him splintered with the force of Donovan's strike, but the ward saved Jamie from an attack that should have killed him. He landed awkwardly, grabbing a wall for balance with the hand that had held the cuffs a moment before.

Before Donovan realized that Jamie had survived, the Inspector leveled his gun back down the hall and opened fire.

The first heavy silver round missed completely, shattering the antique hawk cuckoo clock into pieces. The second clipped Donovan's shoulder, and the Mage stumbled as the silver disturbed whatever spell he was working on.

The third hit the ward Donovan finally managed to raise and was deflected aside into the wall. The fourth shot had barely left the barrel when a bolt of flame flashed across the hallway. The heat and pain, even through the ward, forced Jamie to drop the gun.

Instead, he conjured a shield of force, interposing against the next bolt of flame. He intercepted a third bolt and flicked it aside. In the back of his mind, he sensed the fire hit the antiqued-wood walls and ignite them, but he focused on the Mage before him.

Dodging sideways, he smashed back at Donovan with a hammer blow of pure force. The doctor staggered backwards then tossed another bolt of flame at Jamie as he ducked back into his office.

Tossing the bolt into the walls of the house, Jamie charged after Donovan, weaving a stronger hammer of force as he did. Turning the corner into the office, he unleashed his strike. So did Donovan.

Jamie's shield collapsed under the sheer power of the Third Circle Master's strike. A lance of pure force, it struck Jamie dead center in the chest, where even his wards could only do so much. He never registered leaving the ground, but he *did* register smashing through the remnants of the cuckoo clock—and the wall behind it!

Bruised and battered, Jamie rolled back up to his feet, facing back into the hallway. Donovan had only just regained his own feet from the shattered ruins of his desk. Blood streamed down the Mage's face, distorting it into an inhuman monster's.

"Hurry up and die like your precious mundane," Donovan snapped at Jamie. "He was a mewling weasel, an anchor dragging down one of ours. His death was a blessing to us all."

Jamie's answer was wordless. He stretched out with his magic and tore the roof above Donovan down. Plaster, wood, electrical cabling, and a solid oak armoire came crashing down through the ceiling, filling the room and covering Donovan in debris.

It bought Jamie precious seconds to stabilize and re-anchor his wards, seconds that saved his life when Donovan emerged from the debris, his magic lifting it all into a tornado of flaming pieces of house that he threw at Jamie.

Jamie's ward-aided dodge got him beyond the reach of the debris tornado but crashed him into a burning wall that collapsed under his weight. Fire singed his clothes and skin as he struggled out of the wreckage, realizing at last that the wing of the house was on fire—and starting to come down around them.

Donovan didn't seem to have realized that, though he casually tore a wall out of the way with magic as he bore down on Jamie.

"Shame, really," he said almost conversationally. "These days, I can recognize a Trial in someone. If I let you live, you'd be proof of some of my theories. Oh well." He shrugged.

Jamie felt the lance of power, strong enough to punch through his wards and kill him before he could escape the broken wall he was pinned in, leave Donovan's hands.

A blur passed between the two Mages, and the strike shattered, scattered by a mobile ward far stronger than any Jamie carried.

Jamie barely saw Adrian Pattakos as his Empowered partner joined the fight. The Inspector had a silver chain wrapped around one hand and his service automatic in the other. Donovan threw another bolt of force directly at Adrian, who interposed the silver chain.

The chain fizzled the spell. Jamie saw, now he had a moment to breathe, that the ward around it was small but extremely powerful—it gave Adrian a shield on one hand that could stop almost any spell.

Three more times, Adrian blocked spells, moving with blinding speed to intercept spells that even Jamie barely saw as he pulled himself to his feet, coughing in the rapidly gathering smoke.

Adrian dodged a new spell and opened fire on Donovan. Three shots rang out, deafeningly loud even over the growing noise of the fire around them, but each was deflected by Donovan's wards.

The Mage charged forwards, words of power wrapping spells around his flesh to Jamie's Sight. Donovan sped up, almost as fast as Adrian, and the duel became a blur. More gunshots rang out. More spells were deflected.

Only a moment more passed before a bolt of mage-fire smashed into Adrian despite the shield. The Inspector snarled, a wound that should have killed him barely marking his skin after destroying his suit, and then returned fire.

More rounds bounced from Donovan's ward. Adrian's supernatural speed and toughness were keeping him alive, but he couldn't hurt Donovan either.

With a deep breath, coughing against the smoke, Jamie summoned his magic and his Sight once more. This time, he didn't attack Donovan —he attacked Donovan's *ward*.

He was almost too late. As he started, Donovan hit Adrian with a blast wave of force that threw the Inspector through the wall of the office the duel had started in. Accompanied by a burst of flaming debris, Adrian landed on the landscaped gardens.

Donovan took a moment to laugh at the battered Inspectors. In that moment, Jamie dug under the glittering pieces making up the doctor's ward in his Sight and pulled.

The ward shattered. Stunned, the Mage spun, the same spells he'd woven to fight Adrian speeding him around to face Jamie.

He hadn't completed the turn or re-raised his wards when Jamie loosed the same lance of force Donovan had used back at the doctor.

Dr. Alex Donovan's chest was crushed instantly, killing him before he finished turning.

Jamie hauled himself slowly out of the burning rubble of the north wing of Donovan's house and used a careful telekinesis spell to pick his gun up as he exited the burning mansion. Fire-engine sirens rang out in the distance as he stiffly crossed to where Adrian was sitting on the lawn. The Senior Inspector hadn't bothered to stand up after Donovan died.

"You look like you've been thrown through four or five burning walls," Adrian observed as Jamie dropped himself on the ground next to him.

"Only three," Jamie replied, an involuntary chuckle escaping him. "You called the fire engines?"

His partner nodded. "And the boss," Adrian admitted. "A cleanup team is on its way—somehow, I didn't figure either of us was going to be up to making up stories to tell the fire department."

"For once, the truth is acceptable," Jamie told him grimly.

"Donovan attacked a Federal Agent, and the house was ignited in the ensuing fight. He was killed resisting arrest."

"I didn't exactly mention *that* to the boss," his partner told him. "Up to the point where I got in there, I was planning on taking him alive."

"Hell, I can't tell you when I *stopped* intending to take him alive," Jamie said. "I expected him to come quietly."

"So did I, or I'd have backed you up when you went in," Adrian agreed, glancing aside from Jamie's gaze.

At that moment, the first of the fire trucks pulled up, saving Jamie's partner from having to say more.

The two approached the leader of the firefighters as they began to set up, and Adrian flashed his FBI credentials.

"We were serving an arrest warrant," he explained quickly. "The resident resisted arrest, and the house was ignited in the firefight that followed. I don't believe there's anyone alive in the house."

The fire captain nodded sharply and then turned away to give orders to his team. Hoses were unravelled and run up the lawn in quick, efficient motions. Water began to spray over the burning debris of the north wing as the firefighters began to contain the fire.

A black van and a dark-green sedan arrived shortly after the second fire truck. The van disgorged four suited agents, men from the Omicron Supernatural Concealment Office—the "clean-up teams" that made sure supernatural affairs stayed out of the public eye.

The dark-green sedan after the OSCO men turned out to be Wilson's personal car. The heavyset OSPI station chief exchanged a quick conversation with the OSCO men, and then they parted ways, the OSCO men to speak to the firefighters, and Wilson to meet her two agents.

Jamie watched her approach with apprehension and then pulled his badge and gun out. Holding them together, he offered them to her wordlessly.

"What's this?" she demanded, glaring at him.

"Donovan is dead," Jamie said flatly. "OSPI policy is a one-week minimum suspension for any agent who kills, well, anyone."

"He attacked you?" Wilson said gruffly, nodding and taking the badge and gun as she did.

"When I tried to handcuff him, yes, ma'am," Jamie replied. He kept his gaze focused just past Wilson's shoulders.

"Adrian?" she demanded.

"I was outside when the fight began," the senior agent admitted. "We were expecting Donovan to come quietly; there was no reason for him to fight."

"I would agree with that assessment," Wilson said, continuing to glare suspiciously at Jamie. "I'll get a forensics team down here to work with OSCO ASAP. Don't think of this as a holiday, Inspector," she continued to Jamie. "A week on the job and already suspended?" She sniffed dismissively but otherwise let the comment stand on its own.

She turned away, pulling a cellphone from her purse as she stalked towards the OSCO cleanup team.

"Come on," Adrian said to Jamie. "Let's get you back to your car." He paused for a moment and shrugged. "For what it's worth, I don't think you're going to be off more than a week. It was the right call, Inspector. Well done."

ONSET SERIES

Murder by Magic is a prequel novella to the ONSET series.

ONSET series:
ONSET: To Serve and Protect
ONSET: My Enemy's Enemy
ONSET: Blood of the Innocent
ONSET: Stay of Execution

STARSHIP'S MAGE:
EPISODE ONE

The first episode in the Starship's Mage series

EPISODE 1

"Welcome aboard, Mage Montgomery," the spacer waiting just inside the starship told him. "Captain Michaels is waiting in his office. If you'll follow me, please?"

Damien nodded as he carefully maneuvered himself through the zero-gravity boarding area. Behind him, a short metal boarding tube linked the central hub of the massive rotating rings of Sherwood Prime to the keel of the container ship *Gentle Rains of Summer*. He checked the personal computer wrapped around his left arm as discreetly as he could, making sure he was on time for his job interview with the Captain.

"Our outer ribs are on a low rotation right now, as some of our thrusters are under repair," the crewman warned Damien as he moved toward one of the doors on the outer walls of the main keel. "We're only under about a tenth gee, so watch your step."

"That will be fine," Damien told the man. He watched the spacer move from handhold to handhold up the ladder to the outer keel, and carefully followed suit. If necessary, he was able to control his own motion even in zero gravity, but Mages learned quickly that blatant, unnecessary use of magic didn't make friends.

Damien was shorter and lighter than the spacer, though, so he was slower and more careful with the handholds until they reached far enough out on the rotating outer keel for the pseudo-gravity to kick in. He settled onto his feet with a carefully concealed sigh of relief, straightening out his clothes and unconsciously checking on the gold medallion settled into the hollow of his throat.

The medallion announced to all who saw it that Damien Montgomery had the Gift and was recognized by the Royal Orders and Guilds of the Protectorate of Humanity as a Mage. A member of one of those Orders would also recognize the symbols on it marking him as having completed a degree in Practical Thaumaturgy as well as being a fully qualified Jump Mage.

The last was why he was aboard *Gentle Rains of Summer*. The container ship consisted of a central steady-state keel with the boarding pod at one end and the engines at the other, around which four "outer ribs" rotated to give the living and working spaces a semblance of gravity. She was a wondrous technological creation capable of accelerating at several gravities while carrying up to twelve million tons of fuel and cargo, but it was the silver runes inscribed throughout the interior of her hull that made her a starship. With those runes, a Mage like Damien could jump her up to a light-year in an instant.

"This is the Captain's office," the spacer announced. He knocked on the hatch sharply and then stuck his head in. "The young Mage is here to see you, sir."

"Come in, come in," the man behind the desk said loudly as the spacer gestured Damien into the room. "Montgomery, right?"

"That's right, sir," Damien answered. "I'm here about the junior Ship's Mage position?"

Most starships that could afford it would have two Jump Mages aboard. A Mage was only able to jump so often without using up so much energy as to fatally burn out their brains, so having two aboard would double how fast the ship would move.

"Yes, yes of course," the Captain replied, gesturing for Damien to sit. "I'm Andrew Michaels, Captain of *Gentle Rains of Summer*. I'm afraid I owe you an apology."

Damien took the offered seat, glancing around the Captain's cabin.

It had the lived-in look of somewhere the occupant spent much of their time. The bookshelves, filing cabinet, and desk were all worn green ceramics, and the floating projected terminal on the desk was a model older than Damien himself.

The only "decoration" in the room was a bronze plaque engraved with the silver runes that channeled mana to create magical effects once charged by a Mage.

"An apology?" Damien asked.

"Yes, I'm afraid we couldn't contact you earlier this morning," Michaels told him, to which Damien nodded slowly. Sherwood Prime's internal communications net was oddly spotty for the main orbital dock of a world of two billion souls. "An old friend called me this morning and I've given the Ship's Mage position to her son. I would have let you know in advance, but once we couldn't, I figured I owed you an explanation in person."

Damien swallowed. "Thank you, sir," he said politely. He'd figured he'd at least get the interview, not be shut down almost before he'd introduced himself. "Is there any chance you'd be taking on a second junior Mage?" he asked carefully.

The Captain had the good grace to look somewhat sheepish. "I've actually agreed to take on two juniors already," he admitted. "Kyle and Grace McLaughlin; I would guess that you know them?"

Damien nodded his recognition of the names of his classmates. The McLaughlin family were the core Mage family of the Sherwood system, traditionally providing the system's Mage-Governor and generally acting as an established aristocracy. Kyle and Grace were two of six members of the family who'd gone through Jump Mage training with him—he knew them both well and had been "close" with Grace.

"Thank you for your time, Captain," he said politely. "If you'll excuse me, I'll be heading back to the station—I'll need to see if any other ships have available slots." He knew perfectly well that none did —and if any did, one of the other McLaughlin youths would likely have already snapped it up.

"I know it's a point of pride not to lean on one's parents," Michaels said quietly, "but you really should see if your family knows a ship's crew who owes them a favor."

Damien focused his gaze on the spell plaque above the Captain's head. "I'm a Mage by Right, sir," he said quietly. "My parents were bakers...and died years ago."

Mages by Blood were born to the core families of the Protectorate, the inherent nobility defined by the Compact that ended the Eugenics Wars of the twenty-second century. Mages by Right were identified by the testing every human child underwent at age thirteen. They had all the rights of Mages born of the main families, all of the powers and all of the official support from the officers of the Mage-King of Mars...but none of the family connections.

"I'm sorry," Captain Michaels said quietly.

The young Mage shook his head in response, his gaze still on the spell plaque as his Gift traced the lines of power and he read the runes. He blinked at it confusedly. "Um, sir, what is that plaque supposed to do?" he asked, intentionally changing the subject.

"It's a security spell," the Captain explained, seizing on the topic change. "It detects if anyone enters the office with hostile intent."

Damien traced the flow of energy through the runes and shook his head again. "You might want to have your senior Mage look at it," he told the Captain. "The scribe used future imperative tenses instead of future-probabilistic. It's actually slightly *encouraging* the chance of violence, not predicting it."

He turned his gaze back down to the Captain, blinking away the lines of magic. "Magic doesn't predict the future very well, sir. If the plaque was detecting hostile intent, it would be obvious to you well before it triggered an alarm."

Michaels looked at the plaque and then back at Damien. "You mean I got scammed, don't you?" he asked.

"A little bit, sir," Damien admitted. "Like I said, have your Senior look at it; I may be wrong—I haven't seen a spell like that before."

As he left the office, though, Damien knew the Captain had been thoroughly scammed. He hadn't misread a rune matrix since he'd started studying his Gift at thirteen years old.

The same spacer escorted him out of the ship but clearly sensed that the young Mage wasn't interested in talking. Damien had contacted Captain Michaels as soon as the posting had gone up on the Sherwood internet—he knew he'd been the first to apply; the Captain had even told him so.

Nonetheless, he'd lost the position before he'd even boarded the ship. He thanked the spacer and crossed back to the twelve-kilometer-long cylinder that was the central hub of Sherwood Prime. He quickly grabbed one of the transit tubes that took civilians up and down the central hub to any of the twelve immense rings spaced evenly along its length, each rotating around the hub to provide the semblance of gravity. The sooner he was off the Hub, the happier he was—he was as comfortable without gravity as anyone born with it could be, but that didn't mean he liked its absence.

His rooms were on Ring Seven. Flanked on either side by five more similar immense rings rotating around the hub once a minute, the central two rings were generally inaccessible by ship. This made Rings Six and Seven the cheapest places to live and eat on the immense space station.

At age thirteen, every child on a planet under the Protectorate was tested for the Mage Gift. For the children born to the noble Mage families that served the Mage-King of Mars and bound His Protectorate together, the testing was a formality, as they were *all* Mages. For the vast majority of the rest of the population, it was also a formality but for the opposite reason—children like Damien who had no Mage parents and became Mages were barely one in ten million.

Damien found himself wandering ring seven aimlessly. He paid for his room out of the small stipend the Mage-King provided every unemployed Mage. While his parents had lived, they'd received a larger stipend—an encouragement to have more children since they'd proven they would likely have Mage children. Damien's younger brother and sister had died in the same crash that had killed his parents, long before either was old enough to be tested.

The discovery of his Gift had changed his life, though. The Royal Testers, men and women who reported to the Mage-King, not the McLaughlin's government of Sherwood, had arranged for his education to expand and for him to eventually attend the elite school of magic that trained the noble children—Mages by Blood, versus Damien's Mage by Right—of Sherwood.

Despite that, the Testers couldn't provide the interlinking web of connections the Mages by Blood—especially the grandchildren, nephews and nieces of a man as powerful as the McLaughlin, recently re-elected Mage-Governor of Sherwood for his seventh term.

Lost in his thoughts, Damien realized he'd wandered off of the central concourse, which was brightly lit and patrolled by security even on as cheap and dingy a section of the space station as Ring Seven. He was still in public corridors, but these hallways didn't have wide-open storefronts and bright lights.

Instead, easily a third of the lights were broken, and sealed doors with small nameplates or even just numbers were the only exits. Finally starting to pay attention, Damien realized that someone had scratched out the corridor numbers on the intersection nearest him, and touched the medallion around his throat for reassurance—no matter how run-down the area was, no one was going to attack a Mage.

Conceding that his funk had resulted in his getting very lost, he brought up the map function on his personal computer, a black plastic band wrapped around his left wrist. Its holographic display flickered in the air for a moment, with a small warning in one corner about connection issues, and then identified his location and a route back to his rooms in the main concourse.

"Nice PC," a voice said behind him. "Too nice a PC for so small a bit, don'tcha think?"

Damien slowly turned around to find four large men, the smallest easily twice his own size but carrying a length of black piping where the others were unarmed. He was hoping that the sight of the medallion would cause them to back off, but the largest man simply grinned at the sight.

"Waay too nice a PC for a tiny Spark, boys," he repeated. "Why don'tcha jes' take it off and pass it over? Avoids anyone getting hurt."

The PC turned off, the holographic display and interface disappearing back into the band around Damien's left wrist as he stepped back away from them.

"None of that now, little Spark," the big thug told Damien. "You PC, you cash, and that lovely gold medallion—or we start breaking limbs. You can't spark with no hands, can you?"

Damien drew on memory for a self-defense spell, reaching for the glove that covered the silver runes engraved on his palms, but a massive fist slammed into his stomach before the glove came off.

"Oops, me fist slipped," the man told the Mage with a grin. "Guess the Spark won't play nice, will he?"

The massive fist wrapped itself around Damien's throat and lifted him off the ground. Damien was small and slight; the man likely lifted arm-bells that weighed more than him.

"Like I said," he said directly into Damien's face, "The PC, the cash, and the medallion."

He reached for the medallion and Damien closed his eyes, finally remembering the spell he was after—and knowing what would happen when the thug touched the gold coin.

The security spell carved into the runes under the collar holding the medallion flared into action as soon as it was forcefully removed from Damien's neck. A blast of super-heated air shot out in all directions, burning the thug's hand and throwing him back with telekinetic force.

Damien hit the ground and released his own spell. A mental baseball bat slammed into the leader's knees, and he heard one of the man's kneecaps *crack* as the spell hit them. His face half-burnt and a kneecap broken, the man fell to one leg with his hands over his face.

Before Damien even started to run, however, the thug was moving again. With one eye closed and his face bleeding from the heat burns, the thug rose on his one good leg and grabbed Damien with both hands. He threw the slight Mage bodily into the wall, crushing the breath out of him.

Still balancing on one leg, the thug slammed one hand around Damien's neck, crushing him against the wall, and then smashed his other fist into the Mage's stomach.

Unable to breathe, Damien began to choke, his vision graying out and pain tearing through his body as the thug struck him again. And again.

Then one of the *other* thugs flew bodily into the leader's back. Still, the man remained on his feet, dropping Damien as he turned to see who was interrupting.

Damien barely recognized the spacer from *Gentle Rains of Summer* before the "liberated" length of black piping crashed into the leader's head. The thug wavered for a moment, and then the piping slammed up between his legs, and the mountain of a man finally crumpled.

Damien's consciousness crumpled with him.

———

Captain David Rice figured he was about to die.

The pirate ship had been waiting for the container ship *Blue Jay* when they emerged from their second-to-last jump en route to the Sherwood system. Compared to the freighter's four spinning ribs wrapped around its core and containers, the hundred-meter-long cylindrical ship was tiny.

Unlike *Blue Jay*, though, the pirate ship had antimatter thrusters, a Mage who hadn't just jumped, and fusion-rocket long-range missiles. The last were the cause of the muscular Captain's sense of incipient mortality.

He stood on the freighter's bridge, watching the display from his ship's cheap but functional sensor suite with one eye, and the video link to the simulacrum chamber at the center of the ship showing his Ship's Mage's exhausted face with the other. The sensors showed the pirate just less than two million kilometers distant—and the missile salvo it had fired several minutes before, accelerating toward them at over two thousand gravities.

"Four missiles," his first officer, Jenna Campbell, reported in a strained voice. "RFLAMs engaging."

The ship had two Rapid-Fire Laser Antimissile systems: defensive turrets containing a dozen rapidly charging gas-chambered pulse lasers. The ship mounted one at the bow, where the four ribs and the central keel combined into the protective shield dome. The second was at the rear of the ship, where it guarded the vessel's immense engines.

"I'll see what I can do," Kenneth McLaughlin told Rice through the video link, the Mage closing his eyes and reaching out. Even from the simulacrum chamber, no Mage could reach very far, and jumps were exhausting. There was no way McLaughlin would save them.

"RFLAMs each got one," Jenna reported grimly. "Two more inbound—*shit*! One's out of the gun's field of fire!"

"Got it," Kenneth said grimly. A third blinking icon on the screen disappeared as the Mage reached out and turned part of the missile into superheated plasma.

It wasn't enough. The immense, multi-megaton mass of *Blue Jay* lurched as the last missile slammed into the forward RFLAM turret. Rice expected to die in that moment, only to blink as nothing more happened.

"What the hell?" he demanded.

"Either it was a dud or a straight kinetic," Jenna told him harshly. "Not that it matters—the RFLAM is gone, as is half the bow dome. We try any major maneuvers and we'll open up like a rusty tin can."

"I am not dying like this," Rice told her, engaging the maneuvering controls himself. He took it gently, trusting the XO's assessment, but he slowly turned the ship so her main fusion rockets—and the last laser turret—faced her attacker.

"We're being hailed," Jenna told him. "Playing it."

"Captain Rice," a sardonic voice told him. "I do believe your ship may be a bit banged up! Please don't run too hard; you might hurt yourself."

"Shit, shit, shit, *SHIT*," Jenna exclaimed as the hull lurched again, this time much less noticeably.

"What?!"

"Asshole painted us with an x-ray laser while we were busy listening to his transmission," she said bitterly. "Now the *aft* RFLAM is gone."

Jenna didn't wait to play the second transmission; she just threw it on when it arrived.

"In the name of the Blue Star Syndicate, I order you to heave to and be boarded," the voice ordered. "Continue running, and I will put a kinetic warhead through your bridge and then collect your cargo and bodies from the debris field."

Rice shared a helpless look with Jenna and McLaughlin. If the Blue Star Syndicate boarded the ship, he was dead. If they blew out *Jay's* bridge, he was dead.

Now Captain David Rice *knew* he was going to die, and his crew with him.

The Ship's Mage took a deep breath and looked him in the eye.

"Not happening, sir," he said quietly. "Ready the ship for jump."

"You just jumped," Rice told him. "You can't jump for at *least* a few hours!"

Regulations said a Mage should jump every six hours. If you had a strong, brave Mage, you could jump after three…once. They'd arrived at the final jump zone short of Sherwood barely twenty minutes before.

"I'm sorry, David," Kenneth said quietly. "I won't let everyone on this ship die."

The camera to the simulacrum chamber cut out, and David turned back to look at the sensor board and the pirate ship closing. Then the indescribable sensation of teleportation took hold, and the whole bridge faded out.

When it slowly faded back in, the sensors were clear. They were a day's regular flight out of Sherwood Prime.

"Get the camera back," he ordered Jenna. "Kenneth, answer me, dammit!" he snapped.

The monitor flipped back on, and Rice swallowed hard. The simulacrum chamber was at the center of the ship. It had no gravity, only the small model that was always, somehow, at the exact direct center of the ship it was a copy of.

One of Kenneth's hands was caught in the model. The rest of him had started to float away when his eyeballs had exploded out of his head.

Blue Jay's only Ship's Mage, the youngest son of the Mage-Governor of the planet they'd just arrived at, was very, very dead.

Damien woke up to bright lights and white walls, blinking as he slowly realized that he could breathe and wasn't in pain, both facts a minor surprise after having a human-mountain hybrid try to choke him to death.

He managed to make it about a quarter of the way into a sitting position before a nurse realized what he was doing, arriving in time to stop him from collapsing back onto the clinic bed he was occupying.

As the brunette clad in light blue scrubs helped him upright, he glanced around a room that any citizen of a Protectorate world would recognize. The Charter defined a minimum standard of health care as a human right for governments to provide, and Olympus Mons helped meet that standard by providing funding and a standard prefabricated clinic-in-a-box with a certain set of diagnostic and medical tools.

"Hold still," the nurse ordered once she had Damien upright. This was followed by a series of scanners, pokes and prods. Apparently finished, she grunted and disappeared out of the clinic room with a sharp "Stay here."

Still dizzy, Damien thought that might have been the most useless instruction ever. The room slowly stopped spinning while he waited, but the nurse eventually returned with three other people.

The last of the three newcomers was the spacer from *Gentle Rains of Summer*. In front was an iron-haired gentleman in a white lab coat reading over a datapad the nurse had passed him as they entered the room. In between was a tall redheaded woman in the dark blue uniform of Sherwood System Security.

"I am Dr. Anderson," the man introduced himself. "This young lady is Nurse Kosta—remember to thank her on your way out.

"You are lucky to be alive, young man," the doctor continued, setting the datapad down next to Damien's bed. "Your trachea was damaged and several of your ribs were cracked. The dizziness will fade, though you will be very tired for a day or two—a normal side effect of the bone-mending process."

The doctor asked him a few questions, ran a more complex scanner the nurse hadn't used over him, and nodded in satisfaction.

"We'll keep you in tonight for observation, but you'll be free to go in the morning," Anderson told Damien. "If there's anything that needs to be taken care of at your home—pets to feed or a girlfriend to let know—let Kosta know and we'll get it taken care of."

"Neither," Damien told him, coughing to clear his throat after he spoke. "Thank you."

"Now Kosta and I will leave you with Captain Harrison," the doctor continued. He turned to the SSS officer. "You have fifteen minutes," he said sternly, "and then I am kicking you out of my clinic, clear?"

"Perfectly, Doctor. Thank you," the Security officer said calmly.

The doctor shuffled out, and Captain Harrison pulled two chairs up beside Damien's bed, gesturing for the spacer to sit.

"I kept Mr. Casey here around, as I figured you'd want to thank the man who saved your life," she said quietly. "Brian Kendall—the thug who worked you over—is known to System Security. Given the number you'd done on him, he was going to kill you. Mr. Casey's intervention prevented that, and his witness statement is going to put him behind bars for a very long time…after the doctors finish fixing his knee. That was you, I presume?"

Damien nodded. "I… didn't think he would keep coming after that," he admitted. "I was trying to calm things down."

"With most thugs, that'll work," Casey told him with a small smile. "But that Kendall…'e seemed a piece of work."

"Thank you," Damien told the spacer. "I'm not even sure why you were there, but Captain Harrison is right—he was going to kill me."

Casey slipped a small paper envelope from his jacket onto the table by Damien. "The Cap'n wanted to give you a little something for your help with the ward," he told him. "'E sent me after you to hand it over. I, um"—he gave a sideways glance at the Security Captain—"pinged your PC for your location…and hurried when I saw where you were."

Harrison was studiously looking at Damien's medical monitor, pretending she hadn't heard the spacer confess to a minor crime. Personal computers were keyed to a user and contained all of their personal information—accessing one without permission was considered a form of personal assault.

After a moment, the Captain turned her eyes back to Damien and tapped her own PC.

"I need you to give me a recorded witness statement," she told him. "After that, I shouldn't need to call you in for anything, but we'll hold on to your contact information in case. Is that acceptable?"

Damien nodded, and Harrison pressed a button on the computer. "All right, let's get started."

———

It didn't take very long for Damien to give as complete a description as he remembered of the incident. Some of his memories were clouded from being choked into unconsciousness, but at least the start of the encounter was clear.

"One last question for the record," Harrison finally told him. "How many spells do you know that would have killed Kendall?"

Damien blinked, confused. "Sorry?"

"I'm aware of at least some of the spells taught in the self-defense portion of the Practical Thaumaturgy curriculum," she said. "Your response was nonlethal, but you were capable of a lethal response —correct?"

Damien thought about it. He'd learned self-defense spells around various forms of energy manipulation—heat, cold, electricity. Even the straight force spell he'd used could have been deadlier if directed at, say, Kendall's neck.

"At least five," he finally answered quietly. "At most basic, a fire spell would have inflicted significant third degree burns if not killed him."

"Thank you," Harrison said, turning off her PC. "That will be sufficient for the courts, I think." She was shaking her head slightly.

"What?" he asked.

"I think you are the first Mage I've ever met to default to a nonlethal level of force when threatened," she told him. "Most Mages go straight for fire or lightning—we spend a good part of the training for the System Security Mages teaching them to use a targeted level of force."

"I thought I could scare them off," Damien admitted. "I was wrong."

"That wasn't your mistake," Harrison told him. "Your mistake was not escalating as soon as you realized you couldn't. Training can fix that—have you ever considered joining the SSS?"

"I'm trained to be a Jump Mage," Damien answered. "That's what I'm going to be—as soon as I find a ship."

The Security Captain looked like she had swallowed something sour.

"Every Mage wants to Jump," she told him. "There are what, ten thousand Mages in Sherwood? Out of two billion people—ten thousand Mages. Everyone, from System Security to the Shipwrights to the damned *power company*, needs Mages. They're desperate for anyone who can cast a spell—and you are sitting up on this station, doing *nothing*, complaining that you can't find a place on a starship?"

Damien touched the collar he wore—the product of years of study and training so that he could Jump. Getting into Jump training wasn't easy, for the exact reasons that Harrison had just thrown at him.

"I earned the right to Jump," he told the cop. "You'll excuse me if I don't give up on that just yet."

Harrison took a deep breath. "I'm sorry," she told him. "It's frustrating trying to recruit Mages and watching there be not enough Mages for anything *except* Jumping—and too many Jump Mages. Just...keep it in mind, hey? You'd make a better cop than most."

"I'll think about it," Damien told her. He even might, if he went long enough without finding work on a starship.

It took six hours to get any of *Blue Jay*'s massive fusion engines working after they'd jumped into Sherwood. Rice had made his way along the ship's zero-gravity core after the first hour to help out—without engines, they were dead in space and unlikely to even show up on sensors so anyone knew they were in trouble.

Finally, the Captain was shoulders deep in a maintenance box, reconnecting wires, when he heard the ship's engineer shout, "That looks like it, Skipper. Get clear; I'm going to open up the hydrogen feeds."

David pulled himself free of the open panel and glanced up at the even-blacker-than-usual face of his senior engineer, James Kellers. "Go for it," he told the man.

"Everyone clear?" the engineer asked loudly. Both of the two assistant engineers responded in the affirmative, and the wiry black man threw a toggle on the datapad he was carrying. The engine room was on the aft end of the gravity-less main core, so they all felt it when the engines kicked. The room had a sudden, very faint sensation of down.

"Well?" David asked.

"It's not much," Kellers admitted. "We've got the thrusters back at about fifty percent, but the main engines are shot to hell. Call it…two percent of a gee."

"It'll get us inbound—and make it so the Fleet can detect us," David told him.

"And if they do, you should be on the bridge, not immersed in *Jay*'s guts," Kellers replied. "We can take it from here, boss."

Rice looked down at his hands, which were covered in ash from the burnt-out conduits he'd been helping replace. It had been years since he'd worked Kellers' job, but he hadn't forgotten which way the circuits went in. He knew from when he'd done that job, though, how filthy his face was after crawling into a burnt-out maintenance panel.

"I don't know; looking like this might get help from the Martian boys faster," Rice observed, but he was carefully making his way up the engine room against the very slight pressure of the ship's acceleration.

For once, he'd welcome "the Martian Boys"—the Royal Martian Navy of the Mage-King of Mars, more commonly simply the Protectorate Navy—showing up.

Given that any Navy ship would have to at least wait until the lightspeed signature of *Jay*'s engine reached them, though, he probably even had time for a shower.

"Captain to the bridge," Jenna's voice echoed over the intercom. "Captain Rice to the bridge, ASAP."

With a sigh, David increased his pace up the core.

———

Jenna had somehow managed to get the main viewscreen for the communicator online, and it was showing an impeccably turned out officer aboard the disgustingly neat bridge of a Navy warship.

"This is Mage-Captain Adrian Corr of His Majesty's destroyer *Guardian of Honor*," the fair-haired man in the dark blue uniform told David as he entered the room and faced the concealed camera over the viewscreen. "You are Captain Rice of *Blue Jay*?"

"I am," David replied. "I have to say I'm glad to see you boys so far out."

He counted in the back of his head until the Mage-Captain responded. He made it to four seconds—the destroyer was still two full light-seconds away. Close in interplanetary terms but still quite a distance away.

"We were doing an outer-system scan as an exercise, and one of my officers identified your jump flare," Corr said in his neatly precise tones. The blond hair with the slightly angled eyes and the soft accent marked the Mage as a Martian, one of the *old* Mage families. "When she did not see an engine signature, she recommended we investigate. My apologies for the delay, Captain—my first officer believed that even an in-system jump was my decision, not his."

"As you can see, Mage-Captain, *Blue Jay* is in no state for me to be complaining about any help present."

"Of course." Corr nodded. "My apologies again—are you in need of medical assistance?"

"We have no significant injuries," David told him. "Only minor injuries and one fatality."

"What happened?" the Mage-Captain asked.

"A pirate ship jumped us at our last jump layover," Rice answered. "Disabled our defensive turrets and was preparing to fire into us when our Ship's Mage jumped us."

The Navy Officer's wince, four seconds later, was small but noticeable. "Early," he said. It wasn't a question.

"We will take your ship under tow when we arrive," Corr informed Rice. "I will pass your report on to System Command. We will investigate this pirate."

David nodded his agreement. "Thank you," he said quietly.

"We serve the Mage-King of Mars," the Martian noble told him. "What does his Protectorate mean if we do not protect people?"

———

Guardian of Honor was unable to tow *Blue Jay* much faster than the battered freighter could move on her own power. While the destroyer's engines were both more powerful than the freighter's and fully intact, the Navy ship had done a full sensor sweep of the freighter— and Mage-Captain Corr judged her only capable of surviving about a quarter-gravity of acceleration.

At that much-reduced rate, it took the destroyer several days to haul the ship into something resembling real-time communication range of Sherwood. David spent most of the trip on the bridge, watching the battered thermal scanners carefully for any sign of trouble. A million-ton warship was a lot of reassurance, but after watching pirates try to blow his ship away, he figured he was allowed some paranoia.

He'd sent Jenna to get some rest earlier, which meant he was the only one on the bridge when *Blue Jay* received the first of the two transmissions he was dreading.

The transmission was a video signal carrying the image of an expensively dressed dark-haired woman with the kind of perfectly imperfect prettiness that spoke of either natural beauty or *truly* expensive cosmetic surgery.

"Office of the Sherwood Governor," the woman announced herself. "Please connect me to Kenneth McLaughlin."

It was phrased as a request, but the tone made it very clear that the woman expected to be obeyed instantly.

"I'm sorry, miss, I can't do that," David told her with weariness tingeing his voice that had nothing to do with having been conscious for over twenty hours.

A few moments later, he could tell when his response arrived. The woman blinked, clearly surprised by his response. "And why not?" she demanded sharply.

"Kenneth McLaughlin is dead," the freighter Captain told her simply.

This time, he could time the lightspeed lag to the microsecond. As soon as his words arrived, the haughtiness took a full-on body blow, and the woman's lips tightened until they were almost white. It took her a few seconds to even minimally recompose herself.

"Hold for the Mage-Governor," she instructed sharply before the screen threw up the eagle and bagpipes of the Sherwood planetary crest.

David waited out the crest patiently. They were slowly decelerating toward the massive station in orbit around Sherwood. Even with *Guardian of Honor*'s tow, *Blue Jay* wouldn't dock for another five hours at their current pace. There was no rush.

Finally, the crest cleared to show a man David had only met once before, though he'd seen the face on dozens of newscasts.

Miles James McLaughlin, patriarch of his clan and seven times elected Mage-Governor of Sherwood, was a tall, steel-haired man with cold blue eyes. He wore a plain black suit, but pinned to the breast pocket of the jacket was a small red ribbon with a golden planet hanging on the end—the Mars Valor Award, given to a much younger Mage-Commander McLaughlin after single-handedly ending one of the nastier anti-pirate campaigns in recent history.

"Where is my son?" he demanded.

"In the morgue of the destroyer Guardian *of Honor*," David told him quietly. "We didn't have the facilities to properly preserve his body." Or the spare manpower to clean up the awful mess Kenneth had left of himself, but the medical team *Guardian* had sent over had taken care of that too.

"What the hell did you do?" McLaughlin snarled. "I sent my son with you so he'd stay *safe*, not so you'd get him killed!"

"Kenneth saved our lives," David told him. "We were ambushed by pirates—he jumped early, saving everyone else aboard."

"Pirates don't find ships at random anymore. What the hell are you involved in, Rice?" the Mage-Governor demanded.

"Your son died a hero," the Captain repeated, his voice even quieter. "I have no idea how the pirates found us."

"Heroes happen when other people fuck up," the McLaughlin said sharply. "You won't be dragging any more children of Sherwood into your disaster, Rice. Get out of my system."

The connection terminated, and Rice stared at the screen wordlessly, glad none of his crew had been on the bridge. Getting out of Sherwood wasn't an option, not with no Mage and the damage *Blue Jay* had taken. Staying in the McLaughlin's system after he'd told you to get out wasn't wise, though.

Before he could begin to come up with a plan, the communicator announced the second call he'd been expecting—this one from his insurance company.

With a sigh, he opened the channel.

―――――

The medallion of a Mage opened a lot of doors—even for an unemployed Mage like Damien. When he'd heard that a new freighter was coming in, he'd made his way down to Sherwood Prime's zero-gravity hub. His medallion had earned him a respectful nod from a security guard as he entered an observation lounge he'd normally be barred from.

There was a neatly marked and signed line between the zero-gravity hub and the luxury lounge. The signs warned Damien, so he was ready when his feet dropped sharply toward the ground when he crossed over the rune-inlaid carpet. Like so much else, artificial gravity could be created with magic, but runes like those woven into the carpet required recharging by a Mage at least once a week. Only warships, with their multiple Mage crews, would expend the resources to have gravity throughout the ship.

Damien reveled in the experience of full gravity for a moment as he made his way to the massive windows. Even the rotating rings only maintained about seven tenths of a gravity, but this lounge was spelled to Sherwood's nine tenths. Weirdly, the slightly heavier weight he was bearing was…relaxing.

The lounge was quiet at this time, roughly midnight by the station's clocks, which was likely part of why the gold medallion at the base of his throat had been enough to get him into the lounge unquestioned. Lounges like this were the only ones in the hub with tables and chairs, and he settled into one by the windows.

The windows were impressive. Normally, an "observation lounge", even on the hub, was just a set of viewscreens, but the Angelus Gravity Lounge had managed to get itself a place right on the edge of the station's hull—and right above the main docking arms. The owners had then paid an astronomical sum of money to magically transform the complex ceramic-and-metal composite of said hull to be transparent.

Damien ordered a small coffee from the cute but tired waitress and settled in. From here, he could see *Gentle Rains of Summer* at a far docking arm, having cargo containers slowly maneuvered into locking positions on the massive ship's keel. Closer, a fast passenger liner rested at another docking arm, its sleek lines suggesting that it, like the Angelus Lounge, had magical gravity.

Eight of the slender docks were visible from the cafe, half of the civilian docking arms on the station. The other eight were on the other side of the hub of Sherwood Prime's ever-rotating wheels. Of those sixteen docks, four were full. Sherwood wasn't one of the Core systems around Sol and Mars, but it was a hub of interstellar trade by MidWorlds standards, let alone the Fringe farther out.

The distinctive star-white flare of an antimatter engine took Damien's attention entirely away from the incredibly good coffee the waitress delivered. No civilian ship used an antimatter torch, and the young Mage stretched his eyes for what he knew had to be out there.

The Protectorate destroyer swam out of Sherwood's corona like a swimmer from the surf, carefully short bursts from its rockets slowing it as it guided its charge home. An even pyramid, one hundred meters on a side, at this distance its hull was a smooth white, the weapons it bristled with invisible.

He was so shocked by his first sight of one the famous Martian ships that he almost missed what the ship was doing. Massive cables, visible only by the occasional glint of sunlight on them, linked the destroyer to a long and rounded container ship. Like *Gentle Rains of Summer*, this ship had a long, solid keel with four rotating ribs arrayed around the keel and cargo like an old eggbeater.

The ship was about a third of the size of *Gentle Rains*, and even from several hundred meters' distance, Damien could see someone had worked the freighter over hard. Scorch marks marred an already dirty gray hull, with the engine so battered the Mage wasn't surprised that the ship had needed a tow.

From the looks of it, the freighter might *need* a Mage, but sadly, he didn't think they were going to be hiring one anytime soon.

Wondering both at the sharp lines of the destroyer and the battered curves of the freighter, Damien sipped his coffee and watched *Blue Jay* arrive at Sherwood.

———

A full day after finally easing *Blue Jay* into the docking arms at Sherwood Prime, David Rice found himself walking the ship with the insurance agent, a thin man in a cheap gray suit. The agent said very little as they walked the docking arm, viewing the exterior damage from the windows. He occasionally took a picture with his PC and spent much of his time making notes on a keyboard visible to him.

When they reached the entrance to *Blue Jay* so they could survey the internal damage, they were interrupted by the agent's PC buzzing,

"Excuse me, Captain Rice," the man told David before stepping aside to answer the call. Only the occasional small exclamation was audible of the conversation, but when the man returned, his closed exterior was replaced with a wicked grin that belonged on a prank-pulling schoolboy, not an insurance agent of a company notorious for nickel-and-diming every claim they ever received.

"I'm pleased to inform you, Captain Rice, that my superiors have confirmed that the damage to your ship is covered under the piracy clause in your contract," the agent told Rice. "As such, only half the usual deductible will apply, as the damage is entirely beyond your control."

"I thought that was what you were here to assess," Rice asked, and the agent shook his head.

"I'm assessing the value of the damage," the agent told him. "I have no authority on my own to confirm or deny your claim—the branch head retains direct control over all claims related to starship damages."

"Ah," Rice observed. "So, if I may ask, what is the joke I'm missing?"

The agent's smile faded slightly but not completely. "Off the record, my manager is the worst I've ever met for rejecting claims on any grounds," he admitted quietly. "But Mage-Captain Corr called the office and let us know that he and his crew would be perfectly willing to supply their professional analysis of your telemetry data if there was need to support the piracy claim—and then reminded him that *Guardian of Honor* is slated to be on-station for the next *two years*, so they couldn't even push it off until the ship left. It feels good to watch that tightwad get stuck in a corner."

"I see," Rice agreed, understanding at least part of the other man's thoroughly unprofessional glee, and grateful for the Martian officer's assistance. Without Mage-Captain Corr leaning on the insurance, it would have taken longer to get the claim cleared, and if they'd managed to declare it an accident, it would have doubled how much of the repairs he had to pay for—a difference that would almost have bankrupted him.

"Shall we go see how much we have to fix, then?" he asked the agent, gesturing back toward the ship.

———

The rest of the tour with the agent was much more pleasant than the exterior tour had been, as if the certain knowledge that he wasn't going to be forced to screw the ship's crew took a large weight off the man's shoulders.

David was finally relaxed for the first time in days when he settled in at his desk to call the Ship's Mages Guild to post for a new Ship's Mage. The video screen on his desk showed the gold icon of the Guild, the same three stars that every Jump Mage wore carved onto the medallion at their throat, and the Guild's Latin motto: *"Per Magica Ad Astra"*—"Through Magic The Stars."

The young woman who answered the call did not wear any such medallion—no one would waste a Mage on reception and booking duty. She did wear a fetching skirt-and-blouse combination in green and white that accented her black hair in a manner that reminded David it had been two years since his divorce.

"Sherwood Ship's Mage's Guild, Melanie speaking, how may I help you?" she chirped cheerfully.

"Good afternoon, Melanie," David greeted her calmly, refocusing his attention where it belonged. "I need to put up a posting for a Ship's Mage position."

Among its many roles and tasks, the Guild maintained the job board on the system communication net. A ship's Captain could be fined for posting a Ship's Mage role on a more general classified board, and none of the Jump-qualified Mages in a system would be looking for jobs anywhere else.

"Of course!" Melanie told him. "That will only take a few minutes. Do you have an account with the Sherwood office?"

Of all the wonders that magic had given humanity, one that the Magi hadn't managed to pull off was any type of large-scale interstellar communications. A few facilities, massive monstrosities of runes and power, allowed a Mage to transmit their voice to a specially built, equally massive receiver, but data transmission of any kind was impossible. It wouldn't matter if David had accounts with every other Guild Office in the Protectorate; he would need an account for Sherwood.

"I do," he told the girl. He'd hired Kenneth in Sherwood, though that hadn't been through the Guild but through a favor to an acquaintance in the government. He reeled off the account number. "Captain David Rice, aboard *Blue Jay*," he concluded.

Melanie cheerfully started inputting data into a computer below the edge of the screen and then stopped in confusion.

"I'm sorry, Captain," she said slowly. "I've never seen this before, but I have a note here that your ship is blacklisted and I can't authorize any job postings or hiring contracts."

The ground fell out from underneath David in a way the rapid rotation of *Blue Jay*'s ribs to create gravity didn't explain.

"I can put you through to a manager and you can try and sort out what it would take to get you un-blacklisted?" she offered, still fully in "help the customer" mode. The girl didn't realize what a system-wide hiring blackout meant to a man like David. The McLaughlin had just killed his ship.

"No," he said faintly. "I will contact them later. Thank you, Melanie," he managed to squeeze out before cutting the connection, staring at the screen as it dropped back to an automatic rotation of the cameras around the docking bays, showing him *Blue Jay* and the other ships in dock.

Miles James McLaughlin, it seemed, did not fuck around. When he'd said that David would drag no more of Sherwood's Mages into his affairs, the Mage-Governor had clearly leaned on the system's Guild to block his hiring any Mage in the system. Since David hadn't committed any of the acts—lack of payment, for example—that would normally result in being blacklisted, he knew it wasn't a Protectorate-wide blacklist. He could send a note on another ship to another system's Guild, hire a Ship's Mage sight unseen and ship them to Sherwood.

The risks and price tag of that option made him sick, and the shifting images on his screen weren't helping. He touched the screen, freezing the picture on a single camera, and then stopped in thought.

Off to the side of the camera view he was watching was *Gentle Rains of Summer*. Four times *Blue Jay*'s size and capacity, the ship likely had more than one Mage aboard, and Andrew Michaels was an old friend of David's.

Maybe they could work something out, at least to get *Blue Jay* out of this ill-begotten system with its vengeful overlord.

———

With his rooms tucked away deep in the cheaper areas of Ring Seven, Damien didn't think that anyone knew where he was staying—he certainly hadn't *given* anyone the name of the cheap hotel or his room number, so when the buzzer for his door went off, he had a moment of panic.

Remembering after a second that he was paid up for a full week and it was unlikely to be the landlord, Damien opened his door. Waiting on him was the last person he expected: Grace McLaughlin, one of the two McLaughlin mages who'd beaten him out for *Gentle Rains'* junior Ship's Mage slot…and his on-again, off-again lover from the Jump Mage program.

"Hi, Damien," she greeted him with a mischievous grin. "Hurry up and invite me in; this is one shithole of a neighborhood you've picked to slum in."

Damien was too surprised to do more than wordlessly step back and gesture her in. The petite redhead ducked under his gesturing arm and closed the door behind her, rapidly finding the room's sole ragged couch and perching on it, eyeing him like a cat with a favorite toy.

"You know, I know you're trying to save money, but would it kill you to have asked for a little help?" she asked him. "I don't know what you're paying, but I'm sure we could have found you somewhere nicer for about the same—the family *always* knows somebody."

"It doesn't work that way for most of us," Damien told her quietly. He'd spent a lot of time around the various McLaughlin scions of his age, and continued to wonder at their view of the world. They weren't *arrogant*, they were too driven to help and serve to be arrogant, but they knew that everyone on Sherwood would happily do them favors at the drop of a hat.

"It works that way for family," Grace told him, locking her gaze on him. "And you went to school with six of us *and* Granddad likes you— you practically *are* family."

Grace, as Damien had not found out until *after* he'd shared her bed, was the eldest daughter of the Governor's eldest son. She was the only adult in the entire *system* that would refer to the McLaughlin as "Granddad". Damien wasn't so sure the Governor liked him—he'd barely met the man after all.

"How did you even *find* me?" he asked finally. "It's not like I even told your Captain where I was staying."

"Casey," Grace answered simply. "First rule of being shipboard—the Bosun can *always* find out what they want to know. I asked her, she sent me to Casey, who apparently lifted your address from your PC while he was saving your life. An incident, I'll point out," she said sharply, "that you didn't mention to me, my sister, *or* my cousins."

As usual when dealing with Grace, Damien was starting to be overwhelmed. He was never sure why the woman had picked him to be her lover, though he would never have dreamed of complaining. She ran at roughly twice his speed on a good day.

"Everyone involved is spending a very long time as guests of System Security," Damien told her. "Beyond that, what was the point of telling anyone?"

Grace sighed loudly and pushed Damien down onto the couch to hop into his lap, snuggling up against him in an *extremely* pleasant way.

"Because, you adorable dolt, we actually care and worry about you when we don't hear a peep for weeks?" she told him. "To hear *about* you getting beaten up from the spacers on my new ship on top of that is not my idea of a good day."

Damien hugged her back, not sure what to say.

"I'm sorry about *Gentle Rains*," she continued after a moment, her voice quieter. "I wasn't expecting Mom to call in favors quite that heavily. If it helps, she promised to make sure the next Captain heard about you first."

Arya McLaughlin was, as well as the daughter-in-law of the system governor, Head Administrator for Sherwood Prime. Her prodding ship Captains about Damien couldn't hurt him, but he felt uncomfortable at the thought of strings getting pulled on his behalf.

Before he expressed that thought aloud, however, Grace laughed and kissed him.

"You, of course, have an even greater portion of pure Sherwood Scot stubbornness than any of the family," she told him. "Which is a small, teensy portion of why I'm spending my last night on the station here."

"You leave tomorrow?" Damien asked, surprised.

"Yeah, we ship out at eleven hundred hours station time," Grace told him. She sat up straight, remaining on his lap but creating some distance between them. "Which, given that I need to be on ship two hours beforehand, means we only have about twelve hours. I'd better get business out of the way."

"What business?"

She slid a tiny data disk out of her cleavage and dropped it on the side table.

"That's from Captain Michaels," she told him. "It's the contact info for Captain David Rice on *Blue Jay*—they're the ship that came in damaged from a pirate attack a couple of days ago. Trick is, they lost their Mage on the way in—but for whatever reason, the Sherwood Guild has blacklisted them. Rice can't post for a new Mage."

"You mean..." Damien said slowly.

"Rice asked the Captain if he knew anyone," Grace told him. "Then the Captain asked Kyle and me if we knew you—and I said I was trying to track you down since we were leaving, and he told me to tell you to contact Rice if you still wanted a Jump job."

For a long moment, Damien was silent, looking at the tiny disk on the table. Finally, he looked up at Grace.

"Thank you," he said quietly.

"You're welcome. Now, I believe I mentioned spending the night?" she continued with a familiar wicked grin.

———

Damien didn't get a lot of sleep that night, but when he did wake up, Grace was gone. He wasn't sure when she'd left, but by the time he woke up, it was only an hour short of when she'd said *Gentle Rains of Summer* was due to leave. Running his hand down the slight indent her body had left in the cheap motel mattress, he realized he could still clean up and make it down to watch the freighter leave.

Making sure to grab the data disk Grace had left with him, he made his way down to the same observation deck he'd watched *Blue Jay* arrive from, slipping into the window table in the Angelus

Gravity Lounge in time to see the last lines drop away from the big freighter.

The *Summer* was one of the biggest freighters the worlds of the Protectorate built, rated for twelve million tons of cargo and massing over twenty million tons fully loaded and fuelled. This close to the even-greater mass of Sherwood Prime, the immense ship moved slowly, running on secondary ion thrusters to avoid damaging the station itself.

Her gravity ribs were locked as she maneuvered out, so Damien could clearly make out the four flattened structures that contained crew quarters, and the hundreds of standard ten-thousand-cubic-meter containers attached to the central keel's cargo spars.

Launching from the central, immobile hub of the station forced the ship to build up her momentum entirely on her own. It took easily ten minutes before the minuscule thrust of the ion thrusters moved the *Summer* out of the station's safety zone and rotated her to face out-system. Once the ship was in position, the massive fusion rockets at the end of the central keel flared to life. The window between Damien and the rockets darkened noticeably to prevent the light of those miniature suns from injuring the patrons' eyes.

Watching the ship burn away from Sherwood, it finally sank into Damien why Grace had been looking for him even before her Captain had asked her to. It would be months, even years, before *Gentle Rains of Summer* returned to Sherwood. If Damien went on another ship, it was exceedingly unlikely that he would be in Sherwood when the ship returned. Last night had been the last time they were likely to see each other.

Damien pulled the data disk out with a sigh and eyed it. The PC on his wrist could read it and place a call. On the other hand, *Blue Jay's* dock was only ten minutes' drift through the zero-gravity section of the station.

———

"David, there's a young Mage here to see you," Jenna told Captain Rice, sticking her head into the office just off the bridge. The bridge and his office, located on Rib Four, had only had gravity restored about two hours before, and David was trying to catch up on the paperwork his insurance agent was inflicting on him.

David suspected he'd never seen this much paperwork for insurance before because he'd never seen insurance work progress so quickly, but the agent was taking an almost-gleeful pleasure in ramming through *Blue Jay*'s repairs before his superior could find some way to argue against the sworn affidavits of the bridge crew of a Martian destroyer.

"A Mage?" he asked to be sure he'd heard correctly. His best efforts to try to track down a Jump Mage without going through the Guild hadn't produce much more than vague promises, and his best hope of poaching a junior Mage from someone had just left port, with Michaels assuring him that "steps had been taken".

"He says his name is Damien Montgomery—and that Captain Michaels sent him," his first officer advised, glancing at the small pile of authorizing data disks on Rice's desk. The stocky blonde flashed a bright smile at her Captain. "I'll send him in, shall I?"

"Any distraction from Mr. Clarke's mountain of helpful paperwork," Rice told her, agreeing with her significant glance. For that matter, David was willing to meet with *any* Jump-qualified Mage, even if they had three heads and spoke Sanskrit.

The "young Mage" that Jenna showed into his office a minute later, though, was barely more than a boy. Dark-haired, short and slim, he was probably older than he looked, but David would have placed him at maybe sixteen years old.

"Captain Rice, I'm Damien Montgomery," the youth introduced himself calmly. Instead of the tie that David would have worn with the dark-slacks-and-shirt combination he was wearing, Montgomery wore a black leather collar holding a gold medallion against the base of his throat. As the youth stood across from David, the Captain recognized the tiny three stars carved into the medallion that marked him as Jump-qualified.

"Have a seat, Damien," Rice told him. "I'd ask if you were here about the Ship's Mage posting, but I'm afraid there is no posting."

"So I was told," Montgomery said quietly, settling into the proffered chair. "The Governor has blacklisted you. The Guild won't let you hire anyone." He paused and shrugged. "I'll jump for you."

Rice regarded him levelly.

"As you said, the Guild has blacklisted us," he said carefully. "Our last Ship's Mage died jumping too early to get us away from a pirate attack. Jumping for us may be risky and will definitely get you in trouble with the Guild. Why?"

The youth shrugged again. "I Jump-qualified in the same year as six children of the McLaughlin clan," he said quietly. "Their families have connections and wealth to buy favors. My father was a baker and died several years ago."

Rice nodded slowly. "What you're saying, Mage Montgomery, is that we are both desperate?"

"Exactly."

The Captain eyed the young man across the desk for a long moment. To qualify as a Jump-Mage, a Mage had to have made at least twenty supervised Jumps, but he suspected that those jumps were the only time Damien had ever cast the spell. He hesitated to put his life—and his crew's lives—into the hands of a youth with no experience.

"Are you prepared to have me review your Jump calculations?" he asked bluntly. Normally, a Jump Mage's work was extremely private, with no oversight except maybe a more senior Mage. After thirty years on merchant ships, though, David knew enough to at least tell if the calculations were wrong.

Damien paused again, then nodded. "I think that might even make me more comfortable," the young man admitted, looking sixteen again for a moment.

"Fine. You're hired," Rice told him. "Jenna will find you a bunk—we only just got our ribs rotating for gravity, so you may have to lend a hand cleaning up around the ship, if that's all right?"

"There is a lot I can do to help 'clean up,' I suspect," Montgomery told him. "If nothing else, I will need to review the rune matrix before we jump. From what I saw of the damage, I want to be sure it wasn't compromised."

That wasn't a thought that had occurred to David yet, and he shivered at the potential danger. Hopefully, the young Mage in front of him knew his job. At best, a compromised rune matrix wouldn't work. At worst…it would scatter the ship in pieces across the full length of the jump.

"What about registering your employment with the Guild?" David finally asked: another unpleasant thought.

"I…would prefer to do that in a system not Sherwood," Damien suggested, and the Captain laughed.

"I think we can both agree to that."

————

Damien took a long, slow look around the tiny room he'd been living in for the last two months. It had never been much of a room, though Grace had managed to add some pleasant memories to the space before vanishing out of both the room and his life.

When he'd left the surface, he'd sold or given away anything large or heavy he'd owned, so it had taken him under ten minutes to pack a single mid-sized bag with all of his worldly belongings. Now the room was sparse and empty, merely awaiting a simple transmission to the landlord to deliver his last payment and cancel his access code.

Once he left this room, it was done—he was leaving Sherwood and unlikely to return. Even if he switched ships later on, the McLaughlin was unlikely to forget that Damien had defied his blacklisting of *Blue Jay* and returning to Sherwood would be unwise.

From the moment he'd tested positive for the Mage Gift and his life had changed forever, Damien had known he wanted to be a Jump Mage. He'd failed the entrance exams for the Protectorate Navy—by the skin of his teeth, in a year when no Mage on Sherwood *had* passed the exams—which meant the merchant ships were the only way to Jump.

His family had passed on before he graduated with his degree. Grace had left aboard *Gentle Rains of Summer*. Nothing held him to Sherwood, but he still hesitated for a moment.

But it was only a moment. He sent the transmission to the landlord, shouldered his bag, and headed for *Blue Jay*.

Jenna was waiting for Damien when he reached the transfer tube to *Blue Jay*, a zero-gravity transfer cart waiting by her. She glanced at his single bag and arched an eyebrow at him.

"I brought the cart to help carry your stuff, but I see that wasn't necessary. Light packer?" she asked.

"I lived alone; I didn't have or need much," Damien admitted. "Anything specific I should make sure to have?"

"Not really," the heavyset officer told him. "Food and such are included in your pay. Grab the cart; let's get aboard."

Damien grabbed the cart and pushed it forward, keeping a hand on it as it drifted through the zero-gravity boarding dock. Not much more than a metal tray with clips for keepings objects attached to it, the cart was useful to keep things from drifting away while moving through zero-gravity zones such as the central hub of Sherwood Prime, and the transfer tube that linked it to the keel of *Blue Jay*.

"*Blue Jay* is a *Venice* class freighter," Jenna told him as she kicked off into the tube. "We're rated for three megatons of cargo—three hundred standard ten-thousand-cubic-meter cargo containers at their max mass."

"To carry that, she's almost a full kilometer long, with four rotating gravity ribs. With a crew of eighty-five, we have quite a bit of cubage to give people living space." She paused as they entered the main lock and gestured to a storage rack on the side of the plain room. "Since you've just the one bag, stow the cart there."

Damien obeyed, carefully propping himself as he slung the bag back over his own shoulder.

"Through here is the rear access point for the ribs," Jenna continued, launching skillfully and catching the handle by the open door out of the loading zone. The room beyond the door held four "elevators" that would spin up to match the ribs, and then slide into tubes heading out to the edge of the ship.

"Your cabin is on Rib Three," she told him, "the same cabin as the last Ship's Mage.

"Don't worry," she said after a pause, "we already sent all of his stuff onto his family."

"What happened to him?" Damien asked, following her into one of the elevators

"We were jumped by pirates," Jenna told him grimly as she carefully oriented herself feet-first toward the outside of the ship before hitting the button to start the tiny cab rotating around the ship. "Kenneth jumped us before he should have, and burnt himself out."

Damien wasn't sure if the bottom fell out of his stomach due to the memory of the lectures he'd had on overexerting his magic, with attendant pictures of the results, or the sudden acceleration-induced shift in apparent gravity.

"Are pirates common?" he asked slowly, holding onto the safety railing and determinedly ignoring his inner ear's confusion.

"In the Fringe and the UnArcana Worlds where the Navy is sparse, they can be," she said quietly. "But normally, a major MidWorlds system like Sherwood is so safe as to be boring."

The sensation of gravity changed again as the elevator stopped accelerating sideways and Damien's stomach lurched as the pod shot outward toward the rib.

When it finally came to an apparent halt, there was a comfortable sense of about half a gravity of centrifugal force, and Damien breathed a sigh of relief.

"The elevators take some getting used to," Jenna told him with a grin. "But you *do* get used to them."

She led the way out of the elevator, pointing out the stairs leading "down" toward the outside of the ship. "Each rib is arranged in four decks," she explained. "The outermost deck is storage, systems, and radiation shielding. Quarters are on the inner two decks, and working spaces on deck three. Follow me; I'll take you to your cabin."

Damien's cabin, it turned out, was on Deck One of Rib Three—the innermost deck.

"The ribs are about two-thirds the length of the overall hull," Jenna told him as she led him along the corridor. "Even after curvature, shielding, and the rotation motors, there's about five hundred meters of usable length on each one, so we have no shortage of space. There's a saying in the merchant fleet—'cubage is cheap, mass is expensive.'" She gestured at the doors they were passing. "We have individual cabins for one hundred and sixty people, almost twice our crew, but crew are restricted to less than one hundred kilos of personal possessions."

"Do we ever carry passengers?" Damien asked.

"Sometimes," she confirmed. "We keep Rib Four's cabins empty for just that purpose, actually. I'd say we have passengers maybe a quarter of the time—we're no luxury cruise liner, though."

She palmed the scanner by one of the cabins and the door slid open. "Put your palm on the scanner," she ordered, and Damien obeyed. After a moment, the device beeped at him.

"It's now keyed to you," Jenna told him. "The Captain or I can override it if we have cause, but no one else can enter your rooms."

Damien almost missed the plural until he stepped into the cabin. The room was bigger than the space he'd rented on Sherwood Prime, though it only contained a single, extremely lightweight couch, an entertainment screen, and a desk.

"Bedroom to the right, bathroom straight ahead," Jenna told him. "You can pick up some furnishings on the station if you want, but, like I said, one hundred kilos max. The Captain and I have the same restriction—mass is expensive," she concluded with a grin.

"Thank you," Damien told her, looking around the living room with a small degree of shock. "Are all the cabins like this?" he finally asked.

"This is an officer's cabin," she admitted. "The crew cabins are only a single room and the workspace requires you to sit on the bed, but they still have the couch and entertainment screens. *Blue Jay's* first owners outfitted her for the long runs in the Fringe—it makes sense to keep the crew in style if you're in the boonies for months at a time."

The Mage nodded, dropping his single bag—*much* less than a hundred kilos—on the bench and looking around for a moment.

"Where is the simulacrum chamber?" he finally asked, figuring getting to work was probably a good idea.

Jenna laughed. "You've been on the ship less than ten minutes, and we aren't leaving port for at least three days," she told him. "In any case, I have to get back to the bridge for a conference call with the repair company and our insurance agent. How about you get unpacked and grab a bite to eat, and I'll give you the grand tour at eighteen hundred hours?"

Damien looked around the somewhat excessive cabin and at his tiny bag. Unpacking wouldn't take him long, but he could probably order some useful items through the communications net for delivery if he had three days.

"Call it a plan," he agreed.

————

Damien took about forty minutes to unpack his few belongings and lock them away in the drawers set into the wall of his bedroom next to the lightweight bedframe. The bedroom shared the front room's lack of any major pieces of furniture, containing only the bedframe and two sets of shelves set into the wall. A handful of the drawers contained the multi-point clips that substituted for hangers when you were traveling in zero gravity, so he placed his two dress jackets and the eight half-necked dress shirts that were formal wear for Mages in them to keep them unwrinkled.

Fully unpacked, he found himself with over an hour before he was supposed to meet Jenna for the tour of the ship, so he pulled up a map of the ship on the screen in his sitting room and began to study it.

His stomach allowed him long enough to locate the mess hall on Rib Four before loudly growling at him, and he realized he hadn't eaten since before Grace had arrived at his hotel. With a grin at his own forgetfulness, he took mental note of the location of the mess and headed out into the ship's passageways.

The half-gravity that *Blue Jay* maintained wasn't much lighter than the inner area of Ring Seven where he'd been staying and the layout of the Rib was straightforward—each floor had a single passageway down the center, and the mess hall spread from one side of the hull to the other at the end of that corridor on Deck Two.

There was no one in the mess hall when Damien entered it, giving him a minute to take in the plain, lightweight table bolted to the floor, and the similarly lightweight magnetized chairs. One of four mess halls on the ship, this one had enough tables and chairs for sixty people—half again the number Jenna said would live on a rib, and almost three quarters of the crew.

There was a kitchen, set up to function in gravity but be easily secured for zero gravity, and a number of reasonably high-quality food prep units. They were glorified vending machines, but they happily spat out a sandwich and a cup of coffee for Damien with only a little coaxing.

He had half-finished his sandwich when someone else wandered into the mess. A bulky, dark-skinned man with a black turban wrapped around his head, the newcomer flashed bright white teeth at the sight of the gold medallion on Damien's throat.

"So! The Captain did find us a Mage!" the stranger boomed, stepping over to Damien and offering his hand. "I am Narveer Singh, First Pilot aboard *Blue Jay*. May I join you?"

Damien shook the big man's hand and gestured to the several empty seats at the table he'd taken.

"Feel free," he agreed. "I'm Damien Montgomery—the new Ship's Mage, as you guessed."

"The Captain, he is a lucky man!" Singh boomed as he conjured a stew-like dish from the food prep units. "Rumor I heard was that the Governor blacklisted us!"

"I had my reasons to ignore that," Damien told him. "I also never officially heard about it, so I don't think it counts as breaking it."

Singh boomed laughter, echoing off the previously sterile and silent walls of the mess.

"I like your style, Montgomery!" he told the young Mage. "It isn't disobedience if you didn't hear the order—'communications failures' are good for that in shuttles!"

Damien was about to ask about the First Pilot's role when the ship's public address system clicked on with a slightly noticeable, almost definitely artificial buzz.

"Now hear this, now hear this," Jenna's voice rang clearly throughout the ship. "We have confirmed loading times with Sherwood Prime Docking and will have a twelve-hour loading shift commencing at oh nine hundred OMT. Please secure all items for zero gravity.

"I repeat: we will have twelve hours of zero rotation in the ribs starting at oh-nine-hundred Olympus Mons Time tomorrow. That is all."

Singh pumped his fist exuberantly. "Brilliant!"

"What is?" Damien asked, thinking through the announcement. It made sense, though he'd never thought about it, that they'd have to stop rotating the ribs to load the cargo. *Blue Jay*'s ribs were two hundred meters out from the ship's center, which meant they rotated around the ship three times every two minutes, preventing anyone from attaching cargo to the central keel.

"We have a cargo—with the blacklisting, we might not have found one," the dark pilot explained. "The Captain, he is brilliant!" He paused, swallowing down some of his spiced stew. "I'll need to check on the shuttles," he continued after a moment. "We've been using them to help with repairs, but we'll need to get the beasts set up for cargo handling again."

With a shudder at the thought, Narveer Singh started inhaling his food so he could get started. Damien simply watched in amazement and nodded goodbye to the pilot as he left, charging toward the aft of the ships and the shuttle bays.

———

"And this is your working area of the ship," Jenna told Damien as she drifted up to a handhold near another hatch. They'd started their tour of the keel of the ship at Singh's shuttle bay at the rear end of the ship and worked their way down the central corridor of the keel in zero gee. "The last Ship Mage called it the ship's 'Sanctum.'"

Damien followed Jenna through the hatch and saw that the central corridor doglegged ahead around a chamber he knew would be exactly one hundredth the length, height, and width of *Blue Jay*'s exterior structure. Even if Jenna hadn't warned him what he was approaching, that dogleg would have suggested he was approaching the starship's simulacrum chamber.

Runes coated the outside of the chamber: swirling patterns of silver inlay that Damien knew cut through the wall and were visible from the inside as well. From here, they linked into other patterns that marked carefully calculated routes out to the outer hull of *Blue Jay*.

"Your workshop is over here," Jenna continued, gliding neatly up to a side hatch leading off the doglegged main corridor. "Watch your step," she warned, "Kenneth put gravity runes in the workshop, but they've been finicky since..." She trailed off.

"They likely haven't been charged recently enough," Damien told her as he joined her by the workshop door. "Runes like that need to be renewed weekly."

Jenna hit the panel to open the hatch, and it slid aside to reveal what Damien judged to be a relatively standard Mage's workshop—a Wonderland-esque cross between a research lab, a jewelry workshop, and a private office. On the far wall, a centrifugal casting unit occupied the center of a workbench, surrounded by soldering irons and etching tools.

Another wall held a desk with three massive workscreens, touch-driven interfaces that were currently combining to show a pseudo-three-dimensional view of the space around Sherwood. The opposite wall held a spectrometer, a microscope, and a set of micro-scale manipulators—for the *really* fine rune work.

The floor plating was the same plain steel as the rest of the ship, but here someone—Kenneth, presumably, or possibly an even earlier Ship's Mage—had inlaid the silver pattern of runes that provided artificial gravity equivalent to the spinning ribs. They were a common luxury for a Mage's work room, providing a sense of "down" even the Simulacrum chamber lacked.

Even from outside the room, however, Damien could tell that *these* runes were almost uncharged, spitting out tiny bursts of gravity that would make the entire room a tripping hazard.

"Hold up a moment," he told Jenna, and focused. He needed to touch the runes without worrying about spinning off, so he oriented himself with the floor of the workshop and slowly created a gravity field underneath himself. He drifted downward and then settled his feet onto the floor in a comfortable half-gravity before kneeling and removing the glove on his right hand.

As soon as the rune on his palm was within a few centimeters of the runes on the floor, both began to glow gently. Damien focused on that glow and fed energy into the gravity runes. The glow rapidly spread out from his hand, and Jenna's gasp behind him suggested that it was bright enough that the ship's first officer saw it.

After about fifteen seconds, the entire room's floor was glowing brightly to his eyes, and Damien closed his hand into a fist, cutting off the connection between his own power and the runes on the floor.

He rose to face Jenna, standing in his own personal field of gravity as he met the gaze of the officer floating in zero gravity beside him. "It'll be safe to enter now," he told her. "It doesn't take much to maintain a room this small; it just has to be done regularly."

"You don't actually need to deal with zero gee," she answered accusingly, reminding Damien of what he was doing.

He released the spell, though without motion, he remained standing on the deck initially.

"Not really, no," he admitted. "We're taught not to show off magic, though," he explained. "It tends to attract unfortunate attention."

"I can see that," Jenna agreed. "Is there anything you need to check in here?"

Damien took a glance around the workshop. All the equipment looked relatively standard. "Nothing that I can check quickly," he told her. "I'll need a few hours to get used to the gear and the setup before I do much of anything, but you said we have a few days?"

"We do," she confirmed. "Enough of the crew is living aboard that we need to rotate the ribs during the night, so we can only load for one of Sherwood Prime's twelve-hour shifts each day. Even with all of their gear, it takes two full shifts to attach three hundred ten thousand-ton containers to the keel."

"That'll give me time to review the gear and go over the ship's rune matrix," Damien told her. He had never had a chance to inspect the rune matrix of a jump ship in detail before. He saw and identified power flows and purposes better than any other Mage he knew, but it still took time to examine as complex a spell as a jump matrix.

"Speaking of which"—Jenna gestured carefully toward the simulacrum chamber—"the rest of your Sanctum awaits you."

Damien didn't wait for her to catch up with him once he'd kicked off, and touched the panel next to the hatch. It slid gently open, and he slipped into the only space from which he would be able to jump the ship.

The same runes that coated the room on the outside were visible on the interior as well, continuing up onto the roof and the floor and coating the room on all sides. The inlaid silver runes stood out against the thousands of tiny optical diodes around them that projected the image of the outside of the ship. Right now, Damien saw the docking arms and the base of the hub of Sherwood Prime, but beneath him fell away the black of space, and if he looked carefully up and to the side, Sherwood itself was visible past the bulk of the space station.

In the exact center of the room, unsupported yet utterly incapable of moving from that position, was the simulacrum. Forged by magic from molten silver when the ship was built, it exactly mirrored every part of the ship's exterior. *Blue Jay*'s four ribs rotated around. Her forward radiation shield still showed the damage where the last repairs were being done. Damien drifted, unthinking, to the model— exactly one thousandth the size of the ship itself, catching himself on the immobile engines. His hands on the simulacrum, he *felt* the ship, and with the screens around him, he saw what *Blue Jay* saw.

"This place is always awe-inspiring to me," Jenna said quietly from the edge of the room, and Damien glanced up from the impossibly perfect model of the ship to look at her. "I don't understand *any* of how what you do works, but this room...this is the key to the stars."

"That was the Compact," Damien half-whispered, reveling in the power pulsing around him. "Peace between Mage and Mundane, between Mars and Earth...and in exchange, we gave you the stars."

———

"How's the firewood loading going?"

Captain David Rice turned around, carefully, in the bridge's zero gravity to face his executive officer.

"I think the company paying for a million tons of premium hardwood would be…displeased if it was used as firewood," he observed drily. "Or were you referring to the forty-five containers of luxury furniture made from said hardwood?"

Jenna shrugged, grabbing a handhold and positioning herself to review the video screen Rice was watching. On it, the dozens of manipulator arms of a major docking station were carefully maneuvering the Protectorate's standard ten-by-twenty-by-fifty meter, ten-thousand-ton-rated mass cargo containers onto *Blue Jay*'s keel.

"Did you follow up on the secondaries?" he asked her.

"Yep," she confirmed. "Corinthian is just major enough that people are shipping there, and just minor enough that no one has shipped out for two months."

There were dozens of cargos to be shipped between the worlds under the protection of the Mage-King of Mars, but few of them would justify filling even a three-megaton freighter like *Blue Jay*. The usual policy was to book a standard container, fill it with your cargo, and list it as a secondary cargo on a station like Sherwood Prime. As soon as Rice had the contract to ship a hundred and forty-five containers to Corinthian, he'd had Jenna put in a notice to Prime of which world they were shipping for.

All secondary shipping contracts to Corinthian would now be loaded onto *Jay*, along with a massive data upload to be transferred to the other system's communications net. The data transfer fees alone were a hefty part of the freighter's operating costs, but it was the primary cargo contracts that paid the bills.

"How's our young Mage working out?"

"He seems dedicated and smart so far," Jenna told him. "I showed him around Kenneth's lab—he fixed the gravity in about two seconds flat. Last I saw, he was going over the runes in the simulacrum chamber with a magnifying glass."

"He thinks they may have been damaged?" Rice asked, remembering Damien's comment to that effect with a shiver.

"I don't *think* so," she replied. "From what he said, I think it's the first chance he's ever had to really examine a jump matrix, and he wants to make sure it all…'flows right' was how he described it."

"Good." David let out a breath he hadn't realized he'd taken. "We'll have all of the rest of the repairs finished by the time the primary cargo is loaded. We'll hang out a day or so after that for any new secondaries, but then we need to get to Corinthian."

"That wood isn't exactly going to rot in our hull, Skipper," his executive officer pointed out.

"No," David agreed, looking around the empty bridge carefully before continuing quietly. "But I don't think our pirate friends are deaf and dumb either, and I've got an itchy feeling between my shoulder blades. The sooner we're out of Sherwood, the happier I'll be!"

———

The Martian Runic script defined a spell matrix in the same way that a programming language defined the 0s and 1s that allow a computer to function. With seventy-six characters and fourteen different ways of connecting them, the script was complex and difficult to read—and *Blue Jay*'s jump matrix contained the equivalent of sixteen million lines of code.

Damien read Martian Runic fluently, but he couldn't go over that many runes in detail with less than a month of solid reading. Unlike every other Mage he'd ever known, though, he didn't need to. He saw the flow of energy along the patterns and read the purpose and flow of entire blocks and sub-matrices at a single glance.

On a small matrix, like the "warning spell" in Captain Michaels' office, he often read the entire structure of the spell, from its triggers to its actions, in a few seconds. Larger spells would take him some time, but it was minutes where another Mage would spend hours.

He'd never done it on a spell matrix as large as *Blue Jay*'s jump matrix, though, so when he hit the first utterly wrong sub-matrix, he assumed he was misreading it.

The sub-matrix was at the core of the spell, one of the seventeen that linked into the simulacrum at the center of the ship. The other sixteen sub-matrices fed energy out from the simulacrum, but the seventeenth interfaced with the others and changed the energy flow somehow. On certain criteria, it redirected energy away from the main matrix.

Damien spent an hour reading the runes on the sub-matrix and then took another long, hard look at the energy flows. Sub-matrix clusters came in primes and squares, so it was theoretically possible that the seventeenth sub-matrix was unnecessary, but it made no sense. Shaking his head, he made a note on the matrix diagram he'd inherited from the ship mages before him. It was the only current notation on the file, all the previous notes were "sub-matrix in this location damaged by crate impact, repaired" or similar minor fixes.

Still confused, he moved on, following the rune matrix forward toward the prow of the ship.

———

At the front of the ship, where the lengthy connecting sub-matrix expanded into the runes that covered the inside of the immense radiation shield, he found another "wrong" sub-matrix. Four of the sub-matrices made sense, channeling the power of the jump spell out into space, but a fifth, again interfacing with the other four, siphoned off energy if criteria were met. The criteria didn't make sense to Damien, the runes basically redefining the standard teleport spell that the matrix would amplify.

From the empty, echoing void beneath the radiation cap, Damien made his way into Rib One, following the chains of runes that linked together the major sub-matrices into the locked-down decks. At the far extreme of the rib, the links broke apart to create seventeen sub-matrices, spread along the length of the outer rib, the extreme exterior of the ship. The central matrix, the one linking all seventeen together, was "wrong" again. Like the runes in the simulacrum chamber and the radiation shield, it channeled away energy on criteria that read like a description of a jump spell.

By the time Damien had followed the rune matrices around to the central part of Rib Two, he wasn't surprised to find almost the exact same rune matrix as he found in Rib One. He noted the slight differences on his matrix diagram. It almost looked like all three of the matrices were redirecting energy toward the same place if it met the same criteria.

In Rib Three and Rib Four, he didn't even try to follow the linking matrices, heading directly to where he knew he would find the strange matrices. Each was basically an if-then line of code, redirecting energy to a single point in the jump matrix if their criteria were met.

He floated in an empty maintenance space on Rib Four with his personal computer up, reviewing his notes on the sub-matrices. The six patterns had more to do with each other than with the hundreds of other sub-matrices and millions of other runes that made up the jump matrix, and they made no sense to him.

All six redirected energy away from the matrix, where the entire purpose of the runes was to multiply a spell that would transport Damien, personally, roughly ten thousand kilometers at best into a spell that would transport an entire ship a full light-year.

The calculation he'd set to run finally finished, and the computer spat out an answer—all six runes were directing energy to the same place, likely a seventh and final sub-matrix. If his calculations were correct, it was in Engineering.

———

Drifting into the engineering spaces in zero-gravity almost got Damien crushed as a load of containment cylinders of some kind swung through the space just inside the door. Only an instinctive jerk of magic pulled him back from a dangerous collision, and a voice bellowed across the cavernous space at the rear of the freighter.

"*Watch* what you're doing, you dimwits! That's the only damn entrance; let's *try* not to kill ship's officers, eh?"

Damien remained motionless for a long moment as a white-faced assistant engineer caught up to his wayward cargo. The man gave Damien an apologetic glance before regaining control of the floating cart from his datapad. Tiny jets flared on the cart, redirecting the cylinders—which he now noticed had a WARNING: EXPLOSION HAZARD sign on them—away from the Ship's Mage.

A dark-skinned man, not much bigger than Damien's own slight frame, appeared out of the depths of the engineering space, zipping across the empty space and grabbing a support loop with practiced skill, turning bright blue eyes on the Mage.

"Only one person on a ship like this wears that gewgaw," he said gruffly. "Welcome to Engineering, Ship's Mage Montgomery. Chief Engineer James Kellers."

Damien carefully shook the engineer's hand, keeping his feet and spare hand carefully wedged to keep him in place. Releasing the handshake, he looked around the engineering room in awe. There were no rooms, corridors or dividers in the working space at the rear of the ship. Designed for function in zero gee, the space around the engines was festooned with hundreds of devices and consoles that he didn't begin to comprehend.

The room stretched to the exterior of the hull on all sides, and on the far edges of the room Damien saw the graceful looping patterns of the runes of the jump matrix.

"What brings you to Engineering, Mr. Montgomery?" Kellers asked.

"Looking in awe right now," Damien admitted. "I did my jump tests on a much smaller ship, and they had the life support and other equipment separate from the engines."

Kellers nodded. "Probably ex-military," he admitted. "The Navy likes to space important bits out through the keel; minimizes the point failure sources. Concentrating all of the important gear in one place allows three of us keep everything functioning, though."

Damien took a deep breath, inhaling the faint scent of burnt plastic and fused hydrogen. "Is it safe for me to move around in here?" he asked. "I need to review the runes and make sure nothing was damaged when we got banged up."

"The Shipwrights had a pair of Mages in here day before yesterday, checking all of the runes," Kellers told him, scratching the stubble on his chin. "But if you're careful, you should be fine. My boys are not normally quite that dumb," he finished loudly, glaring at the assistant who'd nearly flattened Damien.

With a nod to Damien, the engineer kicked off toward one of the many strange machines in the cavernous space. Damien took a moment to orient himself against the map he'd put together on his PC, and then kicked off himself.

The runes he was looking for weren't on the exterior hull, but as he approached the strange device they were carved on, he saw that they were close. A massive block extended in from the "'bottom" of Engineering, with grills and strange conduits all over it. The runes ran in from the sub-matrices that connected the matrix to the rear of the ship, and Damien looked at them, tracking their energy.

The links that flowed out to the matrix on the massive metal block were barely even connected to the main spell, tying directly back to the other strange matrices throughout the ship. Whatever the other runes were doing, it focused here.

The runes on the center of the block were different from the other six weird matrices. Those had all been roughly the same, criteria-triggered redirects. This just took all of the energy that flowed into it and cast a simple…fire spell?

"Kellers?" Damien called. After a moment, the engineer rejoined him, a worried look on his dark face.

"Something broken in the runes?" he asked quickly.

"I don't think so…" Damien said quietly, eyeing the matrix. "What's this block?"

"Block?" the engineer said slowly, blinking at the massive piece of technology in front of him before smiling brightly. "Oh, *that*—sorry, I've never heard anyone not know what it is. That's our primary heat exchanger—takes the excess heat from the reactor and life support and dumps it into space. Without it, we'd eventually cook ourselves just with our body heat, let alone the engines!"

The Mage eyed the runes. A spell to create heat in something that had the purpose of getting rid of heat still made no sense.

"How much extra capacity does it have?" he wondered aloud. If this was something wrong, at least it probably wouldn't cause too much damage.

"A lot," the engineer told him. "The only thing on the ship more overengineered than the heat exchanger is the main reactor core. You could fire one of the main engines at this baby and it would dump the heat to space. Whatever you're thinking, this gear can take it."

Damien nodded, eyeing the runes again. Whatever they did, it clearly wasn't new—the runes had the permanently rubbed-in layer of dirt over them that came from being as old as the ship itself. The jump matrix was a standard set of runes; no one ever changed it. Whatever these runes were, they made sense to experts with a lot more experience than Damien.

But the pattern of energy to them…didn't fit.

———

The strange matrices didn't quite leave Damien's mind over the next few days, but they weren't the focus of his attention as *Blue Jay* loaded its cargo for its journey to the Corinthian System. He'd helped arrange the loading of supplies onto the freighter for the crew while keeping one eye on the overall loading process, and spent his spare time checking the rune matrix for any damage.

The last day before they left the station, he and Captain Rice spent three hours going over the calculations for the fifteen jumps it would take them to travel to the other system. They'd worked out a relatively sedate three-jumps-a-day path that would deliver their massive cargo in just less than five days without straining Damien much on his first-ever voyage. Including the two and a half days of maneuvering clear of the gravity wells at the beginning and end of the trip, it would be a ten-day voyage to cross fifteen light-years.

Finally, after three days of chaos, he waited in the simulacrum chamber as *Blue Jay* began to slowly accelerate out of Sherwood Prime. The chamber had a small platform just "beneath" the simulacrum in the acceleration-driven gravity, allowing him to keep a hand on the magical token, sensing the gentle rush of power as the freighter accelerated at one twentieth of a gravity.

Around him, he watched the station rotate around the ship as they spun to face open space. On a part of the bubble of screens that surrounded him, he had a video link open to the bridge. Jenna sat at the navigation console, her face composed as she fed the computer the series of maneuvers that would get them clear of the station.

On the screen of the PC strapped to his wrist, Damien reviewed the calculations for the jump. He kept one eye on the world around the ship, though, and saw when they were finally clear, the last gantries falling behind them.

A few more minutes passed in silence, and then Rice spoke on the bridge link.

"Link to Sherwood Prime," he ordered. A moment later, a triple click announced an open channel.

"Sherwood Prime to *Blue Jay*, our screens show you clear of the station safety zone," a space controller's voice informed them. "Please confirm."

"Sherwood Prime, this is *Blue Jay* Actual," Rice replied. "We show five-kilometer separation; requesting permission to fire main engines at seven hundred thirty eight Olympus Mons time."

"We confirm five-kilometer separation and authorize main engine firing," the controller informed him. "*Cair vie, Blue Jay.*"

"*Na h-uile la gu math duit,* Sherwood Prime," Rice replied, the old Gaelic flowing smoothly off his tongue. The channel shut down and his next words were for the crew.

"All hands, hear this, all hands, hear this," he said into the PA. "All ribs are secured, all cargo is secured, prepare for one-gravity burn in two minutes."

At seven thirty-eight AM on the faraway clock of the mountain the Protectorate was ruled from, *Blue Jay*'s main engines burned to life, the tiny stars sending a surge of entirely nonmagical power through the simulacrum under Damien's hands.

Standing on the acceleration platform, Damien breathed deeply, standing against the firm acceleration and reviewing the calculations on the datapad again. There was no computer assistance for the final jump—he had to know the vectors and energy levels in his mind and move the ship entirely with his magic.

———

Blue Jay accelerated for twenty-four hours, building velocity, and then coasted for another day, drawing clear of the gravity well of the planet behind them. Damien calculated and recalculated his first jump. Rice reviewed it once more, the morning of the third day.

It finally came down to it late that afternoon. Damien checked the sensor readouts, and they were clear enough of gravity wells for the spell to function.

"Captain, we're ready to jump," he said quietly into the bridge link, and Rice nodded.

"Note for the log," Rice ordered. "It is seventeen forty Olympus Mons Time, and I am authorizing the jump."

"Noted for the log," Jenna replied, though Damien knew the computer would be recording after the phrase "noted for the log."

Rice looked through the link directly at Damien, holding his gaze. "You may jump when ready, Ship's Mage," he said firmly.

Damien nodded, and turned his attention from the link screen to the simulacrum floating at the heart of *Blue Jay*. The tiniest of kicks launched him away from the acceleration platform, leaving him floating in zero gravity, held in place only by his hands on the silver icon of *Blue Jay*'s essence.

With a deep breath, he slipped the runes on his bare palms into the exact places carved for them on the simulacrum, and let his power become part of the rune matrix of the ship. The screens around him allowed him to see as the ship saw, and now he *felt* the ship.

He reached out with his mind, confirming through the simulacrum what the sensors had already told him—that the space-time here was sufficiently unbent by gravity to allow for a jump.

He touched the reservoir of power in his core, mustering energy up into his hands and through the connection into the ship. The rune matrix greedily sucked up his power, reflecting it around the ship in an ever-building net that would have been almost blinding to someone who saw the magic in the rune matrix.

Without conscious thought, Damien knew the calculations were perfect, and he held them in the center of his mind.

Then he released his breath and his power and *moved*. He touched a blip in the probability of reality, and all of his energy fled his body in a single exhalation.

Blue Jay jumped.

———

"How are we looking?" Rice asked Jenna as soon as the indescribable sensation of being transported trillions of kilometers through space in an instant faded.

"Checking position now," she replied, running a series of programs on her console before looking back up at him. "We are bang on target, dead center in jump zone one of the Sherwood-Corinthian sequence."

Rice turned to the monitor showing him the simulacrum chamber, taking in the utterly drained expression on his new Ship's Mage.

"Well done, Mr. Montgomery," he told the youth. "Shall we schedule the next jump for oh three hundred Olympus Mons time?"

That would give the young man over nine hours to rest—nine hours it looked like the Mage desperately needed. He and Damien had scheduled to jump every eight hours, but after the new Ship's Mage's first jump, he figured they could spare the time.

"I'll be ready," Damien promised; his voice soft with fatigue.

"Get some sleep, Damien," Rice ordered. "We'll talk before the next jump."

With a nod, the young Mage turned off the video link, and Rice turned to Jenna.

"Scopes clear?" he asked quietly.

"All clear so far as our sensors can read," she replied, equally quiet. "No one has come through here in a week at least."

Rice considered the screen showing the thermal signatures around them. The thermal scope was the most reliable method of detecting ships, seeing as how any vessel under power blazed like a tiny sun against the backdrop of empty space.

"Three degrees Kelvin as far as our eyes can see," he muttered to himself. "Why does that not make me feel better?"

"Because you're rightfully paranoid, sir," Jenna replied.

"Which is why I want you to send the maintenance 'bots out to check over both of our new turrets," Rice told her.

———

For ninety quiet minutes, Rice slowly relaxed as no sign of pirates or technical difficulties materialized. Both of the new Rapid Fire Laser Antimissile turrets checked out as fully functional, and he took some comfort in the fact that he'd paid to upgrade them heavily from the previous weapons. Each of these turrets was rated to take down a four missile salvo like the last one they'd faced on its own.

Ninety-one minutes after arrival at the jump zone, all of his quiet hopes for a peaceful trip shattered as the distinctive heat and radiation flare of an incoming jump appeared on their screens.

"Jump flare!" he barked, grabbing Jenna's attention from her focus on the maintenance 'bots. "Get me something, Jenna," he ordered as she pulled up the rest of the sensor suite. Heat would tell them only so much.

"Single ship, three million kilometers," she reported, then double-checked her figures. "Damn, their Mage must have blown his numbers —I bet they were planning on coming out right on top of us."

As if to prove her comment, the heat signature on the new contact flared with a sudden, massive brightness.

"Boss, if I'm reading this right, she just lit off a fusion rocket at six gees," Jenna said quietly, and David winced.

"Time to missile range?" he asked steadily.

"If they're using the same birds as last time, about an hour," she admitted. "If the turrets hold up, it'll take them just over five hours to match speeds and rendezvous with us to board—that's if we start burning now."

Five hours. That would make it over six hours since Damien had jumped, which meant that, if they could make it, the young Mage would be able to jump them *before* the pirate ship boarded them.

"Sound the emergency acceleration alert," Rice ordered, "and let's burn directly away from them. Let's buy as much time as we can."

A klaxon began ringing through the ship, and the bars on his screen showing the rotational speeds of the ribs rapidly shrank.

"All ribs at full stop," Jenna reported. "Initiating emergency burn...now."

The four massive fusion torches at the rear of the ship lit up, and a large man sat down on Rice's chest as his ship began to accelerate at two full gravities.

———

It seemed like Damien had barely closed his eyes when the klaxon woke him up. He certainly didn't have time to wake up or prepare at all before the rib stopped rotating and the motion of his waking up sent him drifting away from the bed beneath him, into the safety straps included for just that occurrence.

Then the engines engaged, and two gravities of force slammed him into the back wall of his cabin, crushing the breath from his body. He struggled against the gravity to regain some measure of breath and then wove magic around his body to reduce the force to something he could move in.

"Captain, this is Damien," he said as he opened a link to the bridge. "What's happening?"

"We've been ambushed," Rice said shortly, his breath strained. "They missed their jump, though, and we should be able to stand off the missiles until you can jump us again. How long?"

Damien focused for a moment, testing the reserve of energy buried deep inside of him. It had recovered somewhat during his hour-long nap. The gravity spell wasn't a major strain, and from the feel, he could handle anything that wasn't major.

Of course, a teleport spell was the definition of *major*.

"At least a few more hours," he admitted. "I'm still shot to hell."

There was a long pause, during which Damien pulled on a shirt and grabbed a folded-up emergency pressure helmet.

"We're running," Rice said finally. "But he's got four gravities on us, and he'll be in missile range in under an hour. Anything you can do?"

"I can knock down some missiles from the simulacrum chamber," the Mage told him. "Not sure what else…"

"Any little bit helps," the Captain told him.

"Then I'll be in the simulacrum chamber," Damien promised.

———

Blue Jay was not a small ship, and there was no direct route from Damien's quarters in the middle of Rib Four to the simulacrum chamber at the center of the vessel. The two gravities of acceleration didn't help, though at least the ship had fold-out stairs and other tools to function with acceleration-driven gravity.

By the time Damien made it to the chamber, struggling up a ladder to the small platform beneath the simulacrum, the pirate ship was just drawing into missile range. He opened a video link to the bridge, as well as several windows that showed him sensor data on the area and the ship.

"There he was," Jenna said suddenly, as a spike of hour-old light showed up in the sensors. "Bastard was sitting a full light-hour out of the jump zone with his drives dead—not even the Martian boys would have picked him up at that distance—but he'd have seen everyone jump in. He IDed our signature as soon as it reached him, took half an hour to be ready, and then jumped us. If their Mage hadn't overshot, we'd have been dead or boarded before we even knew they were there."

Damien replayed the sudden burst of energy and saw her point. Up to that moment, now a full hour earlier, there had been no sign of a ship in that bit of space. Then the jump flare appeared, marking the pirate's disappearance in the jump they'd ambushed *Blue Jay* from.

"Missiles," Jenna reported calmly as four more signatures lit up on the thermal scope. "They look the same as last time—two thousand gravities acceleration, seven-and-a-half-minute flight time. I'm taking evasive maneuvers—hold on!"

The missiles were anemic compared to the antimatter-driven weapons the Protectorate Navy would use, but they were still a thousand times faster than *Blue Jay*. Damien focused the sensor screen on them, using it to focus in and zoom on the missiles.

Through the simulacrum, Damien could affect the space around them with his magic, but all it did was let him see as the ship saw. His power and range for his normal spells were almost the same, unlike using the jump spell.

One of the spells he knew, however, was explicitly intended for just this situation. It was draining, but it had a range of forty or so thousand kilometers. Normally, that was utterly useless, but here and now, he could take down a missile in its last six seconds or so of flight.

"Sixty seconds to impact," Jenna announced. "RFLAMs engaging."

The lasers were invisible on the visual screens that surrounded Damien, though they lit up the sensor feeds. Their results weren't. One missile and then another disappeared in fireballs that were clearly visible in the zoomed-in screen.

A third missile detonated, and then the last came within Damien's reach. His power flicked out through the simulacrum's matrix and conjured a tiny fireball, not much more than a spark.

Conjured *inside* the missile's fuel cells, it triggered a reaction that blew the missile apart.

***

Even as Damien breathed a sigh of relief, something was bothering him. A niggling thought at the back of his head. The spell he'd cast hadn't felt right. It wasn't a spell he'd cast many times before, but most of the time he had he'd been in deep space, casting through a window or viewscreen on the side of a ship.

This wasn't the first time he'd cast it from the simulacrum chamber of a starship—but it was the first time he'd done so only a short while after casting the jump spell. The feel of the two spells should have been very different to his mind. The jump spell was tied into and amplified by the rune matrix throughout the starship, but the defense spell was only using the simulacrum to allow him to see what he was aiming at.

Both spells had felt *exactly* the same when he'd cast them. His energy had fed into the matrix that ran throughout the ship, and he swore that the defense spell had started the same amplifying feedback loop that the jump spell had...and then it had simply continued on as normal, as if that loop had broken.

He ignored the pursuing ship as he dove into the ship's operating system, looking for something he knew had to be there.

"More missiles incoming," he heard Jenna's voice report. "I think the RFLAMs have their measure now, but keep your eyes open, Damien."

The missiles were still two minutes out when he found what he was looking for. The usage level of the main heat converter popped up on his side screen, tracking back in time…to a massive heat spike when he'd cast the spell.

He stared at the spike in shock, understanding what the strange matrices he'd found did at last. There was no difference between a jump matrix and the spell amplifier a warship would carry—except that those seven sub-matrices would break the amplifier loop for any spell *but* the jump spell.

His moment of realization shattered when *Blue Jay* leapt under his feet. Five megatons of mass jumped like a startled puppy, and then he was in zero gravity.

―――――――

"What the hell happened?" Rice demanded. The RFLAM turrets had only just started to engage—the missiles had been tens of thousands of kilometers out, nowhere near close enough to actually hit the ship.

"Three of the missiles were decoys," Jenna said grimly. "They were augmenting their radar signatures, and we nailed all three. The fourth was an x-ray laser. It blew up at twenty thousand klicks and hit the engines."

X-ray laser warheads were rare and expensive—so expensive that even the Martian Navy didn't use them normally. A small atomic bomb triggered a lasing reaction in specially treated crystals, providing a deadly and precise standoff weapon.

Rice flipped up a link to engineering. "Kellers, how bad is it?" he demanded.

"We've a giant hole through the main conduits for Two and Three," the engineer snapped back. "The conduit for One got clipped—that *might* be repairable, but if we fire up Two or Three before a shipyard's been at them, we may as well just set off a nuke back here."

"Get me at least one engine back, Kellers," Rice ordered. He turned back to Jenna, and she answered his question before he asked it.

"It's gained them forty minutes," she said quietly. "Maybe as much as a full hour."

An inexperienced Mage jumping with anything less than a six-hour wait between jumps risked the same fate that Kenneth McLaughlin had suffered. Rice looked at the link to Damien, knowing that the youth would likely risk it. If they pushed it close enough, it might even work—assuming the pirate didn't open them to air and let them suffocate. The bounty on Rice's head would be paid as happily for a vacuum-preserved corpse as for a live prisoner. He met the young Mage's eyes and saw something there he wasn't expecting: hope.

"Captain, I have an idea," Damien told him.

He ran for the front of the ship, power flaring through the runes in his palm as he formed his own "down" in the zero gravity of the ship. A bag of tools, soldering irons and silver wire, banged against his side as he dodged around Singh, who was trying to make his way backward along the keel. The big Sikh stared at him in surprise, then flashed him a thumbs-up.

"Whatever you're doing, Montgomery, good luck!" he shouted after Damien, who barely heard him as he caught a support bar and redirected his personal gravity.

With a bruising thump, Damien slammed into the underside of the ship's radiation cap, where the sub-matrix diverted energy away if it wasn't a jump spell. He focused his gaze on it, following the lines of energy and noting where they detoured.

With a deep breath, he pulled the soldering iron and embossing tools out. With a single slash of the iron, he severed a rune. Molten silver followed, new runes taking shape that looped the energy back into the general matrix.

One link done, he slid sideways and repeated the process. Runes were something to carve carefully, with time, precision and detailed calculations. Without time, Damien relied on his sight, on knowing how the energy would flow.

The forward matrix took him fifteen minutes to disconnect, and then he ran again, redirecting gravity to speed him toward Rib One.

He had mere hours to change the entire nature of the rune matrix, and all he could do was pray he was doing it right.

————

Damien had made it to Rib Four when the ship lurched out from beneath his feet, his spell failing to compensate for the entire kilometer's length of the vessel jerking a full meter sideways. He slammed into the wall, gouging his hands and cracking his jaw.

Carefully feeling his jaw for any major injuries, he opened a link to the bridge.

"What the hell was that?" he demanded.

"They have a laser," Rice said shortly. "And we no longer have a forward turret. You're out of time, Damien. Whenever that thing recharges, we lose the rear turret, and then we either jump or die."

Damien looked at the sub-matrix for Rib Four. Most of the runes were severed, with only one rune chain still linking it. With a deep breath, he focused on the lines of energy and slashed with the soldering iron. If he'd judged it right, he'd broken the rune without creating a dangerous feedback loop, but at this point, he could only hope.

"Computer, connect me to engineering," he ordered his PC as he charged rearward for the simulacrum chamber.

"Kellers, it's Montgomery," he told the engineer, focusing his gravity spell so that he fell toward the rear of the ship.

"I'm a little busy trying to keep us from blowing the fuck up, kid; this better be important," the engineer snapped.

"You know those runes on the main heat exchanger?" Damien asked, grunting as he slammed into the ladder leading to the keel. He hadn't slowed himself enough, but he hadn't broken any bones.

"What? What about them?" Kellers demanded. *"Watch that hydrogen line,"* he bellowed at somebody else. "Do *not* connect that thing to the conduit yet; hold off till I *tell* you to hook it up."

"I need you to break the rune chains connecting them to the rest of the ship's matrix," the Mage told him.

There was silence on the other end of the line as Damien forced his bruised, weary legs to carry him toward the keel.

"And how the fuck am I supposed to do that?" Kellers finally demanded.

"It shouldn't matter," Damien told him honestly. He was pretty sure that destroying the other six matrices would render the one in engineering utterly ineffectual—but he couldn't be certain. "Weld it, gouge, burn it—take an ax to it for all I care, but I'll be in the simulacrum chamber in two minutes, and I need those runes disconnected when I get there."

Another pause. "You owe me one hell of an explanation, Montgomery, but I'll see what I can do," Kellers finally said.

"If we live, I'll explain with diagrams," Damien promised, and then redirected his gravity spell toward the simulacrum.

As long as he made it to the simulacrum in time, he didn't care if he broke something anymore.

———

Leaving the door to the simulacrum chamber open had been one of his better ideas. He fell through the door, barely slowing himself at the last moment. With a deep breath and steeling himself against the result, Damien grabbed onto the simulacrum to slow himself.

The simulacrum *couldn't* move. He barely held his grip, and one of his arms was clearly going to make him pay later, but he stopped.

He looked up at the bridge link and met Rice's eyes.

"They have a six-minute recharge on the laser," the Captain told him. "It's no Navy gun, but it's plenty for their purposes. We are now out of defenses, so I hope your idea works."

"We'll see," he said quietly, opening a link to engineering. "Kellers?"

"It's done," the engineer replied. "You have no idea how scared shitless I am right now."

"Join the club," Damien told him. "Everyone hold on."

With a deep breath, he placed the runes on his palms on the model and became the ship.

This was the true purpose of the matrix. He knew it the moment he linked in. Before, only trying to cast the jump spell had linked this completely to the ship. Now, just completing the matrix changed everything.

He saw as the ship saw. Felt as it felt. The scars where the turrets had been burned away hurt as badly as his own strained limbs. The broken engines burned as if his own skin had been seared with fire.

And *Blue Jay*'s eyes were his eyes. He saw in radiation and heat as clearly as day, and saw the pirate ship closing on them, certain now that it had disabled its victim—so certain they hadn't even demanded their surrender.

This time, he had no intention of scaring anyone off. The simple self-defense fire spell every Mage learned leapt to his mind, and power flowed from his hands into the runes of the ship. He sensed the power loop through the ship, repeating and building so quickly no one outside the spell would have sensed it.

Fire lit the darkness of deep space as his magic lit a tiny sun and flung it across the void. His senses and power followed it the entire way, waiting for the pirate to try to dodge.

They never even saw it coming. Superheated plasma ripped through their hull, tearing a hole through the length of the ship, until the fireball reached the antimatter storage that fueled the pirate's engines.

The ship vanished in the searing white flame of annihilating matter.

———

As *Blue Jay* drifted in space, the senior officers gathered on the bridge. Damien joined Kellers, Jenna and the Captain, and found himself the center of attention.

"What did you *do*?" David asked.

"I turned our jump matrix into an amplifier," Damien explained. "There were limiters built into the spell matrix to make it only amplify the jump spell—I removed them."

"That's *possible*?" Jenna exclaimed.

"A week ago, I would have said no," the young Mage said. "We're discouraged from looking too closely at the jump matrix—messing with it in flight is illegal. I just had no choice."

"Can we still jump?"

"Yes," Damien replied unhesitatingly.

"Good enough," Captain Rice replied, turning to Kellers. "What about the engines?"

"We've fixed the conduits for One, but Two and Three are gone until we get to Corinthian."

The Captain nodded, looking around at the officers.

"Then whenever you're ready, Mr. Montgomery, let's be on our way."

STARSHIP'S MAGE

This was the first episode of the five contained in *Starship's Mage*

Also available in Starship's Mage series:
Starship's Mage
Hand of Mars
Voice of Mars
Alien Arcana
Judgment of Mars
UnArcana Stars
Sword of Mars
Mountain of Mars
The Service of Mars (upcoming)

Starship's Mage: Red Falcon
Interstellar Mage
Mage-Provocateur
Agents of Mars

FAE, FLAMES, AND FEDORAS

A Changeling Blood universe novella

FAE, FLAMES AND FEDORAS

Joe Costa sighed exasperatedly as he filled the date in on the form—September 8, 1948—and accepted the detonators and wires he used to do his job every single day. Stacking them and several boxes of explosives on his cart, the burly sewer worker quickly caught up with his team as they headed into the new sewer tunnel heading out west, into one of New York's rapidly growing suburbs.

The six-man tunnel-blasting team lit up their electric headlamps as they passed beyond the brightly lit excavation where the engineers had laid out diagrams of how the sewers were going to look in about six months. Most of the work was being done on the surface, with excavations and pipelines, but Costa's team's job was to blast the massive drain tunnels the rest of the pipelines drained into.

This required them to walk the better part of a mile through the portion of the tunnel they'd already blasted out, in roughly an inch of water that had leaked in from where the tunnel linked to the existing storm system that drained out to the sea.

The group of men laughed and joked as they headed deeper and deeper under the earth, their lights occasionally reflecting off various side tunnels where the other sewers linked to their tunnel. The joking was self-defence—Costa shivered slightly, remembering the first few times they'd made even part of this trek. With only their headlamps to light the way in the dark, it was terrifying.

They reached the end of the tunnel, where they'd finished clearing and smoothing the existing walls the night before.

"Have at 'er, Joe!" the team lead told the demolitions man.

With a big grin, Joe started pulling explosives off of his cart and setting them on the rough rock face where the tunnel would soon extend. Even though he'd gone over the placements with the engineers the previous evening, he'd served in the War and could have done it himself by feel.

For the first hour or so, the other five men were mostly only there to keep the demo man from going insane in the dark, though he happily used them as grunt labour, running wires and holding charges in place. If nothing else, the other sewer workers' expressions when holding the charges were always priceless.

"Right, boys, stand back," he finally ordered once the first set of charges was in place. Joe wasn't technically in charge of the team, but no one argues with the man holding the detonator.

The big man lit a cigarette as he backed away with the rest of the team and rolled out the wire from his detonator until they were clear.

"Fire in the 'ole!" he barked and hit the button.

He expected a shockwave of air, a blast wave of heat, and then a shortness of breath for a few minutes while the air refreshed in the tunnel.

There was a shock and blast of heat, but then his cigarette was torn from his hand by a massive backflush of air as it rushed into the space opened by the explosion. The sound of the explosion echoed, along with a clatter of stone falling into an empty space that shouldn't have been there.

Joe carefully picked up his cigarette as the rest of the team ran forward to see what had happened. No demolitions man would ever leave loose flame in an area he was working.

"You've gotta see this, Joe!" one of the men yelled. "We blew into some kind of cave."

"*Madre de dios,*" one of the other workers suddenly swore. "That's *gold.*"

That got even Joe's attention. He jogged lightly forward to join his team. They were well ahead of him, scrabbling down the uneven slope of the massive hollow he'd blown open. Distantly, flickering in the light of their headlamps, he could make out the gold the other man had seen.

It wasn't the veins of natural gold he'd been expecting. It was *coins* —piles of coins. Blinking against the strangely fresh air of the cave, he saw that it wasn't just the metal—the gold lay amidst statues and what looked like the fanciful scrolls from Hollywoodland movies. A giant pile of money and artifacts buried under New York? That was impossible!

Joe stayed at the edge of the cavern for a moment, trying to comprehend what his coworkers' lights were showing him, and that was why he saw the movement before any of them did.

He opened his mouth to shout a warning, and then the hollow was suddenly filled with light. A pillar of flame wider than a man was tall flared through the cave. It lit the entire space as bright as day for a few moments, showing the immense cavern to be filled with gold and priceless artifacts—and the immense winged lizard that had just burnt two of Joe's friends to ash.

There was movement in the dark as Joe stared blankly forward, and then a third light simply disappeared with a cut-off scream, and the remaining two workers who'd entered the tunnel turned to run.

Joe didn't wait for them. His paralysis broke with the scream, and he fled back through his tunnel.

None of the others ever caught up to him again.

———

Talus, son of Korinth, noble of the Seelie Courts of the Fae, had never visited New York before. When he left his birthplace in London for the wilds of Western Canada to escape the Blitz, he'd been carried by the Wild Hunt and had bypassed all of North America's ports.

The nineteen-year-old fair-haired Fae tried not to gawk as the car carrying him and two other young Fae into the city drove through under-construction skyscrapers and other wonders of the energy of man.

An older, dark-skinned Fae drove the car, grinning unabashedly as his three young passengers gawked at the bustling energy of the city around them. In the aftermath of the War, New York continued to grow ever more dramatically. That growth had left the Fae Courts in the city under-strength and overwhelmed, so both the Seelie and Unseelie had sent out calls for new blood to support them.

Talus was still, technically, the ward of his uncle Oberis, the Fae Lord of the western half of Canada, but he'd argued that as a fully trained Fae Noble, one of the most powerful beings in the world, he was doing the Courts a disservice by remaining in what was, supernaturally, a complete backwater.

So he and the other three youths in the car, all of them Seelie Fae Nobles, all of them under the age of twenty-five, had answered the call of the New York Court. Clad in trench coats and fedoras against the autumn chill, they'd met their driver on a train platform and now were seeing New York for the first time.

The black car eventually pulled into a loop around a massive oak tree next to a four-story brownstone building on the edge of Manhattan Island. The driver turned to look at the three youths and smiled gently at them.

"This is the Manor for New York," he told them. "Keeper Owen should be waiting for you."

The sign above the door the oak shaded declared the brownstone the Galahad Inn. All Fae were required to meet with the Keeper, the neutral arbiter of Fae law in an area, when they arrived in a new town. In turn, the Keeper was responsible for providing three days of room and board—formally "succor"—to them, so most Keepers ran a hotel as their Manor.

The driver easily offloaded the three suitcases from the trunk, and then the car drove off, presumably to some hidden parking lot behind the building. With a grin at the other two Fae, Talus grabbed up his suitcase and entered the hotel.

The lobby looked more like a museum than a hotel. It was a double-height room that stretched the full length of the building, with glass display cases shaping the space into clear areas and serving as the reception desk.

Each of the display cases contained weapons. Some were clearly crude, historical artifacts from the history of firearms. Some were new, likely used in the World War a few years before. Pride of place in the room was taken by a stacked display of what Talus recognized as bazookas, with an odd, multi-barrelled weapon set up on a tripod on top, out of reach of even the tallest without climbing.

Around the display cases with their impressive arsenal, the interior of the building was panelled in plain light wood, and cheap but sturdy furniture filled a clear hotel waiting area. A dark-skinned man, similar enough to the driver of the car to have been his twin, sat behind the reception counter—a display case of no fewer than fifteen tommy guns. Two men and a woman, dressed in the same trench coat and fedora as Talus—and, truth be told, about half of New York—occupied one of the seating areas.

Like Talus and his companions, the receptionist and all three guests had their hair cut roughly shoulder length, concealing their ears. The receptionist lacked the high pronounced cheekbones of most of the Fae, but the guests all shared it.

Talus approached the desk.

"I am Talus," he told the man simply. "I believe we are expected."

The dark-skinned Fae ducked his head minimally, checking a list. "Yes, Master Talus, Master Caleb, Master Andre. Keeper Owen is unfortunately out of the Manor, dealing with a Covenant issue. He will be returning shortly and asked me to hold the six of you to meet with him."

"The six of us?" Talus asked, glancing over at the other three Fae.

"Yes, Masters Michael and Morgan and Mistress Celia are nobles of the Unseelie Court," the lesser Fae explained. "Keeper Owen wished to speak with all six of you since we rarely get quite so many nobles arriving at the same time."

"Thank you," Talus told the man, raising an eyebrow in question for the man's name.

"I am Isaac, sir," the dark-skinned Fae offered. "You met my brother Abraham on the way here."

"Thank you, Isaac. We will await the Keeper's pleasure."

Behind him, Talus felt Caleb and Andre bristle, but they remained silent. They might object to him taking the lead, but the truth was simple.

Whether they wished to or not, they would await the Keeper.

———

Talus considered avoiding the Unseelie Nobles for a few moments, but there was only one large sitting area in the hotel lobby, and it would be impolite to blatantly sit apart from them. The split between Seelie and Unseelie Fae was more on the order of a family feud than a conflict between nations. Some sub-species exclusively hewed to one side or another, but in the main, Fae were Fae, and if the race was challenged, Seelie and Unseelie would stand together. That was why the Keeper existed, after all.

Concluding the only polite thing to do was to introduce himself, he crossed to the sitting area in the shadow of the pyramid of rocket launchers and offered the three nobles a slight bow, that of a Noble to an equal.

"Good day," he said genially. "I am Talus of the Seelie Court of Western Canada."

The same standards of politeness that had forced him to join them forced them to their feet. The woman, a petite platinum blonde with pitch-black eyes, bowed first, slightly deeper than required to better expose a flirtatious amount of *décolletage*.

"I am Celia, of the Unseelie Court of San Francisco. Greetings," she returned before allowing her two male companions to speak.

"Greetings," the largest of the three Unseelie Fae rumbled. He was easily six inches over six feet, and an ugly scar crossed the man's face. "I am Morgan, most recently of the United States Marines."

The last of the three Unseelie grinned at Morgan's self-description. "I'm Michael," he said simply. Michael was the smallest of the six Fae present, barely over five feet tall, but there was an air around the fair-haired man that suggested this was *not* a Noble to mess with.

"I am Caleb, of the Seelie Court of London," the first of Talus's fellow Seelie joined the introductions. Caleb was a slim Fae, almost as tall as Morgan but far slighter than the massively bulky ex-Marine. He was also, so far as Talus could tell, a cousin on Talus's mother's side.

Andre had opened his mouth seconds too late to pre-empt Caleb, which left him introducing himself last. From the corner of his eye, Talus could tell that the redheaded Noble was unenthused, but he introduced himself gamely.

"I be Andre, of the *Teutha* Courts," he said simply, declaring himself a Noble of the homeland, one of the Irish Fae beholden directly to the Council of Lords and Ladies that ruled their race.

The formalities observed, Talus and the other Seelie joined the Unseelie in the sitting area. None of the six seemed to feel overly pressured to make conversation, and the time passed slowly.

After a few minutes, he found himself examining the odd revolver-like launcher at the top of the pyramid of anti-tank weapons in the middle of the lobby. Almost as long as he was tall, it was made of nine tubes surrounded by a metal ring at two points. Standing and crossing to it, he could only make out a single trigger mechanism. It was designed to fit over the shoulder in much the same way as the US Army-issue bazookas stacked beneath it.

"That's a *Luftfaust*—or *Fliegerfaust B*, depending on who you ask," someone said behind him. "One of Hitler's people's many brilliant ideas that never quite got produced in enough quantity to make a difference in the war. I ended up with three, but as you can tell, I collect weaponry."

Talus turned to the speaker, who turned out to be a dark-tanned older man, his skin weathered by the sun and his eyes a glinting, gleeful blue. The typical Fae features that were so stark in the Nobles were muted in this man, though the feeling of oak strength and iron will that radiated from him suggested that even they should take him seriously.

"I am Owen, Keeper of the city of New York," he introduced himself. "I am a Gille, for those of you who were wondering, not a Noble."

Talus nodded his understanding. The Gille were one of the races that mostly joined the Seelie Courts, but they were bound to trees in a way that tended to keep them outside Court politics even when they joined a Court. The immense oak outside, for example, was likely bonded to the Fae in front of him. While they both lived, they would both draw strength from the other. Of course, Owen would survive the tree dying—and the reverse was *not* the case.

"Welcome to my Manor," the Fae continued. "If any of you are in need of the traditional three days of succor, you are already booked into rooms—just ask Isaac for your key.

"I apologize for holding you up as I have, but something came up in my meeting with the city's mortal authorities. It appears that a number of workers have gone missing in the city's sewer construction project," he explained. "What little information I could extract from the survivor was inconclusive but enough for me to know that his companions are dead—and that it wasn't an accident or any ordinary creature that claimed the lives of his compatriots."

"What does this have to do with us?" Morgan asked, his deep voice surprisingly curious rather than challenging.

"This city is not really under the control of any supernatural faction," Owen told them, perching on the edge of a display case. "Until a few years ago, the vampires ran New York—and it was mortals that drove them out, not us.

"This means the Covenants between us, the Shifters, the Magi, and others in the city are still in negotiation," he explained. "Any action we can undertake that shows us to be capable of handling incidents like this in which others couldn't or hadn't will help us seize a position of primacy here. I want to be sure that this beast, whatever it is, dies. That's where you six come in."

"Isn't six Nobles a leetle much for some poor beastie in the sewers?" Michael asked, glancing around the group. "Wouldn't just one of us be more than enough?"

"We don't know what's down there," Owen reminded them. "There are many creatures in this world that could threaten a Fae Noble alone. There are even creatures that would pose a real threat to two or three Nobles. There are very few things in this world short of the Powers that could threaten *six* of you."

"We're all new to the city," Celia purred into the conversation coquettishly. "We lack arms or any assets beyond our own powers."

Owen gestured lackadaisically at the display case of tommy guns that served as a reception desk. "I would not allow you to take on this task without aid," he declared. "Each of you should take a Thompson and a couple of drums of silver, salt, and iron rounds.

"I will also pay each of you ten thousand dollars to complete this task," he finished. "That should help you get set up in New York while you find places at the Courts."

Something about the situation seemed off. Fae were not normally so free with promises and offers, even the Seelie, and *especially* not Keepers.

Duty to the race, however, was duty to the race. With a nod at his fellow Nobles, he settled his fedora back on his head then nodded at the Keeper.

"I think you'd best be getting us those guns, then, milord," he said politely. "Looks like we're going monster-hunting."

———

Abraham and Isaac drove the Fae nobles, once again divided between cars by Seelie and Unseelie Courts, down towards the under-construction districts where the sewer workers had encountered the beast.

They drove past a busy worksite assembled around a large excavation—the entry point for the deeper tunnels, according to the map that Owen had provided—and then parked several blocks away.

Talus left the car then opened the trunk and passed out the Thompson sub-machine guns that the Keeper had given them, along with the drums of ammo. The guns were in webbed carrying harnesses designed to hold the spare ammunition drums.

A bitter wind coming in off of the Atlantic made Talus grateful for the trench coat he was wearing, but he had to admit that the heavy coats did nothing to conceal the heavy guns on any of the six Fae Nobles. Abraham looked askance at the lot of them.

"How are you planning to get through the streets like that, let alone the worksite?" the man asked.

Talus grinned at the man and wordlessly wrapped a glamour of invisibility around himself, disappearing from even supernatural eyes that weren't looking in the right way. Abraham looked at the apparently empty space where he'd been standing, blinking for a moment.

"You can all do that?" he asked slowly.

"We are Fae Nobles," Talus replied, dropping the glamour and checking that the webbing was cinched properly. "If we could not summon glamours—of invisibility and the archetypes of man's mind —we would not be Fae Nobles."

Even the Unseelie nodded agreement with that, and Talus flashed the lesser Fae another brilliant grin. Invisibility was among the easiest glamours, on a par with calling on "archetypes"—images so woven into the human subconscious that they came easily to even Fae minds. A White Knight of the old Arthurian tales, clad in steel upon a mighty steed, would be a glamour easily woven around himself by any Fae raised in Europe.

"Indeed," Morgan rumbled, the big Unseelie Noble coming closest of them all to successfully hiding the three-foot-long weapon under his trench coat. "This is why your master sends us to hunt this creature in the sewers. Only Lords and Powers are greater than we."

That wasn't strictly true, Talus knew, but the other creatures in the world to equal a Fae Noble were few and far between.

With the tommy gun and its webbing firmly cinched into place, he glanced around the others. The two Seelie Nobles were both ready, eyeing the Unseelie impatiently. He raised an eyebrow at Celia, who was watching the two male Unseelie to make sure they were ready.

She gave him a wink and a nod as she met his gaze.

"Let's go," he said. A suggestion, not an instruction. Among Nobles, you always had to be careful how you phrased such things.

The others nodded, and a moment later, Abraham and Isaac stood alone in the bitter wind.

———

It was always disconcerting to walk down a street veiled from sight by glamours. While the streets weren't filled with the packed crowds of downtown, there were still enough people walking through the autumn afternoon to force the six Nobles to continually dodge around mundanes who didn't know the heavily armed Fae were even there.

Fortunately for the oblivious mundanes, Nobles had superhuman reflexes to go along with more unusual abilities. Dodging around the shifting pedestrians was only amusing for the first half dozen or so, but it was hardly difficult for any of them.

As they approached the worksite, the tenor of the people around them notably changed. The trench coats and fedoras of the middle class petered out in favor of the heavy coveralls and hard hats of men on shift. By the time they reached the fenced-off area around the excavation, the group of Nobles would have looked out of place if not concealed from view.

A tiny bit of Power allowed Talus to see the other Nobles, mostly because they weren't trying to hide from him. Even against other Nobles, this glamour would be effective unless they were looking for it, and he could have concealed himself from them if he chose to.

The worksite was fenced off, but no one had bothered to close the gate. Workers streamed in and out of it almost constantly, starting and ending shifts, moving to different worksites, and loading and unloading the trucks of materials that were arriving and leaving almost as constantly.

Talus and the others slipped through a momentary gap in the crowd following the entrance of a truck full of smooth stone blocks. He stopped just inside the fence, stepping out of the way of the crowds, to survey the site.

There were multiple open manholes around the excavation, and several tunnels of various sizes heading off in different directions from the excavation itself. Two were in the process of being fitted with pipes to seal them off, and one tunnel, at the very bottom of the excavation, dwarfed the rest.

"I think that's our storm drain," Celia observed drily, joining him in the quiet spot he'd found. "It's the only one big enough and deep enough."

"I'm guessing we can't hope that our beastie is too big to sneak out," Talus observed, eyeing the gaping hole in the earth. The big storm drain was wide enough to drive a small truck through. "Let's check it out."

As they began to climb down the side of the excavation, as carefully as possible so as not to disturb debris to call attention to themselves, they slowly began to overhear an argument at the bottom of the pit.

"Joe said there was some kind of monster down there," someone with a thick Eastern European accent exclaimed loudly enough for everyone to hear. "I'm not going in there!"

"Joe is an idjit who blew up five men," the foreman snapped back. "His brain gone and snapped when he realized what he'd done! And you lot of fools went and *believed* his ravings?"

"'e don't screw up like that," another worker replied. "Joe's the best. He wouldna blown up his guys."

Reaching the bottom of the pit, Talus saw the foreman, distinguishable from the workers only by the clipboard he was carrying, glaring at a clot of eight workers who were obviously refusing to enter the looming dark of the storm drain.

"Well, *someone's* gotta check and see what damage Joe did," the foreman told his workers angrily. He grabbed a handlamp from the cart. "*I've* gotta go in. You bunch of old women can wait out here if you're so scared!"

After a moment's hesitation, two of the hard-hatted workers blocked the foreman's path, shaking their heads.

"Nah, nah boss," said one of them, the heavily accented Romanian Talus had first overhead. "We ain't letting you get et either!"

With a shake of his head and a momentary shiver at the impenetrable dark of the sewer, Talus slipped past the arguing workers and into the darkness under the earth.

———

Fae vision was far better than that of ordinary humans, so Talus and the other Nobles didn't need to reveal their presence to the men gathered around the entrance of the tunnel as they walked deeper under the earth.

The light behind them grew fainter even to their eyes and eventually disappeared. Around him, Talus could tell as the other Nobles dropped their glamours of invisibility. In the utter darkness, only the faint glow of their body heat allowed him to see them regardless.

After another dozen or so steps, Celia cursed under her breath as she stumbled, then she conjured a tiny blue faerie flame to light their way.

Talus blinked against the sudden glow. He quickly realized the light was far too faint to be seen from outside but was enough light for them to see where they were putting their feet on a floor that had been carved by dynamite and pickaxes and never really smoothed afterwards.

"Douse that bloody light," Andre snapped. "Do ye want to bring the beastie down on our heads?"

"It's barely light enough for me to see my feet with it, you Irish twit," Celia snapped back. "We won't be able to do much if we break our necks on this floor."

"*Quiet,*" Talus hissed. "We need the light, Andre," he told the Irish Fae. "And we need to be *quiet,* or the humans will hear us before our 'beastie' does," he finished, glaring at them both.

Both of them glared back. Celia opened her mouth to bark back, but Morgan stepped between her and Talus, fixing his gaze down on the tiny Noble.

"He's right," the big Unseelie rumbled. "Anything down here is more likely to *hear* us than see that little light, so let's keep it down."

With Talus staring down Andre and Morgan staring down Celia, the argument quieted. The dark around them seemed to press in, and Talus could understand the tempers fraying in the dark.

As they continued to move down the massive tunnel, which seemed to stretch on forever, he carefully unclipped the strap holding his Thompson in the harness, stretching his hearing for the slightest hint of movement.

They walked for what felt like an eternity, and the only sound Talus could hear was the soft tromp of his companions' feet and the shifting sounds of cloth as, one by one, the darkness drew each Noble into drawing their weapons.

The sound, when it came, was thunderous to hyper-attuned Noble ears. *Something* shifted, a leathery slithering sound up ahead. Rocks fell, clattering across the ground in a rattle quickly buried by gunfire.

Talus was never sure who fired first or last, but he was shouting for them to stop after the first few bullets flew out.

The cacophony of multiple machine guns spitting .45 caliber bullets down the tunnel buried any remnant of the sound they'd all heard, and when the gunfire finally ceased, the silence was deafening.

"Did you see something?" he demanded. Silence answered him. "Whatever the hell it was, it wasn't close enough for us to shoot," he told the other Nobles, "so we just wasted bullets and lost any chance of tracking it by sound."

"You are *not* in charge here," Celia snapped back. "Who do you think you are to be telling us what to do?"

"The only one with a damn *brain*," Talus snarled, the darkness pressing on his nerves and his impatience with the Unseelie in the group.

Celia lunged at him in a blur mortal eyes would have completely missed. He caught her dagger-wielding fist in his free hand and bashed aside the butt of her Thompson with his own weapon. Fractions of a second later, she twisted out of his grip, swinging her gun in a heavy slam towards his skull.

Calling on his Power, he flung her away from him, overwhelming her physical strength and shields with a burst of kinetic force.

"This is not helping," Morgan told Celia, stepping in to block a repeat of her charge. "Talus speaks sense," he continued, turning a flat glare on the younger Noble. "Let's hunt this thing as a team—not try to kill each other."

The big Unseelie helped Celia to her feet. Her gaze remained locked on Talus as she nodded slowly, wiping a speck of blood away from an already-healed split lip. Her eyes, barely visible in the dim light from her faerie flame, were unreadable.

"Let's kill this thing, then, so I don't have to keep looking at these stinking Seelie," she spat and stormed forward into the darkness.

———

Celia's unthinking rush forward into the darkness killed Andre. The group spread out in a long line, barely able to see each other even with Fae eyes, and none of them saw the tripwire across the tunnel until Celia broke it.

Fae Nobles were faster than humans. They were faster than any mortal creature that ever lived and many supernatural creatures too. They were *not* faster than electricity.

The explosives the tripwire detonated were fifty feet back from it. Chunks of the wall shattered, spraying stone debris across the immense sewer drain. Talus dove to the ground as a larger chunk shot through where his head had been.

For a single half second, he thought that was it. Andre had been hit by more debris than the rest, but mere stone wouldn't do enough damage to kill a Noble.

Then the tunnel collapsed.

It came down in slabs the size of tanks, stones heavy enough to crush elephants, and smashed Andre, Noble of the *Teutha* Courts, into dust even he could not survive.

———

The tunnel was somehow darker in the following moments, until Talus threw up a faerie light of his own to mirror Celia's. Moments passed, and then three more faerie lights lit up, and the five surviving Nobles, shaken and bruised by the explosion, gathered in the flickering light of their magic.

"That was no beast," Caleb finally said, speaking what they were all thinking.

"That was demolitions work," Morgan agreed. "The same explosives they've been using to dig the tunnel, at a guess."

"Did one of the workers set a trap?" Michael demanded. "Is all of this… a trick to lure someone like us down here?"

"The mortals wouldn't bother," Celia snapped at the three men. "Even those in the know would be more worried about vampires from what the Keeper said. No… this *was* our beast."

"There are creatures the mortals would describe as monsters that could do that," Talus reminded the others. "They are... the deadlier ones we could face. Gryphons. Minotaurs." He paused and swallowed. "Dragons," he finished.

Dragons were the deadliest of the supernatural "beasts" of the world. Immensely intelligent, with a limited kind of omniscience, true Power of a kind few supernaturals could match, fiery breath, and deadly wills, they were terrifying to anyone. Only their strange life cycles that kept them asleep for decades or even centuries kept them from being a greater threat—but their powers of knowledge meant that they were well aware of what happened while they slept.

"This city has been here for centuries," Morgan said slowly. "A dragon sleeping under us would have awoken and devastated it years ago."

Talus released a breath he hadn't realized he'd been holding as he realized the big Unseelie was right.

"It doesn't matter," Caleb said quietly, the Seelie Fae effortlessly gathering their attention to him. "*Something* a hell of a lot smarter than we thought is down here—and we're trapped in with it."

All five Nobles turned to face the tunnel out and saw the truth of Caleb's words. The blocks that had crushed Andre to death had blocked the tunnel completely. Even their Power could not move enough of the stones to clear a way back.

"Whatever it is, it has to have a way out of its own," Talus reminded them. "And the smarter it is, the more dangerous it is—our duty to the Race means it *must* die. And going through it may be our only way out."

The five Fae stared at the cave-in behind them for several moments, and then they set off down the tunnel again.

For the first time since Owen had asked them to take on the task, Talus began to truly feel afraid.

———

The only light in the now-sealed tunnel came from the faerie lights that the five Fae had conjured to light their way. The mingling of five lights caused shadows to jump and flicker across the walls, and each flicker hit already twitchy nerves.

No more shots were fired into the dark, but Talus knew he'd come close a few times, and he doubted the others were any calmer.

"Douse your lights," Celia suddenly snapped from the front of the line. Talus started to snarl back at her but controlled himself.

Dousing his own light, he also poked Caleb with a tiny spike of tele-kinetic force. The London Seelie turned to glare at him, diverting his attention from Celia for long enough for the Fae to draw a deep breath and calm down. Caleb nodded carefully at Talus and then doused his light.

"What did you see?" Michael asked in the sudden darkness, barely penetrable to the vision of the Fae Nobles.

"I'm not sure, but I think we're getting close to where the workers found the beast," Celia answered. The vague silhouette Talus could see of her was studying the floor. "Can one of you *just* light the floor?"

Theoretically, Talus knew, any of them could have done it—if they had that level of control of their power, which most Nobles at their young age wouldn't have. Celia clearly couldn't. After a few moments of silence from the others, Talus stepped forward. His uncle was a Fae Lord, his father the disappointment—a Noble born to a family of Lords. Oberis had made sure that his nephew was skilled enough with what power he had to not shame his family.

He stood at Celia's shoulder and focused his power carefully. A faint glow began to illuminate the floor, invisible from more than a few feet away but showing the ground.

The trail of running footprints leading back the way they'd come appeared first, and then the two Fae continued down the corridor. He focused on maintaining the light, letting her follow the path to where it led.

"Detonator," she said shortly, stopping and pointing. Talus looked down and saw the wires leading away to the side of the cave. A tendril of the faint illumination followed the wire, rising and lighting up the equipment.

"That would only be left down here if they were in the middle of blasting when the beast attacked," Morgan observed.

"Exactly," Celia murmured, following the trails forward with Talus still at her shoulder, providing light.

"Blast hole," Michael told them as they reached a rough ridge in the floor, uneven and marked with scattered debris. "This should have been smoothed with pickaxes and smaller blasts."

"They must have blasted through into something," Talus said. "Let's keep moving forward."

The blast gave way to a sloping path downwards and a slight breeze. The new space seemed to be large enough to have air moving around inside it, which helped reduce the stuffiness Talus had been noticing.

"Blood," Celia suddenly snapped, pointing to the edge of the pool of illumination Talus was spreading.

Talus focused his faerie lights around it and then swallowed hard. There wasn't a lot of blood, just spots scattered in an area a yard or so wide around a pair of feet that ended at just about the ankles. Gobbets of ragged flesh still clung to bones sheared through in perfectly straight lines.

"What. The. *Fuck*." Caleb uttered, his voice low.

"He was eaten," Michael told him, his voice flat. "Almost whole."

"Can you spread the light out without it being seen?" Celia asked Talus.

"A bit farther," Talus told her. He wove a veil over the light so that only those inside the glamour could see it, and then spread both workings out thirty feet down the slope.

The ankles belonged to the worker who'd made it farthest. The slope beneath them was churned to dust by running feet, and gobbets of flesh were scattered across it, marking the places where the other workers had died.

"What's that?" Morgan finally asked as the Fae took in the site of the slaughter before them. It took Talus a moment to realize the Unseelie was pointing at an odd black shape at the edge of the light.

"Check it out," Talus ordered, focusing the light to spread slightly forward as Morgan carefully stepped through the killing ground to check it out.

"One of them's been *burned*!" Morgan shouted in surprise. "Almost to ash. The rest are torn t' shreds. What the hell could *do* this?"

An iron ball seemed to materialize inside Talus, dragging his stomach down to his ankles.

"We all know," he answered shortly and dropped the veil. The faerie flame shot together from the pool on the ground, shooting to the roof of the cavern to illuminate its full contents.

They stood halfway down the sloping side of an immense cave, easily two hundred feet at its height and a thousand feet across. The center of the cave was a hollow four hundred feet on a side and unknowably deep, as it's center was piled fifty feet higher than the rest of the cavern with gold and silver coins and artefacts.

One side of the cave contained rows of chests and bookshelves, all overflowing with scrolls and books. Another contained a collection of brightly painted statues that it took Talus an instant to realize were Greek marbles. The far side of the cave held the original exit, a Power-carved tunnel angling out at a smooth and consistent grade.

"What the hell did we *find*?" Caleb demanded.

"A dragon's lair," Celia said grimly. "It couldn't be anything else—*that's* what they dug up down here."

The light of the Faerie flame Talus had conjured to light the cavern shone over the faces of the five Fae Nobles, variously lit with greed or fear.

No single Fae could defeat a dragon, so those who successfully killed one split the dragon's hoard. The contents of a dragon's lair, even split five ways, would be wealth beyond any possible need or desire, even for a Fae Noble.

"You said it couldn't be a dragon!" Caleb shouted, turning to Morgan.

"I was wrong," the big ex-marine Unseelie replied simply.

"We are going to be so rich," Michael muttered, a considering grin spreading over his face.

"We are all going to be so *dead*," Celia snapped. "Veil yourselves. *Kill that light.*"

She was too late. Even as Talus released the faerie light he'd held for too long, the dragon erupted from the mound of gold in the middle of the room.

———

To the superhuman eyes of the Fae, the sheer warmth of the dragon's internal fire lit the room like a small sun. Talus blinked against the brilliance of the creature and then stumbled as fire blasted across the room from the great beast's mouth.

They were taken completely by surprise, utterly unprepared, and faced with one of the greatest creatures to walk the Earth—but they were *Fae Nobles*.

Five shields of telekinetic force flashed into existence before the fire reached them, and the burst of fire, hot enough to burn bone to ash, scattered across the cavern.

"Run for the exit," Talus snapped, diving forward with a sprint that any Olympic athlete would have envied.

Gunfire echoed through the room as Caleb and Morgan ignored Talus's words, emptying their tommy guns into the monster. Silver, salt, and cold iron bullets bounced from the dragon's scales, and fire hammered the two Nobles' shields.

Michael had discarded his gun, though, and Talus felt the entire cavern chill as the Fae called Power to himself. Glamour and telekinesis wove protections around the Unseelie Noble, and he struck the dragon with a bolt of ice forged from will and power.

The ice pierced the dragon's scales, drawing a single drop of ancient blood.

For a moment, Talus allowed himself to slow, to believe that they might have a chance. Then the immense wyrm, easily a hundred feet long and wrapped in scales of gold that glittered in the fire, drew itself on up its hind legs and wrapped its wings around itself such that it appeared to be wearing robes.

Then Michael died.

Talus sensed but did not see the bolt of pure power that ripped through the Noble's defenses like tissue paper. It latched around the Unseelie's heart and ripped it from the man's chest.

"Run!" Talus yelled back at Morgan and Caleb. Celia had reached the exit from the drake's cave, and he was only a few steps behind her.

The Seelie and Unseelie tried. The dragon turned on them, fire scattering from their shields as it began to close in on them. Talus stopped at the edge of the cave, turning back to watch them in helpless rage as Celia ran on.

Power rippled through the cavern again, lashing out at Caleb. For a moment, Talus though the last of his Seelie companions was dead, but then he emerged from the burst of shattered stone where he'd stood, continuing to run forward. He'd changed his shields—while running—to deflect the dragon's attack to the side rather than stop it.

Neither of the two Fae was going to make it, and Talus began to tense, ready to rejoin the fight, when Morgan made the decision for him.

The big ex-marine Unseelie took a look behind him, realized how close the bounding monster was, and closed his eyes in a moment.

When he opened them again, his gaze locked on Talus's.

"Hey, Seelie!" he bellowed. "*Catch!*"

Caleb had no warning or chance to react. A shovel-sized hand scooped him off the ground and spun him around in a perfect javelin throw that sent the Seelie flying straight at Talus.

Surprised, Talus caught the other Fae and set him on the ground, his gaze still on Morgan. He realized what the Unseelie was going to do.

"Run yourself," Morgan ordered and then turned back to face the dragon, armed only with the power and wrath of a Fae Noble.

Talus ran, dragging Caleb after him. Against most opponents on Earth, that power would be more than enough—but here, in its lair, the dragon was unbeatable.

———

They caught up with Celia after a few moments, the Unseelie woman redoubling her speed as they caught up with her.

"You're *alive*?" she exclaimed. Despite maintaining a sprint that the greatest Olympic athlete would have turned white with envy at the sight of, none of the three were out of breath.

"Let's see how long that lasts before we start cheering," Talus told her, releasing Caleb as the other Fae finally got his feet under him. "I can *hear* that thing following us now."

Morgan had bought them almost a full minute, which was about five times as long as Talus had expected but infinitely less than he *wanted*.

"Watch for side-tunnels," he told the other two Nobles as they ran. "There's got to be one too small for the beast to follow us."

They ran in silence for a few moments, the rough ground shifting unevenly under their feet as the loose rocks slid.

"There!" Celia shouted, pointing to a gap in the side of the tunnel. A ball of light flashed forward from her pointing finger to illuminate what *had* been a side tunnel barely big enough for a man.

About twenty feet back from the main tunnel, the side tunnel was collapsed, the roof brought down by the weight of the city above it.

"Damn," Caleb barked. "Keep running!"

Talus heard faint crunching noises behind them as they continued to run, the dragon beginning to close in on them as it followed them up its escape tunnel.

"Another side tunnel!" Caleb shouted, taking the lead of the three Fae, only to curse and try to run faster as he passed it.

Talus saw that one had been blocked too, the roof collapsed just back from the main tunnel. When they passed a *third* blocked tunnel, even he was starting to grow short of breath.

"We're being *herded*," he gasped out to the others. "The bloody thing has us trapped—and it's *catching up*."

The crunching sounds of the dragon's running feet were growing closer, and Talus growled, slowing to a stop.

"This won't work. We need *time*," he told the other two. "Help me."

He was actually surprised when the other two Fae stopped and joined him. "Those side tunnels gave me an idea. Focus your power— we should be able to bring the roof down."

Suiting actions to words, he reached out with the telekinetic strength of a Fae noble and began to splinter the stone of the roof. A few pieces fell down, and then more as the other two nobles joined in.

Sparks lit the tunnel as the dragon turned a corner, coming into view of the three Fae nobles. It was a majestic creature even to Talus's terrified eyes.

It had the long snout of a lizard, surmounted by bright, humanlike eyes that were currently lit with rage. The dragon's wings, feathered in black and gold, were slightly spread, allowing it to balance as it ran forward on its two massively powerful legs. Twice the length of a train car and more, its half-spread wings stretched from one side of the tunnel to the other, and its aura of Power filled what space its body didn't.

Panic lent Talus strength, and he focused his power on the earth above them. A massive surge of Will coursed through him, and he felt the mighty stone above him crack. For a moment, he was convinced the dragon was going to reach him, and then the roof of the tunnel gave way.

Stone and earth crumpled down. The dragon reared back, the first of the stones striking it before the collapsing tunnel hid it from view.

Then the tunnel collapse continued towards them, and the nobles had to throw their power into holding the same roof they'd broken up. For a few seconds, it seemed their success was going to crush them.

Stones collapsed towards them, the tunnel reaching out to crush them, and finally, finally, stopped a few feet away from them.

A stone the size of a man dropped from the roof last and rolled slowly towards them to stop inches from Talus as it hit his shields and wards without enough force to drive through.

He looked at the rock, which would have crushed him had it fallen closer to him or faster, and breathed a sigh of relief.

As the sighs of the three Fae nobles faded, he heard another sound. A scratching, crunching sound.

The dragon was digging through.

———

"Keep going," Celia said to the two Fae desperately, and Talus laughed.

"What *else* were we going to do?" he demanded before taking off up the tunnel after her.

Caleb was running hard, to the point where Talus was, with what energy he had to spare, worrying about what the Noble was going to do to himself. It took a *lot* for a Fae Noble to do the equivalent of "pulling a muscle"—but it was also a lot more severe of an injury.

The other Seelie Fae passed Talus and Celia, conjuring a bright faerie light to bring the tunnel to the brilliance of day. Talus was about to tell him to shut down the light and then realized it didn't matter—nothing they could warn they were coming could be more dangerous than what was chasing them, and until the dragon was through the cave-in, it didn't matter.

The next several side tunnels were the same as the ones before, collapsed several feet back from the entrance. Talus said nothing to the others, just watching his steps before him, but it didn't ring right to him—if the dragon had closed off the side tunnels, the beast's magic would have left no trace of them, but there was no way the tunnels had *all* been sealed by natural process.

His paranoia kept him watching the tunnel ahead of them, which was why he saw the tripwire before Caleb ran into it.

"Stop!" he snapped, filling his words with the command of a Fae Noble. Caleb, despite being a Fae Noble himself, stopped in his tracks—inches from the tripwire.

"There are traps in the tunnel," Talus told him, pointing at the trip-wire. It was a thin wire, painted black to disappear in the gloom of the underground tunnel, and suspended at about the level of Talus's abdomen—ankle-high on the dragon.

"That's set for the dragon, not for us," Celia observed. "What the fuck is going on?"

"As soon as I work it out, I'll tell you," Talus snapped. "Just watch for more traps—I want to escape the dragon and find who set them, *in that order*, not be crushed or blown to smithereens."

Caleb took the lead again, a stormy look on his face as he ducked under the tripwire and took off again. Talus watched Celia follow, making sure she made it under, and then ducked through himself.

He was the last to start running again, and he heard a sound behind him he thought the others missed—the rhythmic thumping and fluttering of the dragon's odd run.

With a muttered curse, he took off.

Another fifty or sixty meters up the tunnel, Talus had to leap another tripwire at chest height to a man. Two more came along afterwards, and now he could *smell* the cordite and explosives they were set to trigger.

He ducked under the fourth then rounded the corner into an open chamber, only half the size of the dragon's lair but still huge for under the city. Roots of a hundred trees were woven together across the roof, helping explain the size and the presence of the strange chamber torn from the earth. Globes of faerie light illuminated the room, filled with boxes and the tableau of figures in front of him.

He stopped dead in the entrance to the chamber, facing down the barrel of a Thompson sub-machine gun trained perfectly on him, Celia, and Caleb by Owen, the Keeper of New York.

"You built this chamber," Talus said simply to the Gille, whose powers over trees answered how a new cavern had opened over the dragon's escape route. "How did you know his tunnel came here?"

Celia and Caleb were still silent, focused on the gun. Talus focused on Owen. Somehow, the Keeper had set this up. He recognized weapons woven into the tree roots now, trained on the entrance into the root-supported cavern. Either the bazookas from the display cases in the hotel or their very similar sisters had been mounted in niches custom-formed for them around tree roots, and then linked together by some very professional demolitions work to be fired by a single trigger—in the corner of the room, where an extremely shaken but quite large dark-skinned man stood.

"I asked the trees," Owen said simply. "I didn't expect so many of you to survive. I'm impressed," he admitted.

"*You betrayed us,*" Caleb snarled, and Talus felt the other Noble gather Power to himself. "*I am a noble of the Summer Courts. Mine is the wrath of the coming storm, and you betrayed…*"

Power coalesced around Caleb, a glittering sphere of light and flame, only to shatter as Owen calmly pulled the trigger. The tommy gun had the same load as the ones he'd sent them into the tunnels with —rock salt, silver, and cold iron.

Rock salt shattered the construct of Power that Caleb had gathered. Silver and salt overloaded his wards and defenses, breaking the shields that guarded the Noble's flesh. Cold Iron, the ancient bane of the Fair Folk, pierced flesh that could withstand tank shells and ripped apart a heart that could heal any other wound.

Caleb didn't even finish his righteous proclamation before the Thompson's heavy bullets ripped his chest apart. He crumpled wordless, dead before his body hit the ground.

"Why is it that no Noble of either court ever knows when to shut the fuck up?" Owen asked conversationally, training the gun back on Talus. "Now, are we going to play nice now?"

"Four Fae Nobles are dead by either your hand or your lies," Talus said quietly. "Both the Courts and Council will hunt you to the end of the Earth. The Queen will have your head. What makes you think you're going to get away with this?"

"Because you're the only witnesses," the Keeper replied, "and a quarter of a dragon's hoard is one hell of a bribe. You need my weapons—and I could use the two of you to help hold the drake in place."

Tradition stated that all Fae involved in bringing down a dragon split the hoard between them—obviously, Owen was including the mundane engineer he'd drafted. A quarter of a dragon's hoard was wealth beyond imagining, enough to buy small countries. It was as he said—one hell of a bribe.

Talus caught Celia out of the corner of his eye, slightly shifting her weight to slowly sidle away from him. If she kept it up and he kept Owen distracted, the Keeper would only be able to point the gun at one of them.

"The weapons are already here, Owen," Talus reminded the Keeper. "Your man over there has wired them. I'd say, in fact, that you need us—and we don't need you. And you murdered our friends."

The Keeper laughed.

"You are Nobles, and you barely met each other," he told Talus. "Your kind doesn't *make* friends."

"You sent six Nobles down here without telling us about the dragon, planning for us to die," Talus wondered aloud. "Why take that chance? Why not just *tell* us what we were hunting?"

"The six of you might have been enough to kill it," Owen said simply. "Plus, a seventh didn't seem like enough to be worth the risk."

The Keeper still held the heavy sub-machine gun perfectly steady, lined up on Talus with an inhuman precision. Talus knew that Celia had moved away, possibly enough to surprise the Keeper but not enough to save his life if she did.

"My uncle hunted dragons," Talus told Owen. "He said our tradition of treachery had let more of the creatures survive than any action the dragons took."

"You're a preachy fuck, aren't you?" the Keeper said conversationally and gestured slightly with the gun. "Are you going to work with me or not?" he demanded.

Talus hesitated and heard, behind him, the thumping steps of the dragon. The great beast was getting closer—almost as close as…

"You should have worked with us from the beginning," he told Owen sadly.

The dragon hit the first tripwire.

———

Owen's root-supported cavern shuddered as the explosives in the tunnel behind them went off, dropping tonnes of stone on the dragon behind them. A bellow of anger echoed down the tunnel, the floor shifted, and the gun he had trained on Talus shifted off target.

The Fae Noble dived sideways, and Owen fired, a stream of bullets tearing through the air where he had stood. Talus hit the ground then popped back up onto his feet as a burst of telekinetic force ripped the front half of the tommy gun away, leaving Owen holding only a trigger and stock.

Celia followed up with a series of blows of pure force directed at the Keeper himself, which the oak-solid old Fae ignored as he bore down on the Unseelie Noble. Celia blanched at the lack of effect of her strikes, each strong enough to blow holes through concrete.

Talus charged forward before the Gille reached her, conjuring glamours of armor and weapons around himself. A yard-long sword materialized in his hand as he struck, slicing down at Owen's wrists as the Keeper reached for Celia.

The preternaturally keen sword bounced as it hit him, but the strike threw Owen off balance, allowing Celia to escape. Talus focused more Power into the blade of illusion and force and then struck again.

Owen disappeared before the strike could land. Talus watched the old tree Fae flow into the root network that encased the cavern then reappear twenty feet away, standing by the strange multi-barrelled German weapon Talus had seen in the hotel.

He scooped up another rocket launcher as Celia closed on him. The Unseelie Noble wrapped her fists in flame and power and struck at him. He ignored the first blow, letting it land solidly on his flesh, which sizzled under the magical flame.

Celia's second blow was intercepted with the bulk of the bazooka, her fists leaving inch-deep dents in the metal structure of the weapon. The old Fae sidestepped the third blow and caught her fourth with a free hand.

For a moment, Celia exerted the full strength of a Fae noble, a physical might matched by few creatures in the world, against the ancient oak resistance of the Gille. Then Owen released her, allowing her strength to send her flying at the sudden lack of resistance.

The Keeper used the force from releasing Celia to turn around and level the bazooka on Talus. He'd almost reached the fight, losing precious moments to cross the distance the Gille had travelled through the roots.

The barrel of the bazooka seemed large enough to swallow worlds, and the Keeper's timing was perfect. The rocket blasted out as Talus started to move, and slammed into him with the force of a hundred hammers—and then exploded.

A lesser creature would have died. A different creature would also have died since the rocket was laced with silver shrapnel that would have ended a vampire or werewolf. Pain was Talus's world for a short eternity, his flesh seared and his bones broken as he was thrown across the room by the force of the blast.

Celia screamed wordlessly and charged Owen again, her fists now encased in an icy-blue aura that sucked all the heat from the air around them. The Keeper met her with the oak-solid resilience of his kind, absorbing and blocking her strikes, but slowly gave ground.

Talus slowly, ever so slowly, regained some measure of consciousness and realized the Keeper was tricking her. He was giving ground towards another box of weapons—one with a loaded Thompson gun sitting on it.

The Seelie noble was grievously wounded. Even he would take time—hours at best—to recover from a wound of this magnitude. Forcing through the pain, he dragged himself forward, only his Power sustaining him.

He reached the box moments before Owen, pulling the gun to himself with telekinesis. The Keeper, having fallen back far enough, dropped his defense and dived backwards for the gun.

His hands closed on empty space, and he barely turned in time to face Talus before the Seelie leveled the gun.

Only an Unseelie or a madman taunted the defeated. Talus simply fired. He emptied a sixty-round drum into the old Fae, and even his oak-solid flesh yielded before the ancient iron bane of their kind.

———

The ground rumbled again as Owen fell, and Talus collapsed against the crate he'd grabbed the tommy gun from, looking around.

The big dark-skinned man standing by the detonator rigged to fire the bazookas looked at the two remaining Fae with his hands spread.

"Third tripwire," he told them gruffly. "You all got about a minute, and then that *thing* is here. You got a plan?"

"Where are those aimed?" Talus asked, gesturing at the rocket launchers wired up to fire. The motion caused his splintered ribs to spasm, and he involuntarily whimpered. The engineer stared at him in a horror for a moment before replying, his voice uneven.

"There's a set of three big black stones by the entrance. They're all aimed at that."

"He promised you a full share?" Talus asked as Celia moved to check out the stones.

"And got me out of a one-way trip to the asylum," the mundane agreed. "Name's Joe—Joe Costa. Didn't know he was setting no one up."

"You'll get your share," Talus promised him.

"Found the stones!" Celia shouted. "And I can hear the big bastard coming!"

A fourth explosion rippled through, dumping more stone on the dragon. Now Talus could hear the slam of stones on scaled flesh as the roof caved in once more.

"You'll have to lure the bastard onto them so Joe can fire the rockets," Talus told her. "I can't move enough."

The blonde Unseelie sighed and turned her gaze on Joe. "Don't fuck this up, mundane. Believe me, I can kill you before the beast guts me."

"Just get him on the stones," Joe told her.

With that, a spray of debris from the cave-in announced the dragon was free, and the immense creature lunged into the cavern Owen had torn out of the guts of the earth.

———

For the first time, Talus saw the dragon in full light. The black and gold feathers on the wings, spread to stabilize it as it ran, glittered like precious metals under the brightness of the faerie globes entwined in the roots above. The scales that clad the beast's mightily thewed legs glistened like freshly oiled steel. The fangs Talus could see, the smallest easily the length of a child's leg, were iridescent black, rainbow colours flickering along their surface.

The eyes were bright silver in the dark-grey scales of the long-snouted face, their expression surprisingly humanlike—and easily read. Wariness and annoyance lit the great creature's face, and it trained its snout on Celia, who was standing in the center of the chamber with the focus of a determined hunter.

The Unseelie noble held her ground atop Costa's marker stones for several moments, and Talus couldn't help but be impressed by her courage. His own wounds hammered him as he moved, trying to get into a position where he could do something—*anything*—against the dragon.

The dragon huffed, and a ball of fire burst out from between its front fangs, blasting towards Celia. She didn't move fast enough. Her trench coat burst into flames. For a moment, Talus thought she was gone, and then the glamour collapsed.

Dropping the other glamour concealing her from view, Celia loosed a bolt of flame of her own from where she *actually* stood—a good thirty feet back from the marker for the rocket launchers.

Finally prepared and expecting her enemy, Celia attacked with the power of a Fae Noble. Ice and lightning and fire blasted from her hands, the fury of the worst winter storms man had ever seen.

The dragon stopped in its steps, sparks playing over its metallic skin and frost framing its iridescent feathers. The hammer blows of force pushed it back a step, then another. The great beast awkwardly half-hopped, half-flapped back a third time and then stopped Celia's attack in its tracks with a sudden shield of pure force between it and her. The storm blasted against the force for a moment, continuing to chill the entire chamber.

Then a blast of force from the dragon picked Celia up and threw her across the chamber. The storm cut off instantly as she threw her power into slowing her flight and managed to land on her feet, though Talus could hear her heels gouging out trenches in the ground.

A ball of flame followed her, which Celia batted aside with a wave of force. With a surge of power, she coalesced water and chill into a long spike that she spun and hurled like a javelin. Fueled by her Power, it punched through the dragon's shield and slammed into its shoulder.

The dragon screamed, a terrifyingly human sound but with a volume to break eardrums and shatter several of the magical faerie light globes above. Lowering its head, it charged forward.

Talus took a breath, waiting for the creature to approach the black stones marking Costa's targeting point, and then hit the beast with a stiletto-thin line of force. The telekinetic strike stabbed through the dragon's shield and slammed into its other shoulder. It wasn't enough to hurt the beast—but it was enough to draw thick, black-looking blood from where it struck.

The dragon turned its face as it ran, then it slowed to a stop as its gaze found Talus and locked onto him. Grimacing against the pain of his still burnt and shattered torso, the Fae Noble threw it a thumbs-up and a huge grin.

It was on the marker stones.

Talus heard the solid thud of Costa slamming the detonator down, and then the chamber was filled with noise.

Owen and the engineer had mounted dozens of rocket launchers on the wall, and the gap between the first and last firing was only barely perceptible even to the inhuman senses of a Fae Noble.

The impacts were one long explosion, a rippling pyrotechnic of orange and blue as silver and salt lit up in the explosions of the rocket warheads. Smoke and flame obscured the dragon, and it screamed again, a long, agonizing sound.

Celia never saw it coming through the smoke. It emerged right on top of her. Its black and gold plumage had been burned to ash, and massive gouges were torn out of its flesh. The mighty beast oozed thick black blood from a dozen and more wounds, and its right eye was gone.

It screamed in rage that gave it back any speed its wounds had cost it, and a mighty wing swung out with brutal force. Celia never had a chance to dodge, and Talus heard her spine snap from across the room as that burnt and mangled limb slammed into her torso.

Despite all the arsenal of human ingenuity, the dragon was alive—and it was *angry*.

Talus's wounds were probably as bad as the dragon's, but Celia was going to *die* if he didn't act. He forced himself to his feet somehow, casting about for a solution.

Owen's corpse showed him the answer—the Keeper had fallen almost on top of the strange multi-barrelled launcher, the *Luftfaust*. A flick of force brought the heavy eleven-barrelled weapon to Talus's hands.

The dragon reared up over Celia where she'd collapsed on the ground, unable to move, and presented him a glorious target.

He fired.

Only the inhuman strength of a Fae Noble kept the weapon on target as the first six rockets blasted away, slamming into the dragon with more orange and silver fire. The creature screamed again, but as it turned to attack Talus, the remaining five rockets blasted forward.

They hit the dragon in the center of its chest, tearing aside the mighty armor that the dragon had grown there, exposing flesh and organs… and still the creature screamed. Pain and fury lit its remaining eye, and it charged at Talus.

He could feel the power the dragon wrapped around itself, the mighty magic that created a bowfront of force that would pound him into paste and shatter the cavern around him. In answer, he did the only thing he could.

Talus charged back.

The Fae Noble started on foot, his entire body screaming with pain, but he reached for his glamours as he charged, wrapping an ancient archetype around himself. Armor and arms of illusion and force materialized around him as a horse of the same raised him up off the ground.

The ancient archetype of the White Knight encased Talus as he charged, and he threw all of his power into the point of the archetype's mighty lance.

His lance point and the dragon's wave of power met and passed through each other. The crashing force of the dragon's magic hit him, and only the harsh training his uncle had put him through let him hold the glamour, let the armor he'd woven around himself shed the dragon's might, and let him hold the lance on target.

All of his power, all of his fear, his rage, and his pain, focused onto one six-inch lance point forged of illusion and magic.

It struck where the *Luftfaust*'s rockets had torn apart the drake's armor and exposed its great heart, and exploded with power.

Fire and ice and lightning exploded inside the dragon as the lance point came apart and took the dragon's heart and lungs with it.

The glamour-horse lasted long enough to carry Talus past the dragon, and then his strength failed him. His entire glamour of the Knight came apart, dumping him unceremoniously on the floor, grinding gravel and dirt into the still exposed wounds on his chest.

Behind him, the dragon collapsed to the ground, its death throes shattering the remaining boxes of weapons and throwing more gravel around the cavern.

Finally, with an all-too-human whimper, the dragon died.

———

It seemed like a very long time before Talus was able to move under his own power. Joe managed to get him up, leaning against the wall so he was at least not rubbing more dirt into his wounds, but sheer exhaustion held him immobile.

The big Italian had to carry Celia. Even a Fae Noble would take days to recover from injuries of her magnitude. By the time Joe laid her down next to Talus, she was unconscious, her breathing slow and shallow.

"She'll be fine," Talus told the worried-looking engineer. "She's in a healing hibernation—it'll be a day or two until she wakes up, but she'll be mostly healed."

"*Mostly healed?*" the mortal half-squeaked. "I'm no doctor—but I was a soldier. Her pelvis is shattered and her spine *crushed*."

"And she is a Fae Noble," Talus told him. "Joe, I have an inch-deep *hole in my chest*, and I'm still talking to you. She'll recover."

The human dropped next to him.

"What happens now?" he asked.

"When I can walk, we do just that out of here," Talus told him. "With the Keeper dead, I'll have to directly claim audience with both Lords, both to claim the hoard and to explain how Owen died. You know the way out?"

"Yeah," Joe told him. "It comes out in a cave in Central Park."

Talus poked at his chest and winced. The ribs had finished reknitting, but the skin was still half-missing and exceptionally sore. "I'll need a coat to not be obvious."

Joe looked at him in shock as he slowly rose to his feet.

"There should be one around here somewhere," he said.

————

Two days later, a fully healed Talus wished Joe goodbye in the front hall of the Plaza, one of New York's expensive and luxurious hotels. The heavyset Italian wore a perfectly fitted suit but still looked uncomfortable. The initial estimate of the assessors of the Seelie and Unseelie Lords on the dragon's hoard was a mind-boggling number.

Much of it would take time to find appropriate buyers for—ancient Greek marbles and scrolls from the Library of Alexandria were not easily liquidated—but Talus had already arranged to cash in a single chest's worth of gold and gems. His one-third share of that chest alone had made Joe Costa a millionaire.

"What will you do?" Talus asked him.

"I have no idea," the Italian told him honestly. "I think I can trust your people to make sure I get the money from the hoard wherever I go, so I think I'm going to go back home to Italy. Buy an estate—maybe a boat. After that, I'll have to think about it. I never expected to be rich."

"You aren't going to be rich, Joe," the Fae Noble told him with a grin. "You are going to be disgustingly, ridiculously *filthy* rich."

Joe shook his head.

"Not what I was expecting when my team got killed on me," he admitted. "I was heading to an insane asylum before Owen came along."

Talus nodded slowly. "I wish he'd told us what was going on from the beginning," he admitted. "Even an eighth share in the hoard would have been more money than he could *possibly* have needed. But once he'd betrayed four of us to their deaths..."

Costa shivered. "Your people scare me," he admitted. "That's one reason why I'm going to go very far away—no offense, but I don't want to be within a thousand miles of any of you that I know about."

Talus considered telling him that there was a Fae population almost everywhere in Italy outside of Rome, then decided against it.

"Good luck, Joe," he said instead, shaking the engineer's hand.

"Enjoy it—you earned it. Not many mortals have ever helped kill a dragon."

With a nod and a firm grip, Joe stepped outside into the rainy street, waving down a cab as he went. With a small smile, Talus crossed to the elevators, heading for Celia's room on the top floor to see if she'd woken up yet.

The penthouse room was the nicest the Plaza had, and a few extra hundreds of dollars had guaranteed Celia her privacy—the last thing anyone needed was the staff realizing how badly she'd been injured before and then watching her walk out.

"Sneaking into my room?" she called out as he walked in. "You should be more careful—Unseelie are notoriously paranoid."

"So I've heard," Talus said with a smile as he saw Celia walk out of the bathroom, drying her hair.

The fluffy hotel bathrobe did a poor job of concealing her lithe figure or motions, though it did preserve her modesty.

"The Lords agreed with the reasons for Owen's death," he told her, "and signed off on the hoard claim. You are a millionaire dragon-slayer, Miss Celia of the Unseelie."

"And it seems I have a Seelie pretty-boy already sucking up to me," she replied, a smile playing around her lips.

"Well, I'm a millionaire dragon-slayer myself, as it happens, so we have that in common," he agreed, crossing to her. "How are you feeling?"

"Like a dragon smashed my spine into pieces and I've been unconscious for two days," Celia told him. "Mostly healed up, though—and not *that* sore in the pelvis, if you're wondering." She winked at him and closed the remaining distance.

Talus kissed her, and she leaned in against him.

"You saved my life," she whispered. "Thank you."

"You're welcome, Miss Celia," he told her formally. She laughed and shrugged off the robe.

"If you care, this is an awful idea, Seelie and Unseelie meeting like this," she said. "Your taste in women will get you in trouble someday."

"I'll have to work on that," he agreed. "Some other day."

CHANGELING BLOOD SERIES

Fae, Flames, and Fedoras is set in the same universe as Glynn Stewart's Changeling Blood series.

Changeling Blood series:
Changeling's Fealty
Hunter's Oath
Noble's Honor

ASHEN STARS

Prequel novella to Exile

1

Captain Isaac Gallant finished reviewing the readiness report in front of him with a sigh. It was the last of the departmental reports for the Confederacy Space Fleet's warp cruiser *Scorpion*, and it matched the pattern of the rest of them.

Isaac studied the terminal screen in his office for several more seconds, then made a decision with a shake of his head.

"Commander Giannovi, please report to my ready room," he ordered over the intercom. A moment later, an indicator on the computer screen tattooed into his left arm changed, informing him that Lieutenant Commander Harris now held the conn.

Giannovi stepped into his ready room—exactly three steps outside the bridge, just far enough that you had to pass through the bridge's security detail to reach it—seconds later.

"You asked for me, sir?" she asked crisply. Lauretta Giannovi was a throwback by the standards of twenty-fourth-century humanity, born in Italy of entirely Italian extraction. She was a permanently tanned-looking woman of barely average height with short-cropped black hair.

"Have a seat, Commander," Isaac ordered. He shared Giannovi's unimpressive height, which meant that sitting allowed her to tower over him—and that wasn't how this meeting needed to go.

"I presume you reviewed the departmental readiness reports," he told her. It was part of the executive officer's job, after all.

"I did," she confirmed, still crisp and efficient as ever.

Isaac concealed a sigh.

"Are you aware of the Liebermann Readiness Summation Metrics?" he asked bluntly.

"They're part of every XO's training, sir," Giannovi said carefully. Some of her calm seemed to slip. "They're…far from perfect."

"Like any summation tool," Isaac agreed. Given that the late Franz Liebermann had been his father, he was perhaps more familiar than most with Liebermann's own assessment of the tool's flaws.

"But it serves a useful purpose for Captains to assess the changes in their command and compare their departments," he noted. "For example, when I came aboard *Scorpion* a month ago, the readiness reports from every department but one were in the mid-eighties, more than acceptable. Review of the detailed reports is required, but it told me that I needed to focus on our warp drive department."

Giannovi nodded slowly.

"We got Lieutenant Commander Catalan's people a refresher course on the warp drive and set up a new cross-training program," she remembered aloud. "It wasn't really a surprise—there are only eight ships in the CSF with independent FTL."

"Agreed," Isaac said with a wave of his hand. The Captain was even darker-skinned than his XO. The Captain's father had spent his adult life aboard ships, but Franz Liebermann had been born on New Soweto. The colony wasn't much less ethnically mixed than the rest of the Confederacy at this point, but its populace did tend towards the coloration of its original African settlers.

"So, imagine my concern when I reviewed the second set of semi-monthly departmental readiness reports and the summation matrices put them all, including Catalan's warp drive people, in the mid-seventies," he noted dryly.

"That was two weeks ago, Commander. Since all of those reports had been signed off on by my executive officer before they reached me,

I expected the problem to be temporary, the normal problems of assuming a new command and that if anything critical had arisen, my XO would bring it to my attention."

Giannovi was silent. Her gaze was fixed on a point behind Isaac, roughly fifty centimeters to the left and above his head.

"So, then I receive *today*'s reports," Isaac said dryly. "Lieutenant Commander Catalan's department has reached eighty percent. I wouldn't hesitate for a moment to engage this ship's space warp drives. The *rest* of her departments, however…"

He could tell from her fixed department that Giannovi had performed the same analysis, or something similar.

"The Liebermann Metric generally regards an eighty percent average as a truly combat-ready vessel," he noted. "Departments in the seventies general require closer evaluation of their reports and touching base with the officers to see where they need assistance.

"Departments in the sixties or below are potentially serious problems," he concluded. "Warp drive remains at eighty-two. Most of our departments, however, are now in the high sixties—except *gunnery*, which has managed to degrade to fifty-seven."

Isaac steepled his hands and looked his XO directly in the eye.

"Review of the actual reports, however, told me that the reason Lieutenant Commander Harris's report was so low was because Mr. Harris was actually honest in his report," he said flatly. "Review of the underlying statistics in the other department reports suggest that everyone except warp drive should actually be five to ten points lower.

"But *none* of my officers appear to think that, for example, a full-minute increase in scramble time for the emergency repair droids, was a point of concern. None, Commander Giannovi.

"Including my executive officer, who signed off on all of these reports before they reached me."

He smiled.

"Would you care to explain your reasoning, Commander?"

Giannovi swallowed and finally met his gaze.

"Permission to be frank, sir?"

"Granted."

"Your mother is the First Admiral," his XO reminded him. "The—if we're being frank—unquestioned military dictator of the Confederacy."

Isaac winced but nodded. Fifteen years ago, then-Seventh Admiral Adrienne Gallant had overthrown a corrupt president and taken "temporary" control of the Confederacy government.

Roughly half a million dead in two attempted revolutions later, it was very clear that "temporary" was no such thing. Even the woman's son couldn't argue with the description.

"Your career to date has been, in every sense, *safe*," Giannovi told him. "I'll grant that your exemplary Academy scores were when the First Admiral was merely *an* Admiral, but your every promotion since has been exactly in the middle of the zone. You made Captain at *exactly* the average age, and the only thing out of the ordinary was that you were immediately given command of a cruiser instead of commanding one of the destroyers first.

"At no point in your career since First Admiral Gallant took control of the Confederacy has any ship you have served on been placed in significant danger," she concluded. "While I doubt your mother has given any instructions to that effect at all, the Fleet has generally taken the attitude that letting the dictator's son get killed qualifies as a *really bad idea*."

That, sadly, had been roughly what Isaac had expected.

"What you are saying, Commander, is that you and the department heads see no reason to push the crew to one hundred percent of their capacity because you see no chance of this vessel being called into combat?" he asked.

She shrugged.

"The likelihood that the Confederacy Space Fleet will risk First Admiral Gallant's only child in any material action is basically zero," she admitted. "While I will admit that professional pride will keep this ship in some semblance of fighting form, there is no *point* to making her the premier ship in Battle Group *Dante*."

Isaac smiled thinly and looked at the display on his wall. Battle Group *Dante* orbited the planet of Horizon in the Epsilon Eridani System. *Dante* herself was at the core of the group, the four-hundred-meter-long wedge of the battlecruiser over twice the size of his own *Scorpion.*

"That may be true, Commander," he told her. "But you are also wrong. We will *not* be keeping this ship in 'some semblance of fighting form.' We *will* bring this ship back up to full combat readiness and keep her prepared to do her duty."

"Sir, I—"

"Commander Lauretta Giannovi," Isaac snapped. "This is a capital ship of the Confederacy Space Navy. Equally important, may I remind you, is that while Battle Group *Dante* has fifteen ships, *Scorpion* is the *only* vessel in the battlecruiser group with independent FTL.

"Every other ship in this formation must use the Eridani Wormhole Station to leave this system. The tactical and strategic value of the Space Fleet's warp cruisers cannot be overstated."

From Giannovi's expression, she wanted to argue that point. *Scorpion*'s grav-warp ring could propel the cruiser at four times the speed of light. Compared to a wormhole station that could transport an entire battle group up to two hundred light years, it was barely a strategic factor at all.

"I will *not* preside over the reduction of one of only eight grav-warp-equipped vessels in the Fleet to a glorified sinecure. Am I clear, Commander?"

She hesitated.

"Regardless of what the Fleet may expect me to do, *I* swore an oath to do my duty," Isaac reminded her quietly. "I will not be forsworn. That means this ship *will* be ready for action. Whatever it takes."

Slowly, Giannovi nodded.

"Convincing the departmental heads of your determination will not be easy," she admitted. "Convincing the *crew* will be nearly impossible without doing *something* dramatic."

"Fortunately, I'd been thinking along just those lines," Isaac told her. "And I think we need to take the ship out for some full-scale live-fire exercises, including of the warp engines."

His XO winced.

"Given our current readiness…"

"Those exercises will *hurt*," he agreed evenly. "And I think that is *exactly* the reminder *Scorpion*'s crew needs!"

———

"YOU WANT TO DO *WHAT*?"

Vice Admiral Hiro Adams was a relatively standard representative of twenty-fourth-century humanity. He had a faded-parchment tone to his skin, notably folded dark green eyes and pitch-black hair buzzed short like every other officer of the Confederacy Space Fleet.

"I want to take *Scorpion* out on a series of live-fire exercises at the New Liverpool Belt," Isaac repeated. "Her readiness has slid badly since I came aboard, and I need to shake some heads to make people realize that she didn't just become the personal yacht of the First Admiral's son."

His bluntness surprised a chuckle from Battle Group *Dante*'s commander.

"I'll admit, your crew might not be the only person needing that shake," Adams admitted wryly. "All right, Captain Gallant, what did you have in mind?"

"I want to do a series of navigational maneuvers heading out to the belt via the Eridani Wormhole Station," Isaac told him. "Then I'll need to carry out some live-fire exercises in the belt, then head into some of the denser clusters for combined live-fire and maneuvering exercises."

Adams nodded thoughtfully.

"If your readiness is as bad as you suggest, the last could be actively dangerous," he pointed out.

"The crew is solid," Isaac replied. "The officers have been letting things slide for a few weeks, but that's not enough to really undermine the competence of my people. The nav and live-fire exercises en route should shake off most of the rust. And, well, frankly, if my crew is rusty enough that we actually let an asteroid *hit* us, *Scorpion* can take the hit...and I'd rather get smacked by a low-vee rock than some idiot pirate's missile."

"And then I'm guessing you're planning on warping back?"

"Exactly, sir," Isaac confirmed. The New Liverpool belt was an eighteen-hour direct flight from Horizon for a warship. With the exercises he was planning, he would double that—but a return under warp drive would take just over a minute.

"We can probably have the crew at Eridani Station throw out some navigation buoys and targets for you as well," Adams said thoughtfully. "I'll speak to Captain Ventra.

"You have permission to carry out your exercises, Captain. I'd appreciate if you could present a plan in advance so we can warn our sensor crews when to expect pulse-gun fire, but I think shaking those heads that expected you to coast on your mother's name is a good plan."

Unmentioned was that one of those heads had been Admiral Adams's, but Isaac nodded his understanding of the Admiral's *full* meaning.

"Assistance from Eridani Station would be perfect," he admitted. "Dancing around in the belt won't give us the opportunity for true high-speed maneuvers and firing passes; those take too much acceleration time. But if we have targets and nav buoys at the wormhole station, that opens up new opportunities."

"I'll make sure Ventra reaches out to you," Adams promised. "It's not like missing one ship will matter if something goes wrong—and if something *does* go wrong, you can be back here faster than anyone else!"

"Agreed, sir. We'll keep our ear to system and Confederacy com networks, just in case," Isaac promised.

Adams waved a dismissive hand.

"You do that," he agreed. "But remember to have fun too, Captain. It's not every day we sign off on one of our captains blowing up a bunch of asteroids!"

———

2

———

Isaac Gallant felt the pulse of his bridge as *Scorpion*'s engines flared, flinging the ship across space toward her destination.

Most of his officers seemed as much confused as anything else, he noted. *Scorpion*'s crew really did seem to think they'd won the jackpot by having the First Admiral's son as their Captain—and now they were being subjected to the kind of intensive training regimen generally reserved for flagships, wartime, and particularly martinet Captains.

He was perfectly willing to let his crew decide if *Scorpion* under him was the first or last of the three options. One way or another, he intended to maintain a *warship*, not a daycare with guns.

Scorpion was well away from Horizon now, accelerating toward the Eridani Wormhole Station. Despite the mediocre readiness reports, her crew had handled getting her underway in a single day with complete aplomb.

The warp cruiser was an oddity in the Confederacy Space Fleet. Roughly the same mass as the missile cruisers that kept company with battlecruisers, she was only two hundred meters from bow to stern— barely longer than the destroyers that made up the majority of the Fleet's hulls.

Unlike any other vessels in the Fleet, however, there was a two-hundred-meter-diameter ring mounted two-thirds of the way along her hull. That ring was mostly containment fields and capacitors to hold and energize the one-centimeter-thick ring of exotic matter that made up the core of her warp drive.

Heavily armored as it was, the warp ring was critically fragile compared to any other part of any other warship in the Fleet. But it also allowed *Scorpion* to outpace light on her own, which meant that the warp cruisers were the Confederacy's fast attack ships.

All eight of them.

For the cost of a warp cruiser, you could get a missile cruiser *and* a destroyer. For the cost of two of them, you could build a battlecruiser. The full flight of the *Tarantula*-class ships had cost as much as the Confederacy's single dreadnought.

Given their price and their unique tactical value, Isaac refused to see his ship sidelined. His crew was just going to have to get used to that.

"Message incoming from EWS for you, sir."

"I'll take it here," Isaac responded. "Engaging the privacy shield."

While the privacy shield wasn't entirely obvious, every officer on duty on the bridge would have received a notice to their tattoo-comps when he engaged it. The announcement was required by regs, however, and given that the shield meant he couldn't hear his bridge crew either, he agreed with regs.

They were still far enough away from EWS to make carrying on a conversation difficult, so Captain Ventra had sent a recording.

The white-haired station commander was lucky that Isaac had taken the call in private. The open smirk he wore wasn't exactly respectful to anyone.

"Captain Gallant," he greeted Isaac cheerfully. "I see you decided to kick your layabouts into actually doing their jobs."

Ventra was very lucky the call was private, Isaac reflected.

"We've set up a series of navigational exercise for *Scorpion* to run as she approaches," Ventra continued. "It starts off easy but then ramps up. I checked them with a simulated 'perfect ship,' and your cruiser is at least theoretically capable of the last few, but your helm officer will need to have nerves of steel."

Isaac smiled. Aisha Renaud was certainly competent, but he wasn't sure she had "nerves of steel." If she could acquire them, though, it would be an asset to *Scorpion* and, not incidentally, to her long-term career.

"It's harder for me to make the gunnery exercises quite so complicated," Ventra complained. "I don't have much in terms of active drones I can spare, so mostly you've just got crates and barrels with beacons attached. The beacons will flicker in a timed sequence to simulate ECM and maneuvers; your gunners will need to hit them while they're active for it to count.

"I have to thank you for the chance to pull this together," the other Captain told him. "It's been all kinds of fun and I look forward to watching your crew punch through it. There's a download packet—"

The message cut off as a priority override shut down the privacy shield. The vague shimmer that blocked Isaac's view of the bridge vanished and he turned to face Giannovi as his XO approached the chair with a grim look on her face.

"Commander?" he asked.

"Wormhole com pulse from the Conestoga System," she told him. "Code Omega."

———

"CODE OMEGA," Isaac echoed back at her, a momentary shock freezing his system. *Omega* meant imminent attack. Conestoga was a calm, prosperous system. What could be going wrong in *Conestoga*?

"Yes, sir," Giannovi repeated, looking at him with concern.

He physically shook himself, well aware it might not look great to his bridge crew, but he needed to re-engage his brain.

"A star system is a large place and Conestoga is no exception," he finally told her dryly. "Do we have any details?"

"There was a general transmission to all Fleet Stations," she said. "Captains-and-above-only; I can only see the flag."

Isaac considered his privacy shield again for all of about half a second.

"On the main screen, if you please, Commander," he ordered. "If we end up involved in this, the bridge crew will need to know. There's no point keeping secrets."

If he couldn't trust his crew, he didn't want them anywhere near a Code Omega.

The primary viewscreen faded from its usual navigation slash tactical display to an unfamiliar control room. An older man with faded tanned skin and shockingly white hair stood in the middle of the video. He wore a plain gray business suit like it was a uniform.

"All Confederacy Space Fleet Stations, this is a Code Omega priority message from Auburn Production Station in Conestega.

"We have detected three destroyer-sized vessels approaching Auburn at high speed. We have requested their identities and in turn were told to surrender the station to the 'Free Worlds Coalition.'"

The administrator managed to turn the group's name into an epithet.

"This is a Class One Strategic Facility," the man concluded. "We have been told that if we do not surrender, the station will be destroyed. We have attached our position and scans; we request immediate relief."

The message ended.

Isaac exhaled.

"Someone tell me what Auburn Production Station is?" he asked calmly. Three destroyers? It had been ten years since the Confederacy had banned the system governments from owning or building anything larger than a patrol cutter, and required existing ships to be destroyed or turned over to the CSF.

Where had someone found three destroyers?

"APS is an exotic-matter production facility supplying Wyrm-Corp," Lieutenant Commander Harris announced immediately. The tactical officer was more on the ball than Isaac had expected. "They produce approximately twenty-seven percent of all exotic matter used to build new wormhole stations."

Twenty-seven percent. That…justified a Class One Strategic Facility designation.

"It's also…a penal facility, sir," Harris added. "Work force is fifty thousand indentured prisoners."

Isaac winced. That was part of the Confederacy current structure he was less than enthusiastic with, though he could see the virtue in extracting value from prisoners.

If only you could be certain the prisoners actually deserved to be there.

"Any word on the network on who is being sent?" he asked Giannovi out of curiosity. The communications between the system wormhole stations went through miniature versions of the wormholes the stations generated for ships.

Transmission was instantaneous to the destination but could come only from a wormhole station, which meant the longest delay in communication was usually getting your message to one of them.

General messages like this would have gone to the battle group's last known positions, which meant everyone else in the Fleet had known about this before Isaac had.

"Sir…take a look at the tactical plot Administrator Paraten included," she told him.

"On the screen," he ordered. The moment the screen switched to the display of the Conestoga System, he saw the problem.

Exotic-matter production involved immense amounts of mass. Artificial-gravity technology was nowhere near up to producing that scale of mass just yet—and required exotic matter to function itself.

A production facility like Auburn used paired gravitational singularities. The tech to mitigate their effect on the rest of the star system existed, but…exotic-matter facilities were kept well away from everything else.

"The platform is a full day's flight from the near Lagrange point," Giannovi pointed out.

Isaac nodded—a wormhole platform could only generate its exit point either in the deep space between stars or at the Lagrange points where a star's gravity was neutralized by its planets.

"And Battle Group *Calypso* is even further," he noted. *Calypso* was the battlecruiser guarding Conestoga. "What about Battle Group *Enterprise*?"

The battlecruiser *Enterprise* led an overstrength battle group permanently kept at a wormhole station, a strategic reserve to relieve any system against danger.

"Vice Admiral Cohen doesn't have a warp cruiser right now," Harris told them. "BG *Enterprise* can jump from their holding position in Sol to Conestoga immediately, but…"

"A full day's flight," Isaac agreed, studying the chart. "Lieutenant Commander Catalan," he said sharply, tapping a command to open a channel to engineering. "Can you pull the tactical data we're viewing on the Code Omega?"

From Giannovi's sharp inhalation, she understood what he was doing. No one else on the bridge seemed to understand why he was talking to the man in charge of *Scorpion*'s warp drive.

"I've got it up, sir," Catalan said carefully.

"Under full warp drive, what would be *our* ETA from the Lagrange Point to Auburn Station?"

A pregnant silent pause filled both the bridge and the intercom link.

"Ten to fifteen minutes," the engineer finally replied. "It depends on how quickly we push the cycle-up once the ring is live."

"Fifteen is more than acceptable, I think," Isaac told him. "Could any of the other warp cruisers make it?"

Another pause.

"They would all need to use their warp drives to get to their wormhole stations in useful time, and then their drives would need to cool before they could jump again in Conestoga," Catalan told him. "That cooldown would take a minimum of six hours."

"Lieutenant Commander Harris, what's our unknown's ETA?"

"Currently just over three hours," the tactical officer replied instantly. The bridge crew was starting to catch up.

"We are twenty-three minutes out from Eridani Wormhole Station," Renaud interjected immediately.

"Isn't that assuming we don't slow down?" Isaac asked.

"Yes, sir," she said crisply. "We'll hit the wormhole at one hundred sixty-five percent of normal recommended velocity. If Captain Ventra's people have it set up at a standard angle, we can do it."

"And the risk?" he asked.

"Minimal." She paused. "More accurately, sir, if we began decelerating now, we would still hit the wormhole at one hundred thirty-five percent of recommended velocity. The risk profile *change* is minimal, and we would need to decelerate at maximum power. EWS would get a dangerous quantity of hard rads and propellant wash, which would dramatically increase their risk profile."

"Understood."

Isaac paused, collating all of the information as his crew waited for his orders.

"Set the course, Lieutenant Commander Renaud," he ordered. "Lieutenant Commander Harris, pull every piece of data you can extract from Auburn Station's download. I want to know what fight I'm picking.

"Lieutenant Commander Catalan, prepare the warp drive for the jump to Auburn Station from the nearest Lagrange Point. Commander Giannovi, touch base with Captain Ventra and make sure his people have the wormhole ready for us.

"If they do it right, it'll make Renaud's job significantly easier," he concluded. No matter what, this was going to require the exact nerves of steel he hadn't been sure his navigator had.

"Yes, sir," his crew chorused.

A moment later, his XO stepped up to his chair.

"Shouldn't you be contacting Ventra, sir?" she suggested delicately.

"In theory, yes," he agreed. "But I need to tell Vice Admiral Adams I'm about to unilaterally take his only warp cruiser out of the system."

Giannovi chuckled sharply.

"Understood, sir!"

———

"ADMIRAL ADAMS."

Isaac faced the recording camera levelly, searching for the words to make clear what he was doing.

"*Scorpion* received the Code Omega from the Auburn Production Facility six minutes ago," he told the Vice Admiral. "We reviewed the data and the last Confederacy Space Fleet readiness reports relayed to us.

"Sir, unless there are units I am not aware of, *Scorpion* is the only warship of the CSF in position to intervene. Even the other warp cruisers are a minimum of approximately seven hours away, with Battle Group *Enterprise* at least twenty-four hours and Battle Group *Calyspo* nearly thirty-six.

"We can be there in forty-five minutes."

Isaac paused.

"I have already given the orders to my crew and Captain Ventra to make it happen. You will receive this message in time to order an abort —I am aware that this operation is only arguably under my authority.

"Nonetheless. Auburn is a Class One Strategic Facility with over fifty thousand people on board. I do not feel we have a choice but to take any option that gives us a chance of saving them.

"Our course projection is attached. I will refrain from informing Administrator Paraten that we are coming until I have either received approval for this mission or have entered the Conestoga System.

"Captain Isaac Gallant, *Scorpion*."

He hit SEND and dropped the privacy screen, watching as the icon representing his ship screamed closer to the Eridani Wormhole Station.

"Ventra says, and I quote, 'You've all got nerves of steel, I see. Gateway will be open on time,'" Giannovi told him quietly.

"Good. Now get yourself down to CIC," Isaac ordered. "We'll go to general quarters as soon as we're through the wormhole. Before we go to warp."

He managed to control a shiver.

Giannovi paused, studying him for a moment.

"Have you ever been aboard a ship in warp before, sir?" she asked.

"No, Commander," he confirmed levelly. "But there's a first for everything."

"Yes, there is, sir," she said with an odd tone, then saluted. "With your permission, I'll get to CIC."

"Carry on, Commander Giannovi."

———

ISAAC'S RESPONSE from Vice Admiral Adams arrived quickly. Faster than he'd expected, in fact. The Admiral's image appeared in his chair screen as he dropped the privacy shield again, and the man's eyes were tired.

"Captain Gallant, I could probably think of a thousand reasons why the mission you have decided to assign yourself is foolhardy and unwise. I could argue that it's far too risky an endeavour for a man many judge, however accurately or inaccurately, to be the heir apparent to the Confederacy.

"Others would argue that as your commanding officer, letting you do this is putting my neck on the block if your mother comes looking for people to blame."

Adams straightened and looked Isaac directly in the eyes.

"We both know all of those arguments and reasons would be distractions at best and personal moral cowardice at worst," he said calmly. "Your assessment of the situation is exactly the same as my own.

"I, however, had not considered the advantages *Scorpion*'s current position provide. Neither, to my knowledge, has anyone else. You are correct in that you command the only ship that can intervene, and that, Captain Gallant, leaves me with only one option.

"Your relief mission to Auburn Station is authorized. The Confederacy *needs* that facility, Captain.

"I don't need to tell you that you're outgunned," the Admiral noted. "Our intelligence suggests you're looking at three Conestoga System Defense Force *Archon*-class destroyers that 'somehow' escaped the scrapyard.

"They're old but capable ships. Two of my own destroyers are seized *Archon*s. I've attached a full data package on them, assuming this 'Free Worlds Coalition' hasn't upgraded them in the ten years since they were supposed to be scrapped."

Adams tapped a command, then shook his head.

"Battle Group *Enterprise* is on the way, but you're the only one who can make it," he concluded. "So, all I can do is tell you to go get them, Captain.

"And good luck."

———

3

The tension in *Scorpion*'s bridge edged up a notch as the timer before wormhole transit began to tick down. It was easy to accept Renaud's calm assurance that the transit would be fine when it was all theoretical, but as the timer ticked past one hundred seconds to the wormhole, nerves were taut.

Isaac kept an eye on the room. Whatever happened, he was confident his ship would survive and be able to take on the grandstanding pirates threatening Auburn Station. He was more concerned about his crew's stress levels this early in the game than with the actual transit.

"This is insane," Harris finally said aloud, clearly voicing several people's concerns. "No one transits at this velocity! It's suicide."

Renaud coughed delicately.

"CSF vessels have translated at velocities in excess of our current speed over fifty times," she told the other Lieutenant Commander. "While I would hesitate to call it safe, it is certainly not 'suicide.'"

"Eridani Wormhole Station has opened the portal," Giannovi reported from CIC. "Commander Renaud, do you have the target profile?"

"I do," the navigator confirmed. "Wormhole is exactly on specification. That'll make this easier."

"We're about to try and hit a kilometer-wide target with a two-hundred-meter-wide dart at a measurable fraction of the speed of light," Harris pointed out. "What's *easy* about this?"

"The fact that the computers are doing nine-tenths of it," Isaac's navigator snapped. "But my tenth of it would be easier if everyone else would be *quiet*."

"Stand down, Harris," Isaac said firmly. "Renaud's right. A lot of people have made transit at this speed before us; we'll be fine." He leveled a gaze on Renaud. "We *will* be fine, Lieutenant Commander?"

She made several more entries on her terminal before responding, but then looked up.

"All corrections complete," she told him. "The computer has it from here." She smiled. "And yes, Captain, we'll be fine."

"Then why does no one jump at this speed?" Harris asked. To Isaac's amusement, his tone was no longer panicking, just curious.

"Oh, that's easy," Renaud replied cheerfully. "Because this is going to hurt."

They hit the window. At this speed, there wasn't enough time on approach to look through the wormhole and see the stars on the other side. There was only the sudden sensation of transition.

Saying a wormhole transit took 7.42 seconds was the equivalent of saying pi was 3.14. It was accurate enough for most purposes but ignored an infinite number of irrational decimals after that point.

The human brain, however, did not comprehend the process. Some people just…lost those seconds. Some people experienced them stretched out a hundredfold.

Isaac Gallant was closest to the former. Transits always seemed to take less than a second to him. They started and then they were over.

This time, someone stabbed a sword through his head in those short subjective moments. Unlike Harris, he'd known why the wormhole stations normally limited transit velocities. He still hadn't expected to be quite so certain that he was dying.

And then it was past, and *Scorpion* emerged into the Conestoga System. From the expressions around him, several of his bridge crew members had experienced similar sensations…and didn't have quite so short a subjective experience.

He hit a key on the side of his command chair.

"General announcement, all hands: we just made a fast and hard wormhole transit and will shortly be going to general quarters and bringing up the warp drive.

"However, to be *very* clear, anyone who has been negatively impacted by the transit is to report to the infirmary immediately," he ordered. "As your department heads and team leads should have briefed you, we will be going into battle shortly.

"I want all of you at your best.

"Gallant out."

————

SETTLING BACK in his command chair, Isaac flipped open a small shield on the left arm of the seat. It was positioned well away from the repeater panels and computer screens used to operate the ship, and protected from accidental impact.

Once the shield was up, he pressed the single red button underneath it—and the general quarters klaxon began to ring through the ship. There were other ways to bring the ship to GQ, but the button on the Captain's chair was the fastest.

Regulations required a ship to be at GQ to enter gravity warp. It wasn't supposed to be much more intrusive than a regular wormhole transit, but it was rare enough, even aboard a warp cruiser, to make sure the crews was ready for it.

"All stations report ready," Glannovi told him from CIC moments later.

"That's...physically impossible," Isaac replied dryly. The expected time for a crew to report to General Quarters was approximately two minutes. One of the reasons for the readiness failures he'd been seeing was that that time had risen to just over *three* aboard *Scorpion*.

The minimum was probably around a minute. Not roughly eight seconds.

"It is when apparently the crew has been voluntarily reporting to their battle stations for the last fifteen minutes," his executive officer told him with a chuckle. "I think you found your wakeup call, Captain!"

"So it seems," he murmured. "Commander Catalan!"

"Sir?" the warp drive engineer replied instantly.

"Is this ship ready for FTL?"

"All departments report general quarters status and the drive is online and charged," the engineer reported. "*Scorpion* is ready for gravity warp in all respects."

Isaac smiled, studying the updated navigation plot on the big screen in front of him. Three glaring red icons showed the ships hurtling toward Auburn Station. Green icons ahead of him showed that Battle Group *Enterprise* hadn't decided to be left out after all, though the eight-ship formation would arrive at Auburn hours after this was over.

Enterprise herself wasn't there. Three destroyers didn't call for a battlecruiser—even the two missile cruisers and six destroyers the Fleet had sent were overkill.

They did make Isaac's job easier. So long as he delayed or diverted the attackers, that task group would finish them off.

"Commander Giannovi, please send my regards to the *Enterprise* task group," he told his XO. "Then…"

He smiled at his video link to Catalan.

"Take us to full warp, Lieutenant Commander Catalan."

———

THE ONLY INITIAL response was an indicator that popped up on the main screen, notifying the bridge crew that the warp drive's exotic-matter ring was spinning up. Twenty percent of target angular velocity. Fifty. Sixty percent.

After ten seconds, it hit seventy-five percent and the air started to feel heavier as a new velocity icon appeared on the screen.

Seventy-five percent was enough to engage the warp drive, wrapping *Scorpion* in a carefully shaped bubble of nonlinear space and immediately accelerating her to just over ninety percent of the speed of light.

By eighty percent, they were well past the universe's normal speed limit and the air had taken on a thick, almost viscous pressure in Isaac's mouth. From the research he'd done, this effect was mostly psychosomatic.

Mostly.

But it was still universal to all humans in a gravity-warp bubble and moderately uncomfortable. Several of his bridge officers were coughing, trying to clear what felt like a clogged throat.

"We are at ninety percent of ring velocity and holding," Catalan announced, then coughed to clear his own throat. "Estimated pseudo-velocity is three times lightspeed." He paused. "It would take another hour for us to accelerate up to full pseudo-velocity safely. This will get us to Auburn Station in fourteen minutes."

"Entirely acceptable, Lieutenant Commander," Isaac confirmed. He'd told the Commander fifteen minutes was fine and had mentally allotted half an hour.

Even at the ninety percent of lightspeed that was the bubble's minimum pseudo-velocity, they'd have beaten the "Coalition" ships to Auburn Station.

The screen in front of him continued to show everyone's positions, but they were estimates and projections now. The grav-warp bubble was blatantly obvious from the outside, shedding energy with nearly star-like brilliance, but from the inside, the rest of the universe had simply ceased to exist.

"Let's get a meal served to all stations," he instructed. "We're going to be at general quarters for a while, so let's take advantage of the fact that they can't touch us in warp."

There were some theoretical weapons that could attack a ship under warp drive, but there were only seventeen warp ships in the entire Confederacy. The CSF had consciously chosen to make sure even the theory of how to attack those ships underway was quietly suppressed.

"Commander Harris?" He turned to his tactical officer. "How is *Scorpion*'s sting?"

"Ready magazines have been loaded and charged for all missile launchers," he reported crisply. "That gives us fifteen missiles ready to go before we need to transfer from the central magazines."

Which would increase their launch cycle time almost tenfold. That was the sacrifice made to give the warp cruiser *any* real missile armament. She had five missile launchers and a hundred missiles, but only three missiles could be held in each ready magazine next to the launchers. The rest were stored in a core magazine buried at the armored center of the ship.

"Pulse-gun capacitors are fully charged. Once we enter action, we'll spin all of the fusion plants up to full power to keep them fed. Missile defense suite is active and running in autonomous mode."

Harris nodded firmly.

"*Scorpion*'s sting is sharp and ready, sir," he reported.

"Have you familiarized yourself with the old *Archon*-class destroyer?" Isaac asked.

"Not yet, sir," Harris admitted. "I was focusing on making sure we were ready for battle."

"Fair enough," the Captain allowed. "But make sure you know your enemy as well as yourself, Commander. Let's not have any surprises."

"Agreed, sir."

———

FIVE MINUTES LATER, Isaac half-wished that no one had sent him the data on the *Archon*-class destroyers. The Conestoga System government, like most in the time frame between the coup and the disarming of the system governments, had understood the distinct possibility that their defense forces could easily be pressed into standing off the Confederacy Space Fleet.

In the end, none of those fleets had prevented the attempted revolution or the mass arrests that had followed. Thousands had died and tens of thousands had been funneled into the Confederacy's prison system. *Most* of the time, Isaac was reasonably sure that there had been that many legitimate members of the revolution to be arrested for their crimes, and that it had been merciful to refrain from executing most of them.

And if he woke up in the middle of the night sometimes, doubting that his mother had *actually* done the right thing, that wasn't something the commander of a capital ship of the Confederacy Space Fleet could admit to.

But the Conestoga System Defense Force had designed their ships to go head-to-head with their CSF counterparts and win one-on-one. No one had built an *Archon*-class destroyer in fifteen years, but the last flights of the ships had been easily equal to the CSF's current *Glorious*-class ships.

They were bigger and slower than a *Glorious* but packed just as many pulse guns and just as much armor as the more modern ship into that bigger hull. Their missile defenses would pale against the firepower of an actual missile cruiser, but *Scorpion*'s missile armament was probably useless.

The warp cruiser outgunned any individual *Archon*, even if they were the last-generation Flight Eight ships. If they were older ships, Flight Five or Flight Six even, *Scorpion* was an even match for two of them.

Three of them, however, unquestionably had the Confederacy cruiser outgunned. The irony was that she actually *outmassed* all three combined, no matter what, but the rebel ships didn't need to haul their own FTL drives around with them.

How the ships had escaped the requirement to surrender or scrap the System Defence Forces was irrelevant. There was no way any wormhole station commander was going to open a gateway for armed ships that weren't definitively CSF.

Which was probably why they were going after Auburn Station. Isaac pulled up the production data and looked at the numbers. There wasn't enough exotic matter in the Station's holding containers to build a modern wormhole station with its multi-hundred-light-year range…but there was enough to build an older-style station. Enough to allow them to cause havoc across a quarter of the Confederacy.

There was no long-term goal there that he could sympathize with.

Whatever high morals this "Free Worlds Coalition" proclaimed, they were looking to build a tool for piracy. Nothing more.

The Confederacy in its current state was far from perfect. Even the Senate didn't pretend it was much more than an advisory body to the First Admiral…but it was, at least, *honest*. The corruption that had drained the interstellar economy and hobbled the outer worlds had been burnt out when Isaac's mother had lanced the boil of the President's office.

He had his doubts about what his mother had done. Doubts about how the Confederacy's government was run now.

But he had faith, above all else, that First Admiral Adrienne Gallant remained a firm crusader against the corruption that had nearly destroyed the Confederacy once before.

He had to.

———

4

———————

"Warp bubble collapse in five…four…three…two…one…*collapse.*"

Isaac coughed, his throat managing to clear at last as the air aboard *Scorpion* finally returned to normal. Auburn Station was suddenly *there,* the massive refinery platform with its mostly tame black holes barely fifty thousand kilometers away.

That was closer than he'd planned on coming out of FTL.

"Was our navigation intended to be *quite* so precise, Lieutenant Commander Catalan?" he asked carefully.

He could hear the engineer swallow.

"We were supposed to emerge three hundred thousand klicks away, sir," Catalan admitted. "That's…maximum emergence variance." He coughed. "We'll recalibrate the ring controls, Captain. That shouldn't happen again."

"That's a good plan, Commander," Isaac agreed. "But well done nonetheless. Thank you."

The channel cut off and he studied the station that was currently causing everyone so much trouble. Auburn Station was clearly an industrial facility, with zero thought or attention given to its aesthetics. The central production facility was two globes half-melted together, almost forming a three-dimensional infinity symbol.

Storage containers hung down from the globes like icicles, each requiring the power supply of a small city to maintain the containment fields holding their exotic matter in place.

A three-kilometer-wide circular safety shield hung "above" the production field, massive artificial gravity generators and power plants scattered at seeming random across its underside. Some exotic-matter stations Isaac had seen had an entire secondary station on the other side of the safety shield, where the workers lived. That station had drives and independent power and atmosphere—allowing the crew to run away if something went wrong with the temperamental process they were operating.

Auburn Station's builders had been stingier than that. The upper side of the safety shield had been used as an anchor to build a city that, except for the lack of streets, wouldn't have looked out of place on any Confederacy planet.

Building it there allowed them to double-purpose the same massive gravity generators that protected the star system from Auburn Station's captive singularities—but it also made the staff much more vulnerable.

He hadn't expected it to be quite so obvious that Auburn Station was a hard labor prison.

"Sir, a moment?" Harris asked quietly.

"Step up, Commander," Isaac ordered. Once the tactical officer was next to his chair, he activated the extended privacy shield, announcing it clearly to the bridge, then turned to the young man.

"What is it, Harris?" he asked. He had a suspicion.

"I reviewed the *Archon* specifications," the tactical officer told him. "We can't fight three of them. I hate to sound like a broken record, sir, but this is *suicide*."

"I won't permit defeatism on my bridge, Commander," Isaac said harshly. "Identifying the odds is acceptable. Saying this is impossible isn't; do you understand me?"

Harris swallowed.

"Yes, sir. But...I don't see a way we can take all three of those ships," he admitted. "They're just over two hours away. If we go out to meet them, we'll reach missile range in an hour and pulse-gun range shortly afterwards."

"Assuming we just go straight at them," Isaac pointed out. "We have a significant maneuverability advantage over them and they don't have missiles."

"But they have more than enough missile defense for the three of them to absorb every missile we have," his tactical officer said. "And while we can control the range, they're just going to head straight at the station. They know we have to defend it."

"They do," Isaac agreed. "I need to talk to Administrator Paraten," he continued. "Then you and I and Commander Giannovi need to sit down and see what we can think up.

"I refuse to accept that a Confederacy cruiser cannot defeat three rebel destroyers," Isaac concluded. "We just have to be cleverer and more determined than they are. People are relying on us, Commander Harris. We cannot afford wormhole-equipped pirates or, Fates forbid, a new civil war.

"Humanity looks to us to provide order and safety. We will fulfill that charge. Understand me, Commander?"

"I do, sir," Harris admitted. "But…right now, the only way I see to buy time for someone else to arrive and support us is to make the bastards take the time to kill us."

Isaac chuckled.

"Let's call that Plan Z," he told the junior. "And try and come up with a whole *list* of options before we resort to it!"

———

ARTHUR PARATEN DIDN'T LOOK any more authoritative or intimidating in real time. He'd relocated from the control room of his earlier message to an even more plebeian space. This one still had displays around him, but there were no bustling technicians or big displays showing the star system Auburn orbited.

"Administrator Paraten," Isaac greeted him politely from his private office. "This is—"

"Yes, yes, the starship captain," Paraten cut him off. "What exactly are you planning on doing with *one ship*? This is a Class One Facility!"

"It's also an exotic-matter production facility, which means you're positioned a long way away from anything we might not want to lose," Isaac shot back. "Additional units are en route, but for now, the protection of Auburn Station falls to me."

Paraten shook his head.

"Are you serious, Captain?" he demanded.

"Despite their best efforts, the Confederacy Space Fleet is still limited by the laws of physics as we understand them," Isaac told him. "We will do all within our power to protect Auburn Station, but you are correct in that my ship is outnumbered and outgunned.

"Have you begun evacuating the station's crew? You do have sufficient shipping for that, correct?"

If they didn't, there'd be some *interesting* follow-up conversations going on when this was over.

"The prison sections have been locked down and the supervisory personnel secured in the safety pod sections of the station," Paraten admitted. "The presence of the prisoners should prevent these scum from firing on the station."

A chill ran down Isaac's spine.

"That was not my question," he said slowly. "You *do* have the capacity to evacuate your crew, correct?"

"Yes, but I'm not going to," the Administrator said flatly. "If there is even the slightest chance that the prisoners' presence will prevent this 'Coalition' from firing on the station, then they must remain. There are always sympathizers and complainers to be arrested; there is no shortage of indentures, Captain.

"This station is *far* more valuable than the eminently expendables who crew it."

Isaac stared at Paraten for several eternal seconds, then smiled.

"I see that I will need to be more clear," he finally said. "I will need to get underway to engage the enemy within fifteen minutes.

"If you do *not* begin a full evacuation of Auburn Station within the next *ten* minutes, I will deploy my Marines to Auburn Station, where they will arrest you and anyone who attempts to stop them evacuating the prisoners.

"And yes, Administrator, they will be authorized to use whatever force necessary to make certain the *fifty thousand* civilians on your station are out of the line of fire."

If his smile was half as cold as he thought it was, he wasn't surprised that the Administrator was frozen.

"*Am I clear?*" he barked.

"You would not dare," Paraten finally replied.

"Do not test me."

"This facility is owned by the First Admiral herself! Why do you think we have access to the prisoner base?" the older man snapped. "Between her direct ownership and what she owns of WyrmCorp, she'd be out billions if you let this platform get destroyed! If you force me to abandon this platform, you will hear from *her*!"

Isaac suspected Paraten wasn't supposed to tell people that. The First Admiral was quite public that she did *not* profit from her stewardship of the Confederacy.

Except that according to Paraten, she did. If she owned a chunk of WyrmCorp, especially…WyrmCorp held a monopoly on wormhole station construction. Many had—quietly—wondered how that monopoly had survived the coup.

Now Isaac suspected he knew, and he could feel a portion of the faith he had in his mother's rule shrivel and die as he met Administrator Arthur Paraten's gaze.

"You should perhaps have let me finish introducing myself," he told the Administrator coldly. "My name, Administrator Paraten, is Captain Isaac *Gallant*. If there is anyone in the Confederacy immune to the First Admiral's displeasure, I rather suspect it is me.

"Which means you now have"—he checked the time on his screen—"nine minutes and twenty seconds to begin that evacuation before I deploy Marines.

"Good day, Administrator Paraten."

He cut the channel before Paraten could do more than gape at him in shock, struggling with the shifting emotional ground beneath him.

FIVE MINUTES LATER, Isaac stood in his ready room with his hands clasped behind his back while Giannovi and Harris took their seats.

They were supposed to be discussing how to fight this battle, but his own focus was on the bombshell Paraten had dropped on his own worldview. *Scorpion*'s databanks were extensive, and while he couldn't look up the ownership of WyrmCorp, he *had* managed to find the holding corporation that owned half of Auburn Station.

FranzLieb Interstellar Assets.

The context he had would have been enough for most people to guess what the name meant, but Isaac had more. Isaac had seen his mother use the same short form of his father's name for a hundred different purposes.

It was a more than sufficient shield against most people prodding, given that he suspected FranzLieb's ownership was supremely convoluted—and anyone who went poking would get an unpleasant visit from Confederacy Security—but a useless one against Adrienne Gallant's own son.

And he was no longer willing to assume his mother wouldn't use ConSec for her own purposes.

"Has the evacuation begun?" he asked his officers calmly. He didn't turn to face them. He wasn't sure he could manage to fake calm if they could see his face.

"The transports are loading," Harris replied. "The first half dozen are away: twelve thousand people or so."

"Has the Coalition force responded at all?"

"Not that we can see. They're continuing on a direct course for the station." Harris paused. "They also have to be aware of our presence. Our arrival was not covert.

"They haven't responded to that, either."

"Ballsy bastards," Giannovi snapped. "They may have us outgunned, but you'd think they'd have *noticed* the CSF dropping a cruiser in their path."

"I wonder if they have simply done the math and know the odds of their victory, or if they cling to the courage of their convictions," Isaac murmured. "I'd almost prefer the latter—the former suggests far too much competence for my taste."

He watched the second wave of transports blast free of Auburn Station, then inhaled deeply and turned to face his officers again.

"What do we know about this 'Free Worlds Coalition'?" he asked. "Have they crossed ConSec's radar before this?"

"Not that's in our records," his XO admitted. "Which makes me wonder—how in Fates did someone manage to steal three destroyers without Security noticing?"

"Conestoga wasn't one of our problem children," Isaac pointed out. "There were systems where we made sure to account for every ship at every stage of the process. Conestoga wasn't one of them: they scrapped the newest flight of ships to make a point, but they gave the CSF half of the older ships.

"Since they were playing mostly nice, I doubt ConSec did more than validate that the final mass out of the smelter was correct," he continued. "I can think of at least six different ways to sneak a ship or three out of that."

"That's not good, sir," Harris said. "If they went to that effort, wouldn't it make sense that they preserved the most modern ships?"

"Yes," Isaac agreed. "We need to assume these are Flight Eight *Archons*, with all of the upgrades that entails. Where would that put them compared to *Scorpion*?"

"No missiles. Seventy percent of our pulse-gun armament each," Harris responded instantly. "ECM would be out of date. Software updates won't be enough; their emitter hardware isn't flexible enough to beat our current penetrator systems on the missiles.

"That said, they've got enough defensive lasers with three ships to make short work of our best salvos. Their pulse guns are older but still a perfectly effective design. We haven't switched them out on our own *Archons*."

"They're physically bigger but have about the same power levels," Giannovi added. "Range is…functionally identical. We have a slight edge, but it's on the order of kilometers."

"We won't have that precise a control of the approach distance,"

Isaac agreed. "So, we know their ships. We'll assume they're Flight Eight—that will make any surprises pleasant ones.

"But we know nothing about this Coalition. Nothing about their captains, their commander, anything."

He smiled thinly. His faith might be shaken, but this was his job. He could make this work.

"I want you two to keep brainstorming," he told them. "What weaknesses are we missing? What options haven't we considered?"

"What are you going to do, sir?" Harris asked carefully.

"I think it's time I saw the face of my enemy," Isaac replied. "I'm going to hail them and see what they do."

———

THE BIG DISPLAY on the main screen continued to show the position of all the ships involved in this mess. The task group from Battle Group *Enterprise* was still over twenty hours away. A new set of flashing green icons denoted an update from the Conestoga Wormhole Station in the last few moments.

"Who do we have?" Isaac asked as he crossed the bridge.

"*Tarantula*, *Mosquito* and *Termite*," the junior lieutenant holding down tactical reported. "Arriving from Tau Ceti, Sol and Procyon, respectively. All three have begun recharging their warp drives, and Conestoga Station reports they will arrive to reinforce us in just over six hours."

That cut the time period he needed to keep the Coalition occupied by sixteen hours. He had no way to speak to those Captains in real time—any wormhole station that knew where he was could transmit to him, but he had no way to transmit back other than regular light-speed radio.

"All right," he confirmed, taking his seat. "Coms, get me a recording for transmission. I want to ping these 'Coalition' ships hard enough to make *sure* they're listening."

"Whenever you're ready."

A flashing button lit up on his command repeaters, and Isaac restored the cold smile he'd given Administrator Paraten to his face before hitting it.

"Approaching vessels, this is Captain Isaac Gallant of the Confederacy Space Fleet Vessel *Scorpion*," he greeted them. "Your actions and the transmissions sent to Auburn Station already arguably constitute treason. Your possession of three unauthorized destroyers is a violation of the Confederacy Senate's Disarmament Act.

"We have identified your ships as *Archon*-class destroyers, built in this system prior to the Act. That they still exist suggests a conspiracy in the Conestoga System Defense Force, a conspiracy that I am certain Confederacy Security will root out now its existence is proven."

And if Isaac was a little sickened by what that might entail, that was a problem for another time.

"Simply by *appearing*, you have failed," Isaac told them. "Whatever plans you have cannot succeed. You have three destroyers—but a dozen warships of the Confederacy are already in motion. You may think you outgun me at the point of contact, but I have the entire Confederacy Fleet at my back.

"The moment you fire a single projectile at *Scorpion* or Auburn Station, your lives are forfeit," he warned them. "Surrender and turn state's evidence, and I swear your lives will be spared. Continue on your course and this can only end one way."

He cut off the recording, sending the transmission as he studied the situation and wondered what he was missing.

Auburn Station was in the local space equivalent of nowhere. In the Sol System, it would have been orbiting on the outer edge of the Oort Cloud—that was, in fact, where the equivalent platform in Sol *was*. The reason there'd been enough time for anyone to intervene was because the destroyers had only been able to hide so much of their approach before they'd been in empty space.

And while you could hide in space if you were good, you needed something to hide *behind*.

Three destroyers could take out *Scorpion*. They certainly could take out Auburn Station, but destroying the platform would be pure vandalism with no long-term benefits for anyone. The only logical target on the board was Auburn Station's holding towers.

But to steal those, this Free Worlds Coalition needed an *exit plan*. And Isaac couldn't see one.

"Sir, we have a return transmission from one of the destroyers…in fact, it's being bounced from all three destroyers," his coms officer reported. "We're close enough that we can get a live channel, though there'll be time delays."

"Do it," Isaac ordered. "Let me see them." He paused, then grinned. "And see if you can pick out which ship is *actually* transmitting."

Bouncing the signal from all three destroyers kept him from identifying the flagship. A sensible precaution, as there was no question that at least one of those ships wasn't going to survive the coming clash. If Isaac knew which one carried the commander, that would give him more options.

A video feed appeared on the main screen, showing an unusually tall man with no visible hair and pale brown skin. He focused ice-blue eyes on his own camera.

"I'm not going to give you my name, *Gallant*," he spat. "You can call me Justice, for that is what I intend to bring to this galaxy—and to the First Admiral.

"Your threats do not intimidate me, and I am *pleased* to think that the head bitch's son is in my targeting sights. There will be blood for blood, Gallant, and I will end you."

Isaac checked to be certain the link was now two-way and live, then turned his coldest glare on 'Justice.'

"Whatever you claim to be, 'Justice,' your actions are those of a two-bit pirate," he told the rebel. "You come here to threaten the innocent and steal the resources forged by the sweat of others.

"You might end me," he allowed, "but then the Confederacy Fleet will pursue you to the ends of the universe. The Fleet will not forgive the loss of a cruiser—and do you really think my *mother* will forgive *my* death?"

Seconds ticked by and he waited. He could see the moment Justice received his response, the snarl tightening as his words echoed in the rebel's ears.

"You'll never find us," he told Isaac. "You could tear apart the entire galaxy and you will never find the Coalition. We have grown in the cracks where you have never looked, the shadows where you are blind. You will die, Captain Gallant, and your Confederacy of murderers will die—and they will *never* see us coming."

"If I am going to die, *Justice*, then I will die between the innocent and those who would do them harm," Isaac told the other man. "Which of us does that make the murderer?"

He could tell when Justice got that message, because the channel cut off with one last snarl. Smiling grimly, he turned to his coms officer, noting the excited broad grin on the young woman's face.

"Yes?" he asked.

"Right-hand destroyer, back of their formation," she replied. "That's the command ship. And, sir?"

"Yes?"

"Their combat systems are locked down tight, but their coms security *sucks*. I pulled ship IDs while I was tracing the relay. That's *Poseidon*, *Michael* and *Uriel*. This 'Justice' is aboard *Uriel*."

"Ah," Isaac allowed. "Well done, Lieutenant. Well done indeed."

He'd reviewed everything on the *Archon*-class now. *Poseidon*, *Michael* and *Uriel* were his worst-case scenario. Not merely Flight Eight ships, but the very last Flight Eight ships. Their edge over the earlier units in the flight was minimal, but…it was an edge Justice hadn't really needed to make this a battle Isaac couldn't win.

It was nonetheless a battle Isaac had no choice but to fight.

"Lieutenant Commander Renaud," he addressed his navigator. "Do you have an intercept course plotted for the Coalition fleet?"

"I do, sir," she reported levelly.

"Then get us underway. Keep our options open; I want the chance to surprise the bastards, but we need to start moving in their direction."

"Understood, sir. Getting us moving."

Scorpion trembled around Isaac and he studied the readiness display showing on his tattoo-comp.

Time to see what the Coalition could do with their destroyers.

———

5

———

"ALL RIGHT, PEOPLE," Isaac told Giannovi and Harris as he stepped back into the ready room. From the way they looked up at him, their brainstorming hadn't been going very well.

"We are underway. We will reach engagement range of the Coalition task group in just over one hour," he continued. "Renaud will keep our potential vector options open as long as possible, but there will come a moment at which we need to commit to a strategy."

He smiled at their discomfiture.

"There are three pieces that will impact what we need to do," Isaac told them. "The first, thanks to our excellent bridge crew, we now have: we know which ship their commanding officer is aboard. We also, though it won't impact our strategy much, know which ships we're facing.

"*That* piece of data we will pass to ConSec once this is over," he concluded.

"The second piece of information we do not have, but we have enough data to infer," he continued. "Harris, I need you to do a data search on Conestoga System Defence Force Officers, the historical records. If we don't have them, Auburn Station will."

"I need to know every space-born officer who held the rank of destroyer commander or above when the Disarmament Act was passed," he told the tactical officer. "Pull that data for me."

"On it," the Lieutenant Commander said, his confusion clear.

"Thirdly is the piece of information we don't have, just the gap where it should be," Isaac noted. "There are three ships heading toward Auburn Station at high speed. At this distance from the system primary, there is no escape route for them. Nowhere to hide.

"Any of those destroyers has enough weapon and engine power to sever and haul all of Auburn Station's holding towers away with them. But it would take them an hour to do so carefully, and it would be a minimum of eight to ten hours before they were anywhere they could hide.

"Given that either the task group from Battle Group *Enterprise* or Battle Group *Calypso* would be on an intercept course, they wouldn't escape—and that's without the Fleet gathering a strike group of our fellow warp cruisers."

"What are they planning?" Giannovi asked.

"That's exactly the piece of data I don't have, XO," Isaac admitted. "I know they *have* an exit plan…but I don't know what it is. Without knowing that, I don't know if this Coalition has potential reinforcements in play."

She nodded.

"We were studying their formation," she told him, nodding towards Harris who was now embedded in the data search Isaac had ordered. "We don't have much of a range advantage, but combined with the width of their formation, we can make a high-speed pass that keeps us completely out of range of one of the three ships."

"If we combine that with prepped missiles, we should be able to punch out one of their ships in a single pass," Isaac agreed instantly. "We can target Uriel, remove this Justice and break up their chain of command.

"We'd only be able to make one high-speed pass, though," he noted. He didn't even need to run the numbers on a computer. *Scorpion* was fast and maneuverable, much more so than the old destroyers, but she couldn't pass them at high speed, turn around and do it again.

She *could* catch up to them before they ranged on Auburn Station, though.

"Sir, I've got that list," Harris reported. "There were four officers who fit your criteria."

Isaac nodded. "Are any of them still with the CSDF?"

"Yes, sir. Two of them."

"They won't be it. Remove them. Are either of the other two in the public eye at all?"

Harris checked his data.

"Not currently…but one was mayor of an asteroid settlement for five years after resigning from the CSDF."

"Show me the last one," Isaac ordered. He was unsurprised when the man appeared on the ready room's big screen. The decades hadn't been kind to him—space-born rarely aged well when regularly subjected to the higher gravities the planet-born insisted on—but it was definitely the same man as Justice.

"Who is he?" he asked.

"He was Senior Commander Daniel Wehr," Harris replied. "Skipper of the *Archon*-class destroyer *Samael*. Born in a belt asteroid mining settlement, but…his cousin was *Jessica* Wehr."

That name Isaac knew.

"She was killed in the revolution, correct?" he asked.

Harris winced.

"Captured, sir," he admitted. "She was the Commodore of a destroyer flotilla that fought against the Fleet. Her force was battered into submission and she surrendered to then-Vice Admiral Cohen."

The tactical officer swallowed.

"First Admiral Gallant promoted Cohen to Seventh Admiral for his victory—and ordered every officer of the flotilla publicly executed."

"Including Daniel Wehr's cousin," Isaac concluded. "So, he hates the Confederacy and, quite personally, my family. Wonderful."

"I don't see how that's helpful to us," Giannovi admitted.

"Oh, it's quite helpful," the Captain told her. "It means he isn't thinking straight now that he knows I'm here. If we set up a pass that's targeting him, he will make it easier on us because right now, that man is conflicted.

"The soldier he was—and probably still thinks of himself as—has a mission he needs to carry out. The *man* wants to avenge himself on the First Admiral and can't help but see my presence as an opportunity to do so."

Isaac smiled.

"We can use that. We have the beginnings of a plan, at least."

"What about your third data point, sir?" Giannovi asked.

"I'm missing something, Commander," he admitted. "Any inspiration either of you have would be appreciated. I have the feeling the answer to that question will be important."

———

THE VELOCITIES that warships reached relative to the effective ranges of their weapons meant that space combat was even more "long stretches of boredom interrupted by moments of absolute terror" than any other type of war.

It would take *Scorpion* an hour to reach missile range of the Coalition ships and ten minutes after that to reach pulse-gun range—and since they were going to skirt the edge of pulse-gun range, they'd be in it for only seconds at most.

"Keep our course directly at the center ship as long as you can," Isaac ordered Renaud as he and Harris returned to the bridge. "We'll want to swing wide at the last possible moment to avoid coming into range of *Poseidon* while we hammer the crap out of *Uriel*.

"Harris," he turned to his tactical officer as the younger man took his seat and resumed control of his systems. "I want a time-on-target launch of our ready missiles once we're in range. Sequence them to arrive as we enter pulse-gun range, targeting *Uriel*."

Isaac studied the tactical screen.

"We'll be in range for about six seconds," he concluded, "and I don't want Mr. Wehr to survive them. They're going to pound us, too," he warned, "but we need to take the hits and keep going."

"Pursuit course as soon as we're past them?" Renaud asked, the young woman's fingers flying across her terminal.

"Exactly. A stern chase is a long chase, but we've got enough of an edge that we can catch up before they reach Auburn Station."

That was when this was going to truly hurt. There was a small but measurable chance they'd make it through the high-speed pass unscathed. The slugging match of a stern chase that was going to follow had no such chance.

Settling in his chair and bringing up his repeater screens, Isaac checked over all of *Scorpion*'s status reports. His ship was as ready for battle as she could possibly be. *More* ready, in fact, that he'd have guessed from the readiness reports he'd been reviewing mere days before.

"Pulse-gun range in fifty-seven minutes, thirty seconds," Harris announced. "Missile firing sequence programmed, and we're spinning up the secondary fusion plants to keep the guns fed."

Isaac nodded wordlessly, his brain still poking at the question of just what the Coalition was planning.

"Giannovi," he pinged his XO. "Send me everything we have on Auburn Station and this region of space. There's something here. Something they're after *other* than the exotic matter. And we're missing it."

———

"Missiles staged. Multi-salvo impact in five minutes," Harris reported softly.

"Course change in thirty seconds," Renaud added.

"Watch their response," Isaac ordered. An hour's study of everything they had on the outer limits of the Conestoga System hadn't given him any answers. There weren't even any new clues, other than potentially the fact that Auburn Station was only five years old.

Most of their data from out there, in fact, came from the station itself and the powerful sensor array it had been equipped with. That fit with the pattern that Isaac had, but it remained just that: a pattern drawn around an answer he couldn't quite see.

"Course change *now*."

It wasn't much of a change, a few degrees of angle and a handful less kilometers per second squared of acceleration. It was enough to change the minimum-distance approach between *Scorpion* and the Coalition ships from ten thousand kilometers to almost half a light-second.

Suddenly, this wasn't going to be a knife fight after all. Isaac focused on *Uriel* like a laser. What would ex-Captain Daniel Wehr do now? *Scorpion* could adjust course if the Coalition tried to use her maneuver to evade action, but the Coalition now had the chance to do that.

Isaac didn't expect "Justice" to do anything of the sort—and he was right.

"All three ships are adjusting course," Harris reported. "Feeding the data to navigation."

"Adjusting to compensate," Renaud snapped. "They can play all they want, but we've got bigger engines. Holding minimum approach at maximum pulse-gun range."

"Missile course adjusting as well. Coalition ships are firing on the missiles."

Anti-missile lasers were invisible to the naked eye but all too clear to *Scorpion*'s scanners. The computers drew neat white lines on the plot to mark the defensive fire from the Coalition destroyers—whose icons rapidly started to resemble porcupines.

"Penetration EW is operating above expected levels," Harris said crisply. "They have *not* updated the software or emitters from the original construction specs. Sixty seconds to impact. Three missiles down."

The missiles were running on their own suicidal electronic brains. The firing pattern for the pulse guns was programmed in.

The only human contribution at this point was Renaud keeping the range open, making sure that *Poseidon* wasn't in position to fire on *Scorpion*. *Uriel* and *Michael* were going to be more than enough trouble for Isaac's ship.

Thirty seconds from the point of contact.

Twenty.

Ten.

The screens dissolved in a blur of light and motion as the warp cruiser slid into range of her enemies. Pulses of pure-white plasma flashed out from her broadside and her enemy responded, the energy weapons going to rapid fire as the four ships blurred past each other.

The hundred-megaton warheads from the pair of surviving missiles detonated first. Out of fifteen weapons launched, only two made it through the Coalition defenses—but that was two more than Isaac had actually expected.

Uriel reeled from the explosions, her pulse guns cutting off after the first salvo. *Scorpion*'s weapons were not so generous.

Plasma bolts worked their way along the hundred-and-twenty-meter length of the destroyer, vaporizing armor and hull plating and working their way deeper and deeper into the rebel warship's systems.

One moment, she was a mobile wonder of technology, testament to the skill and expertise of her builders.

The next, a pulse-gun capacitor ruptured and plasma erupted inside her armor. Chunks of hypertensile ceramics spun off into space as her exterior hull shattered, ripped apart by the explosions that guttered her interior.

Scorpion danced through her own firestorm, red warning lights flashing up on Isaac's screens as plasma pulses struck home. Armor cratered, sensor and ECM emitters vaporized, and the entire warp cruiser jumped sideways under the impacts.

None of that made it through to the calm quiet of the cruiser's bridge. Inertial compensators and safety systems did their job to perfection, and the only reason Isaac even knew his ship was under fire was because his systems told him so.

"Report," he barked.

"We're clear of their range," Renaud told him. "Bringing us about on a pursuit course."

"Target destroyed," Harris noted after a moment's examination of his files. "*Uriel* is gone. *Michael* and *Poseidon* are…changing course."

He paused thoughtfully.

"They are no longer decelerating towards the station," he concluded. "That will extend our chase."

"Accounting for it now," Renaud snapped.

"What's *our* status?" Isaac demanded.

"I hope you liked those missile hits, because that's all we're getting," the tactical officer noted grimly. "Waiting on an update from Engineering on most of it, but we're down three of five missile launchers. Two birds aren't going to ping *anybody*."

"And the pulse guns?"

"We lost a couple on the starboard and upper broadside," Harris confirmed. "About ten percent of our overall firepower, but if we adjust our approach vector, we can still put full broadsides on target. To get all of our guns in play, we'd basically have to fly *between* them."

"I haven't ruled that out as an option," Isaac said dryly. "Engineering, what's our status?"

"Repair drones are in play," his chief engineer replied. "Forty-three-second scramble time, I'll note."

Isaac chuckled. That wasn't just better than the last readiness reports he'd received. That was thirty seconds better than the *original* reports he'd received when he came aboard.

"I'm guessing Harris gave you the spiel on the weapons, but the rest of the news is pretty clean," the engineer reported. "We've got armor burn-throughs in twenty-two places, but the drones will have those covered over in fifteen minutes.

"Engines are fine, remaining weapons systems are fine. Long-range sensors are degraded about seventy percent until we can emplace new sensor emitters, ECM is down twenty percent, same issue.

"I've already ordered the electronic warfare emitters replaced, but I'd like to hold off on the sensors until *after* we're done being shot at," the engineer concluded. "If we'll need long-range scanners before then, we can put them out, but no point getting them vaporized for nothing."

Isaac nodded his understanding, but then his gaze was drawn to the Coalition ships' new course. They were still going to pass Auburn Station, but it wasn't going to be the hour-long stop they'd needed to steal all of the holding towers. They'd probably still be able to sever two or three and take them under tow, but they weren't going to get the full stockpile.

They were heading somewhere *past* Auburn Station, and that…that also fit the pattern.

"I need eyes, Chief," he said quietly. "There's still a question here. Deploy those sensor emitters."

The radio was silent.

"Wilco. I'll pass the orders now."

———

6

———————

Isaac ran a new set of numbers, ones he'd looked at in passing before. Knowing that his mother owned a large portion of Auburn Station explained why it had been built the way it was: First Admiral Gallant hired professional paranoids for her designers as a rule.

Auburn Station was nowhere near well-armed enough to stand off even a single destroyer, but her sensors gave her a near-perfect view of the empty space around her for over a light-hour, and her handful of missile launchers were loaded with weapons with enough reach to cover most of that space.

An armed freighter or the cutters the system governments were limited to couldn't have threatened the station—but at the same time, the station couldn't stand off the Confederacy Space Fleet.

No one had expected someone in the Conestoga government to squirrel away destroyers for over a decade. If they'd hidden them for this long, why strike now? What was so important here as to risk losing a secret fleet over?

What was inside that light-hour radius?

He ran through the reports again, looking for oddities that had shown up in that space…and found the clue he was looking for.

During the surveys to build Auburn Station, the CSF ships

checking out the area had repeatedly suffered from sensor ghosts. They'd thought they'd seen ships, but when they'd gone to check out the signatures, the ships had been gone.

The first captain had thought they were being watched, but a failure to find any actual ships and a drop-off in the reports over the survey had led to the conclusion that the ship's systems had been corrupted. Following through on that, though, Isaac found the records of the ship's refit after the project.

There had been no sign of a software or hardware problem. No one had followed that back to the fact that those ships might well have existed.

Vanishing ships weren't a normal thing. He could see why the survey had assumed it was a system glitch, but what if it *hadn't* been?

Auburn Station had the full records of the survey and its scans, and he looked at the data.

There were no warships among the ghosts. No pirates. Nothing even remotely strange or abnormal, just regular cargo freighters…that had no business being that far out into the middle of nowhere and vanished before the CSF could investigate to see if they were okay.

"Commander Giannovi, I'm sending you a list of sighting reports from the original surveys to build Auburn Station," he told his XO. "I think I see something, but I want you to look at it independently. Compare it to our friends' new course."

"Sir…these are random ghosts."

"Humor me, XO," he ordered.

"Yes, sir."

He leaned back in his chair. If his suspicion was correct, the Conestoga government had some explaining to do…but other than answering the question niggling at the back of his mind, it didn't change his main problem.

Knowing where his enemy was heading would *help*, but he needed to take on two ships that between them outgunned him three to two.

"Time to range?" he asked Renaud and Harris.

"Twenty-six minutes. We'll reach minimum approach just before they reach their range of Auburn Station," his navigator reported.

"The evacuation?"

"Complete," Harris confirmed. "The closest transports are well clear of any range at which the Coalition can range on them." He shrugged. "It'll take them three days to reach the planet, but they're off the board now."

Isaac nodded, considering.

"What transports are they using?" he asked out of curiosity. "Do we have any data on their sensor range?"

His tactical officer looked at him like he was crazy, but looked at his data.

"They're standard Corellian-type ships," Harris noted. "I don't see any evidence of their sensors having been upgraded, so they've probably got the standard suite, which is just mid-range thermals and proximity radar. They wouldn't pick up anything smaller than a warp ship at over a million klicks."

If there was something out there you wanted to hide, the evacuation transports weren't the problem. The Coalition ships needed to take out Auburn Station's sensor arrays.

And, of course, now they were going to need to take out *Scorpion*.

"THERE'S DEFINITELY SOMETHING THERE," Giannovi admitted a few minutes later. "I'm not certain of exactly where, but the areas those ghosts appeared in is unquestionably where the Coalition is headed. I'm just not sure what could possibly be there."

Isaac exhaled, his executive officer's assessment agreeing with his own and filling in the last few pieces.

"Anything humanity can synthesize can, at least theoretically, exist in nature," he pointed out. "Even the things we're used to thinking of as the signs of our mastery over the laws of the universe."

"Wormholes," Giannovi said instantly. "You think there's a natural wormhole out there?"

"Assuming it's permanently open, we'd only detect if we stumbled across it," he pointed out. Only opening a wormhole was detectable at all. A stable, maintained wormhole could be detected only by comparing the radiation passing through it to the radiation coming from around it and realizing that you were looking at the light from a completely different star.

"If Conestoga found it years ago and kept it secret, we'd never have known it was there—and then we put an exotic-matter station right inside its orbit," he concluded. "Auburn Station cut them off from the other side. They needed to either destroy Auburn or reveal their secret colony's existence."

"Which this 'Free Worlds Coalition' definitely wasn't going to do," Giannovi agreed. "But why now? If they've had those destroyers all along, hidden in the asteroid belt, presumably, why attack today?"

"Because *Scarab* went in for a refit five days ago, and *Ladybug* was reassigned from Battle Group *Calypso* to Battle Group *Reliant* six months ago," Isaac pointed out. "This is the first time since Auburn Station was built that there was no warp cruiser in Conestoga or assigned to the rapid-response fleet."

His XO was silent for several seconds.

"That suggests disturbingly complete intel on the CSF," she noted.

"No, just the support of the Conestoga System Defense Force," Isaac replied. "They knew what *Calypso*'s escorts were, and we keep the SDFs informed of the strength of Battle Group *Enterprise* in case they need assistance.

"And our little exercise was unscheduled. If we hadn't been within half an hour's flight of a wormhole station, no one would have been able to intervene before they destroyed Auburn Station and her sensors. They'd steal the exotic matter to 'explain' the attack, and then disappear through the wormhole with it.

"That would give them a secret base in the shadows where we'd never look, just like Wehr said," he finished. "But because we're here and we put this together, they're done. Package up our conclusions in a neat report for me, Commander, and beam it back towards Conestoga Wormhole Station ASAP.

"No matter what happens to us, we'll get this secret out, and this Coalition's efforts are doomed."

Giannovi paused.

"You think there's an entire colony on the other side?" she asked.

"There has to be, or it wouldn't be worth this risk," he concluded. "They're trying to reopen the shipping lanes and communications."

"What'll happen to them now?" his XO asked.

"They'll be invited to join the Confederacy, to come out of the shadows," Isaac told her.

"Invited. Right." The cynicism in her voice was heavy.

He sighed.

"It's not our call, Commander. That will be the Senate's decision. We've done our part—now we just need to finish the job."

———

ISAAC WISHED he could see something useful in the tactical plot. The two destroyers had moved closer together to prevent *Scorpion* attacking one while avoiding the other's range again. Auburn Station's missiles weren't even worth considering as a factor.

The only option he could see was to fly straight up the middle and hammer the two rebel ships as hard as he could. That wasn't a fight *Scorpion* would win.

It wasn't a fight the Coalition would win, either. Their edge in firepower wasn't big enough to carry the day with ease. The most likely result was that *Scorpion* would be destroyed and the two Coalition destroyers hammered into wrecks.

They *might* manage to sneak through their wormhole before the warp cruisers currently cooling their drives at the Lagrange point caught up with them, but that wouldn't matter now. It was all over, bar the screaming.

"Do you think there's any chance they'd surrender if we told them the game was up?" he asked conversationally.

"Not a very big one," his XO replied. "Any brilliant ideas?"

"Shoot them until they stop shooting us," Isaac told her. "You?"

"About the same. I'm wishing they'd given Auburn Station about, oh, ten times as many launchers."

"Then they might have been tempted to get stroppy with the CSF and we couldn't have that," he said. "Besides, lightspeed delays will cause all sorts of problems if we try to control them. Auburn Station may have incredibly powerful scanners, but her computers aren't smart enough to run missiles themselves…"

He trailed off, staring at the screen.

"Sir?" Giannovi asked. "You have an idea, don't you?"

"Someone get me the full specifications on the sensor array on a Flight Eight *Archon*-class destroyer," Isaac ordered. "The most powerful radar array in this star system is on the other side of the enemy from us. There's got to be *something* we can do with that!"

7

———

"THEY HAVE US DIALED IN," Harris reported. "Evasive maneuvers and ECM are only doing so much. I figure I can generate a thirty percent miss rate...but seventy percent of a hundred and fifty percent is still more guns than we've got left."

"Let them keep their eyes on us," Isaac ordered. "We've got a lovely surprise planned for them now."

Even if his plan worked, *Scorpion* was going to get pieces of her hull ripped off and handed to her. There was no way he was making it through this with his ship intact.

What he *might* be able to do was make it through this with his ship intact *enough* that most of his crew made it home—and his enemy didn't.

"Ninety seconds to pulse-gun range," Renaud reported. "We'll continue to close from there, reaching a minimum approach of just under five hundred kilometers in two hundred and five seconds."

One way or another, *that* wasn't going to happen. Pulse guns grew more powerful as the range dropped, their plasma pulses having less time to weaken after leaving the ship. At five hundred kilometers, he'd be better off flying *Scorpion* directly into a star.

"Commander Giannovi?" he asked.

"Program is loaded into Auburn Station's systems. Initiating five seconds before weapons range."

"And our side?"

"Ready to go," she confirmed.

Isaac nodded silently, waiting as the range dropped down. His "prey" had turned to present their broadsides, but *Scorpion* continued a headlong rush. They could bring fully half of their guns to bear on her, and he could only present about forty percent of his…but everyone "knew" he'd rotate before he reached range.

Twenty seconds.

"Commander Renaud?"

"Yes, sir?"

"Execute."

Scorpion's forward acceleration vanished, the ship twisting into a broad spiral that, exactly as he knew his enemy would expect, presented her full undamaged broadside towards them.

What the Coalition ships *wouldn't* have been expecting was that *Scorpion* was now emptying her water tanks. Her waste tanks. Reflective flakes of specialty chaff sprayed out with every drop of liquid the cruiser could spare as Renaud spun her out to create a thousand-kilometer-wide glittering mirror in space.

It wouldn't do much on its own. The Coalition ships already had *Scorpion* locked in, hard radar pulses still reflecting off her hull as she spiralled.

And then the hideously overpowered radar pulse from Auburn Station's scanners arrived. Passing over the rebel destroyers, it temporarily overloaded their receivers, losing their lock for an infinitesimal fraction of a second.

That wouldn't have been enough to cause trouble. Not on its own —but then the pulse hit the massive mirror *Scorpion* had built around herself. For a few seconds, a massive sun of artificial radiation lit up behind the warp cruiser—and she flashed into range of the destroyers.

Pulse-gun fire lit up the empty space on the edge of the Conestoga System again. The destroyers had completely lost their lock, passive and active sensors alike completely blinded by the mirror behind *Scor-*

pion and the repeating, overwhelmingly powerful pulses from Auburn Station.

They could adjust. They could adapt and use Auburn Station's sensor pulses against Isaac—but *Scorpion* was already using the Station's radar for targeting.

Full broadsides tore into *Poseidon,* almost every pulse from *Scorpion*'s guns hitting. The two rebel ships were firing in random patterns, only a handful of bolts striking him.

Warning lights flickered on Isaac's status display as the three ships hurtled toward each other. They were hammering the one destroyer, but she was still with them…and then the Coalition finished updating their targeting computers.

Their trick had bought them twelve seconds.

Twelve seconds was…enough.

"*Poseidon* is coming apart! Switching targets!" Harris barked aloud. Only a single combined salvo from both destroyers hit home before the first destroyer came apart, but *Scorpion* leapt under the impact.

Inertial compensators did their job, but waves of rippling force crashed over everyone regardless as *Scorpion*'s warp drive ring shattered. Even mostly discharged, severing the exotic-matter ring could be felt through the entire ship, and Isaac forced down a wave of nausea.

"Hammer them!" he snapped—and Harris obeyed.

Renaud twisted the warp cruiser through an insane series of acrobatics, forcing the entire next salvo from *Michael* to miss. Harris's guns automatically compensated for her maneuvers, however, and *his* pulses continued to hammer home on the less-maneuverable destroyer.

Ten seconds later, it was over. One of *Michael*'s fusion plants lost containment, gutting the destroyer in a single blast of stellar fire.

Scorpion reeled. Her warp ring was broken in three places. Her armor was leaking atmosphere, and the damage reports on Isaac's command chair told him most of her guns were gone.

She was a wreck.

But she was a *victorious* wreck.

8

"THE THIRD ADMIRAL is waiting for you, Captain Gallant," the polite young Lieutenant Commander told Isaac.

"Thank you," he told her, glancing at the viewscreen behind her showing the massive yard complex anchored on Phobos, the larger of the two Martian moons. *Scorpion* hung in one of the nearer slips, the distance reducing her scars to blurry dark smears on her hull.

There was no sign of the slow and agonizing process of towing his ship home now. From here, he couldn't even see the swarm of shipyard drones flitting around the ship. She might almost have been undamaged—except for the fact that her warp ring was very clearly missing sections, visible even now.

He stepped past the receptionist and through the door into the office of Third Admiral Caroline Riesling, the third-ranking officer of the Confederacy Space Fleet. She was a tall, gray-haired woman who reminded him of his mother in more ways than one.

"Captain Gallant," she greeted him. "Take a seat."

He obeyed in silence.

"What is *Scorpion*'s status?" she asked.

"Battered and broken, but reparable," he summarized. "The fail-safes worked and we retained over ninety percent of our exotic matter.

They tell me they'll be able to rebuild her drive ring relatively easily because of that; it'll just take time.

"Six months or so," he admitted.

"That's better than I was afraid of," Riesling admitted. "Good to hear, though that means you won't be returning if she'll be out of commission for six months."

"I see, sir," he said, concealing his reaction. He thought he'd done well, but they were going to take his ship away?

"Shepherding her through will be Captain Giannovi's task," the Third Admiral continued with a smile. "There's plenty of credit and promotion to go around, Captain Gallant; don't worry. You saved Auburn Station *and* delivered the Waterloo System to us on a platter."

"Is that what they called it?" he asked.

"Indeed," she confirmed. "Sixth Admiral Cohen and Battle Group *Enterprise* have secured the system. The local government was being difficult, but a few demonstration orbital strikes seemed to have sorted that out, per his last reports."

Isaac was getting better at concealing what he truly thought. Before the Battle of Auburn Station, his mental wince might have actually made it to his face. He'd hoped that whatever secret colony Conestoga had set up on the other side of the wormhole would be peacefully brought into the Confederacy.

Clearly, Admiral Cohen had had different priorities.

"I see, ma'am," he said calmly instead of saying what he really wanted to.

"The media is lapping up this story, you know," she continued. "You're quite the hero, and your relation to the First Admiral doesn't hurt—the details of why you had to insist on the evacuation haven't been released, of course, but the high level of you being determined to see everyone safe has.

"You've probably done more good for the government's reputation than an entire battery of PR flacks working for a decade," Riesling concluded. "That, of course, is to your benefit as well as ours."

"Ma'am," he said noncommittally, letting her get to her point.

"You realize, I'm sure, that there was never any problem with your skill, competence or actions as an officer," she told him. "Bluntly, if we hadn't been determined to make sure Adrienne's son had the most average of careers, you'd have made Captain two years ago.

"Now, of course, you have dragged yourself into the public eye and, I and several other Admirals think, have thoroughly answered the question of who Adrienne's heir apparent should be."

Isaac's new self-control was getting a workout, and he could feel his fists tightening under the desk.

He'd saved his mother's prisoner-run industrial facility and enabled the invasion of a system that had just wanted to be left alone. For this, they wanted to groom him to take over the Confederacy?!

Riesling slid a box across the table.

"Your mother signed off on this," she told him, "but, of course, it wouldn't be appropriate for her to give these to you…Rear Admiral Gallant."

Isaac opened the box, looking at the matching collar pins of a single gold star, and all he could taste was the ashes of his faith in the government he served.

Nonetheless, his hands were steady as he removed the insignia and pinned them to his collar.

The Coalition had had the wrong plan. Running and hiding wouldn't change anything. Secret ships and stolen fleets would never be able to make it through the wormhole network.

The only way to undo what had been done was the same way the Confederacy had been corrupted in the first place: from the inside.

EXILE UNIVERSE

Ashen Stars is the prequel of *Exile*, available now.

ABOUT THE AUTHOR

Glynn Stewart is the author of *Starship's Mage*, a bestselling science fiction and fantasy series where faster-than-light travel is possible–but only because of magic. His other works include science fiction series *Duchy of Terra, Castle Federation* and *Vigilante,* as well as the urban fantasy series *ONSET* and *Changeling Blood*.

Writing managed to liberate Glynn from a bleak future as an accountant. With his personality and hope for a high-tech future intact, he lives in Kitchener, Ontario with his partner, their cats, and an unstoppable writing habit.

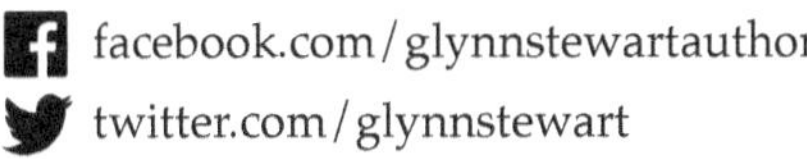

OTHER BOOKS BY GLYNN STEWART

For release announcements join the mailing list or visit **GlynnStewart.com**

STARSHIP'S MAGE

Starship's Mage
Hand of Mars
Voice of Mars
Alien Arcana
Judgment of Mars
UnArcana Stars
Sword of Mars
Mountain of Mars
The Service of Mars
A Darker Magic
Mage-Commander (upcoming)

Starship's Mage: Red Falcon
Interstellar Mage
Mage-Provocateur
Agents of Mars

Pulsar Race: A Starship's Mage Universe Novella

DUCHY OF TERRA

The Terran Privateer
Duchess of Terra
Terra and Imperium
Darkness Beyond
Shield of Terra
Imperium Defiant
Relics of Eternity
Shadows of the Fall
Eyes of Tomorrow

VIGILANTE
(WITH TERRY MIXON)
Heart of Vengeance
Oath of Vengeance

**Bound By Stars: A Vigilante Series
(With Terry Mixon)**
Bound By Law
Bound by Honor
Bound by Blood

TEER AND KARD
Wardtown
Blood Ward

CHANGELING BLOOD
Changeling's Fealty
Hunter's Oath
Noble's Honor
Fae, Flames & Fedoras: A Changeling Blood Novella

ONSET
ONSET: To Serve and Protect
ONSET: My Enemy's Enemy
ONSET: Blood of the Innocent
ONSET: Stay of Execution
Murder by Magic: An ONSET Novella

FANTASY STAND ALONE NOVELS
Children of Prophecy
City in the Sky